THE YEARS AFTER YOU

EMMA WOOLF

AMBERJACK
PUBLISHING

IDAHO

Amberjack Publishing
1472 E. Iron Eagle Dr.
Eagle, ID 83616
amberjackpublishing.com

10 9 8 7 6 5 4 3 2 1

Book design by Aubrey Khan, Neuwirth & Associates

Publisher's Cataloging-in-Publication data available upon request

ISBN 978-1-948705-356
ebook ISBN 978-1-948705-479

To my father, Cecil Woolf (1927–2019)
And my son, Alexander Cecil

PART ONE

THE PHONE RANG AND RANG. STANDING
on the train platform, Lily muttered under her breath, "Pick up,
please . . ."

Finally she heard her sister's voice: "Lil, is that you? Everything
OK?"

"Sorry to call you at work, Cass—do you have a minute?"

"Sure, yes. Let me just find a meeting room."

Lily heard Cassie's heels clicking down the corridor and then the
closing of a door.

"So, what's up? Where are you?"

"You're not going to believe what's just happened. Remember
Harry invited me out to his house today to work on that project?"

"Yeah, right. His wife was out all day and you were going to . . ."
Cassie's voice held a tinge of amusement, "work from home
together."

"Anyway, she came back. You wouldn't believe it, I had to run
out of the back garden and literally scramble over the wall. I'm

waiting for a train back to London now. I'm wearing Harry's shirt. Luckily I've got my bag and phone, although—oh God, I don't know what I've left in his house—I can't call him. Honestly, Cass, she turned up hours earlier than planned. I've never been so scared in my entire life."

Lily heard her sister's intake of breath at the other end of the line, and a snort of suppressed laughter, and found she was laughing too.

"Lil, you two are insane, how could you even risk it? Listen, I have to finish something before the end of the day—but what are you doing now?"

"Right now? I'm standing on the platform at Gerrards Cross wearing a man's shirt tucked into skinny jeans, hair dripping wet, and—oh, wow." Lily's hands closed around a packet of cigarettes in Harry's shirt pocket. "Hallelujah."

"Come and meet me at the office," Cassie said. "I'll be done by six, you can tell me everything over a cocktail."

"Perfect," Lily said, "but I'll need to borrow some make-up." Hanging up, she walked down to the far end of the platform. It was the lull before rush hour and the station was deserted.

Despite her insouciance on the phone with Cassie, she was shaken by the events of the past hour. She had been caught in another woman's house—in her shower—and had made her escape, half-dressed, over the garden wall. It was shameful. She didn't want to imagine what was happening at the house now; she didn't care. She should never have gone to Harry's house—she'd known it was wrong. *Never, never again,* she thought.

Lily felt guilty, but she also felt angry. Damn Harry for making her into his dirty little secret. That wasn't who she was. She longed to be away from the stupid suburbs with their failed marriages and sad lies. She couldn't wait to get back to London and see Cass; she needed a drink. She settled herself on a grassy bank, lit a cigarette with shaking hands, and lifted her face to the sun.

THEY LAY ON THE SOFT GREY CARPET OF Harry's study, Lily's head resting on his chest, arms entwined, gazing up at the skylight.

"I love that view," Harry said. "In summer, it's just an endless blue. It reminds me of this poem called 'Patagonia.'"

He kissed Lily's forehead and pulled himself into a sitting position, reaching for his clothes. "Come on, let's get up. I want to see that flat you were telling me about."

Lily stretched full-length and sat up, her hair mussed from the carpet. "Harry . . . I can't."

"Can't what? Can't show me the flat?"

"I can't accept your offer. It's incredibly generous and I'm touched, but it's so much money. I'd feel wrong accepting it."

"Lil, I've explained. You know that my father left me money in his will, and I'm more than comfortable—think of it as a gift. Or it could be a loan, or an investment, or whatever. You want to buy somewhere bigger, and I want to help you, and . . . show me the flat." He picked up his blue cotton shirt from the floor, shook it out, and draped it around Lily's bare shoulders.

"Come on, at least show me the photos." He flipped open his laptop and started typing. ". . . Let's see, Belsize Park, two-bedroom flat, England's Lane, top two floors. Hey, check out the garden." He shot Lily a grin. "I'll give the agent a call and see if it's still on the market . . ."

Lily shook her head. "I'm going to take a quick shower," she murmured. She knew how it looked, Harry offering her £150,000 for a deposit on the flat. Equally, she acknowledged that it was a small sum out of his late father's legacy, and probably as good an investment as any these days. Standing under the hot water, she resolved to at least go back and see the flat again, with Harry this time. They could argue about the finances later.

Harry walked into the bathroom, smiling. "I've booked a viewing for Monday at midday; we can go straight from that meeting in Camden." He leaned over the sink to open the small bathroom window, and then spun round, his face suddenly pale. "Lil, it's Pippa's car . . . Shit . . . Let me . . . I'll go downstairs and keep her outside, can you—sorry, how quickly can you get out?" Harry was in a panic, gesturing at her with a large towel.

"Don't worry, don't worry," she said. She turned off the hot water and pulled open the shower door. "You keep her outside," she muttered under her breath. "OK, my jeans are in the study, underwear, wait, where's my handbag, and my shoes are in the front hall." Lily was dripping all over the bathroom floor. "Go, Harry, get down there; for God's sake stop her coming in!"

"You know, the back door, out into the garden, then that lane leads along to—"

"Yes, the station, it's fine—just GO!"

*   *   *

There's something going on. I can't put my finger on it exactly, but Harry's been acting weird all evening. And there's something else—the house feels different. I can't work out what's wrong, but I've already broken the no wine on weekdays vow I made yesterday. Can one of you tell me if I'm being stupid?

It started like this: I drove into Beaconsfield for my tennis lesson this morning, then I went and met Trish and Sandra for lunch. We finished around half two, and I had an hour to spare before collecting Daniel and taking him to rugby. So I was in Waitrose, killing time, and bumped into Daniel's best friend's mother. She offered to collect them and give Daniel dinner at theirs, and drop him home later. Which got me out of a boring few hours watching rugby.

So I ended up with a free afternoon. Harry was working from home, so I decided to head back and see if he wanted to help me clear the junk in the garage. (I know, romantic, right?) I'd just turned into the drive when he came rushing out of the house in a bathrobe—this is the middle of the afternoon—saying something about my car making an odd noise and had I noticed anything and maybe we should look under the bonnet. I told him I hadn't heard anything and I wouldn't know what to look for under the bonnet; he was welcome to look at it while I took the shopping in. Then he said had I seen the gravel in the driveway and did I think it needed replacing; all sorts of random stuff, like he didn't want me to go into the house.

After about ten minutes of this, I finally got past him—I was worried about the sorbet melting, it was a warm day—and when I got inside, the back door was open. Nothing unusual maybe, but there was something else—an atmosphere—not a scent exactly, but a feeling within the house. I went upstairs and the bathroom floor was wet, damp towels hanging askew and the caps off my posh shampoo and conditioner. In twenty years of marriage to Harry he's never used more than a blob of his own shampoo, the basic men's anti-dandruff one which sits beside my rather more expensive products. I walked across the landing—our bedroom was as pristine as I'd left it this morning, bed neatly made. But in Harry's study his chinos and socks were strewn across the floor, which isn't like him. Maybe he'd gone to the gym in a hurry? As I was leaving the study I glanced at the screen and saw a website for a London estate agent based in Belsize Park. WTF?

I went downstairs to ask about the bathroom and found him in the kitchen; he was standing at the sink, washing up several plates, coffee cups, and glasses. I was about to mention the estate agent's website but something stopped me. Something was really not right. I noticed that his *hair was bone dry. He hadn't been in the shower at all—or if he had, he certainly hadn't used my shampoo and conditioner.*

So I'm on my third glass of red, and he's down at the bottom of the garden, apparently having a cigarette. I guess the quitting smoking thing is off again. He does that quite a lot these days after dinner, goes outside to smoke, checking voicemails or sending texts, I don't know what. Mobile reception is patchy in the house, but it does make me wonder. I'm probably being paranoid, and the wine doesn't help. It's just this strange vibe—a woman sort of senses that, doesn't she, in her own house? And those unanswered questions about the bathroom and the website. I should have just asked him. Look, Harry doesn't lie to me, so I'm not going to build this up. And I'm not going to become one of those sneaky wives who checks her husband's phone and internet history and bank statements . . .

I just glanced out of the conservatory window and he's on the phone. Who's he talking to at eleven p.m.?

HARRY DRAINED HIS TUMBLER OF WHISKY and set it down on the paving stone which edged the pond. He lit another cigarette and arched his back with a low groan. The pain which had been absent all day had come back that evening, despite the painkillers, red wine, and whisky. The moon was almost full, giving a silvery sheen to the pond and reflecting back a second watery moon.

He exhaled a long plume of smoke and wished he could ring Lily. She hadn't replied to the text he'd sent a few hours earlier, after the initial panic of Pippa's return: *Sorry, Lil, I didn't want to get rid of you—she was meant to be out all day. Hell. Did you get back OK? xx*

He looked at his phone and then glanced back at the house. Pippa was still sitting there, a small figure in the dark conservatory, motionless in front of the glow of the computer screen. Updating Facebook, he assumed, posting photos of her perfect life, their perfect family, scrolling through other people's photos, new cars, houses, holidays. He didn't understand her preoccupation with social media—the boys, fine, they were teenagers—but Pippa was forty-seven, not seventeen. What did she get from it? She saw most of her Facebook friends every day at tennis, for lunch, or at the school gates.

The surface of the pond rippled in the night breeze. Harry found himself remembering ten years earlier, the summer they had bought this house. Back then the garden had been a wilderness. He and Pippa had been full of excitement and still in love, the boys only five and three, and they spent countless weekends out here digging the pond. He could see her now, her hair still long in those days and glossy raven black, brown as a berry from the sunshine, wearing a red bikini and shovelling mud along with him and the boys. Moving to the new house had rejuvenated their relationship. It must have been around that time they conceived their daughter. Where had that Pippa gone? Where had they gone?

He should go indoors. He should go in and switch on the dishwasher and undress and lie beside his wife upstairs, where only hours ago he had lain on the study floor with Lily in his arms. He took out his phone and texted those lines from the poem to her:

. . . When I spoke of Patagonia, I meant
skies all empty aching blue. I meant
years. I meant all of them with you.

"BETTER?" CASSIE SMILED AS LILY SLID INTO the booth.

"Much better! Thanks." Lily handed a small cosmetics bag back to her sister just as the waiter arrived with a tray of drinks.

"And even better now." She took a large gulp of her vodka and lime. "Oh, Cass, what a mess . . ."

"Come on, tell me everything."

Later, after several more drinks, Cassie agreed that the situation with Harry was a mess. But Lily felt better about it anyway. Talking to her sister helped, as did the vodka and lime, and things seemed clearer now. Lily was full of a new resolve as they walked to the Tube station through the dark London streets. She would ignore her feelings for Harry and instead make the right choice. "I'll end it. I was stupid to let it go this far, and even stupider to go to his house. We were lucky today, but it was close. That's got to be a sign, hasn't it?"

"I want you to be happy, Lil," Cass said, "and I worry this will all end in tears. Relationships are a mystery, especially from the outside; we can't really know what's going on with Harry and his wife. But when it implodes—as it probably will—you don't want to be involved."

"And I especially don't want to be standing in his shower, naked! But seriously, Cass, I wonder how people even make marriages work. How can you be sure that you want to be with the same person for the rest of your life? How did you know when Charlie asked you?"

"It just felt right," Cassie said. "As much as he drives me mad sometimes, he's the only man I want to be with. That's not to say that it will definitely last forever—how can anyone be certain they're making the right decision when there are two people's feelings involved?" She paused. "It's a huge gamble, to commit to another person for life. I suppose there's always an element of uncertainty."

"You're right. Nothing's one hundred per cent guaranteed. From what Harry says about him and Pippa I don't understand why they got married in the first place. And he claims their sex life is pretty much non-existent. Although they say that cheating husbands always tell their mistresses that their marriage is dead. Who knows."

Lily reached out and hugged her older sister goodnight as they parted, Cassie to walk the few minutes home and Lily into the Tube station. *Cassie's right*, she thought to herself. She did not want to be there when it imploded.

*   *   *

We made love again last night. It makes such a difference, like we're closer than ever, and now everything's wonderful. We shared a shower this morning and even had breakfast together before I drove Harry to the station. I don't know what all that worry last week was about—me being silly and suspicious and menopausal, I suspect. I've written on this blog before about my hang-ups, how my late forties have hit me, the grey hairs and the saggy boobs and everything going south! Turning forty wasn't as cataclysmic as I'd expected, but forty-five hit me like a ton of bricks. I went from feeling still young at forty-two, forty-three, even forty-four—to suddenly past it.

But I'm not the only woman in her late forties who starts to feel invisible and starts to suspect her husband of all sorts of nonsense. I'm off the wine, at least on weeknights, and I'm going to plough my energies into some kind of start-up; I don't know, an online estate agency, property, or maybe I could train as an interior designer . . . My plans are vague, but I definitely want to get started on something. It's when I sit at home feeling unproductive that my mind goes into overdrive. And I want to focus on the boys and Harry too. And then there's my serve—I really want to take my tennis to a new level, and maybe get involved in the local ladies' tournaments.

It was so good between us last night, tender and passionate, just like when we first met. I know Harry's under pressure at work and it doesn't help when I'm critical and tetchy. Resolution: no more nagging! Even that silly mix-up over the London properties: remember I noticed on his computer he'd been looking at flats in Belsize Park? He explained and it totally makes sense: he was thinking about investing the inheritance from his father, maybe buying a flat for the boys when they're older, but it was only an idea. And there I was inventing all sorts of crazy scenarios—I hate the way I blow things out of proportion! Yet another resolution: don't snoop into your lovely husband's computer or phone!

"SO. AT OUR LAST APPOINTMENT WE TALKED about your father. How are you feeling now?"

Harry shrugged. In these sessions with Dr. Christos he often felt like a sulky teenager, wilfully uncooperative, but what was he supposed to say? "I don't feel anything, really. Our relationship was virtually non-existent for years, now he's dead. It doesn't make any difference."

Dr. Christos jotted something on the notepad in front of him. "And it's been how long now?"

"Five or six months. Honestly, there's not much to say. He was an old man in his nineties, and he was very sick. It happens."

"And yet you're close to your sons. At our last session," Dr. Christos flipped back a few pages, "you said *the only thing stopping me from walking out is being there for the boys.*"

Harry nodded. His voice was low, almost inaudible. "It's true. I doubt Pippa and I would still be together if it weren't for Dan and Joe. I don't love her anymore. I don't know why or when it ended, but it did. Then again . . . I'm not even sure Lily wants me."

"Ah yes. You and Lily."

"Yes, well." Harry's face darkened. "I don't know why I've been fooling myself. She's twenty years younger than me, she's got plenty of other things going on in her life. If she ever was in love with me, I'm not sure she is anymore."

Dr. Christos raised an eyebrow. "Go on."

"Just that I don't think Lily wants me to get a divorce. In fact, I know she doesn't. The cliché is that the married man will never leave his wife for his mistress, right? But this is the other way around. If Lily gave me an ounce of encouragement, I'd up sticks and leave . . . I'd move in with her tomorrow. I'd buy us a house in London." He shook his head and muttered under his breath, "I've even offered to help her buy her own place, for God's sake."

"In your mind, the two are very much connected?" said Dr. Christos. "Or let me put that another way: you trace your altered feelings towards Pippa to meeting Lily?"

Harry let out a sigh. "I honestly don't know. I'd probably been out of love with Pippa for a while but I hadn't really noticed. There wasn't anyone else, if that's what you're asking—I'd never been unfaithful. The one thing, maybe the only thing, I was proud of and cared about was being a good father. You know, a decent husband and provider. But this thing with Lily. I'm just all over the place . . ."

"In what way *all over the place?*"

"I mean, my head, my priorities, my behaviour. What I told you about a few weeks ago, when Pippa came home and Lily was there—you're right, it was risky and reckless. But I almost didn't care. Within minutes of Lily leaving, even while I was trying to hide the signs of her being there—I found her bra behind my study door, for God's sake—even then, with Pippa in the house, I just wanted Lily back. But sometimes—I don't know." Harry shook his head.

"Go on."

"Sometimes I get this moment of clarity and see things from the outside: when she turns thirty next year and I'll be turning fifty—what do I really expect is going to happen? She has male friends her own age, I know she does, plenty of ex-boyfriends sniffing around, and lovers, I assume. I'm just this old guy she works with. It sort of tears me in two. Maybe I'm a father figure to her."

"A father figure?" Dr. Christos looked up. "That's interesting. Can you elaborate?"

"Not really," Harry said. "I don't even know if that's right; she never talks much about her father. As far as I know he died when she was a baby, or walked out, or something . . ." He fell silent.

"I don't want to be her bloody father figure. I don't want any of that shit—I want her to love me back, properly, like a man, not put up with me or pity me or use me. To be honest, the whole thing is making me desperately unhappy." He shot a look at Dr. Christos. "There. You wanted to know how I'm feeling? I feel desperate. When she's with me, I'm so high I don't care about anything, and when she's not, I do dangerous things: I take risks, I drive too fast, I get off my face on drink and drugs. I'm constantly thinking about who she's with and what she's doing. And if she doesn't answer the phone or can't see me, I get angry, really angry. I just need to know what's going through her mind, whether she actually gives a shit about me. Because if she doesn't, I honestly don't know what I'm going to do."

After several minutes of silence, Dr. Christos cleared his throat. "Obviously I'm not privy to Lily's feelings, but we're here to talk about you. You say you're feeling desperate, and I can see that. But you're not powerless—"

"But that's exactly it," Harry interrupted. "I feel powerless. In the rest of my life, I'm in control—or at least, I can make decisions, sort out problems. I've always been on top of things, at work, at home, I don't just wait for things to happen to me and sit around moaning. If something's wrong, I fix it—if the boys are in trouble or colleagues aren't delivering, or whatever. With Lily, it's completely different; I can't do anything to make her want me more, I can't change the way I feel about her. I'm completely fucking obsessed." He shook his head. "And I don't know what I'll do next."

"Harry, we're coming to the end of our session for today, but I'd like to suggest an extra session quite urgently this week. I'm concerned about where this is heading and I'd like us to look seriously at alternatives. I mean, giving you back some sense of agency, getting you back in control. In any situation, it's important to remember that you always have a choice."

"LILY, YOU MAKE IT SOUND LIKE I DECIDED to fall in love with you. But I never intended any of this to happen. It wasn't a choice." That was how Harry remembered it. He and Lily were having dinner in a small French restaurant in Frankfurt, after a long day at the annual Book Fair.

He was talking about her job interview, the day they first met. Harry recalled her walking into his office, and what she had been wearing: "White shirt, navy trousers, bare ankles . . . your hair twisted up in that thing you do" (he meant a chignon). Lily was twenty-seven and it had been her "professional" outfit at the time: slim, dark blue cigarette pants from The Kooples, a crisp white shirt, navy ballet pumps. Smart but not too formal.

The waiter intervened, pouring more wine from the bottle on the table, adjusting their cutlery, fussing with the bread basket. They sat in silence, looking at each other, the air between them crackling. Lily felt as though she were watching this scene from above: both intensely present and very far away. She knew they were getting in way too deep. She needed to change this conversation somehow, to stop it from going any further. The problem was, she believed Harry. When he talked about his marriage, about realising you didn't love someone anymore, about making the wrong choices for the right reasons, Lily knew he was telling the truth.

But then there were his children. Although Harry wanted to leave his wife—they had been growing apart for years, he said—he

15

couldn't imagine leaving his sons. Lily remembered how his face lit up when he talked about them.

"You know the cliché about having children, that it changes everything?" he said. "It's true. If it weren't for the boys I'd have left years ago. Dan and Joe are the only reason I'm still there, they're everything to me." He took Lily's hand. "Before you, I mean."

"Harry, I'm not sure we should be talking like this . . ."

But he continued, lost in his own head, seemingly oblivious to Lily. "I never realised how hard it would be—whatever I do affects the boys. There's such a difference between leaving a relationship and leaving a family. Although divorce is the obvious solution, and of course I'd still get to see the boys, how can I put them through all that pain and confusion? Seeing them at weekends, or a few days on and off, having them come to visit me as some kind of divorced dad set-up, their toothbrushes and pyjamas in their bags, you know it just feels so wrong. I can't imagine not seeing them every morning and night. I live with them. I'd die for them."

"I don't . . . look, Harry, whatever's going on in your marriage, I don't want to break up a family." She took her hand away. "I can't promise you anything. I can't be the reason you leave."

"I know that," Harry said. "I don't want to put you in this position; I know I'm a mess. Just that . . ." He took a gulp of wine, and fumbled for his cigarettes. "Just that I love you."

Just that I love you. Lily always remembered Harry's words. As if love was *just* anything.

IT WASN'T AN "AFFAIR," NOT AT THE START. In fact, nothing physical happened for nearly six months. They talked and talked, closer than colleagues, more flirtatious than friends, the chemistry between them like a live wire. But for all the rumours and suspicion swirling around them at the office, until that evening in Frankfurt they had not crossed the line.

Harry may have fallen for Lily at first sight, but her feelings for him crept up on her. She could see he was handsome, she loved his confidence, his presence, even his smell, but it went deeper than sexual attraction. Whenever she was around him, her body relaxed. If love was an instinct, there was something instinctive between them. When she was in Harry's company, she felt herself resolved, complete. Being close to him reassured her, and their conversations were like thinking out loud.

How could something which felt so right be so clearly wrong? Lily had to remind herself: he was twenty years older, he was married with children. She struggled with this for months—not jealousy of his wife, but an awareness of the fragile situation. Harry was physically strong but vulnerable. He put up a good front in the office, but there were evenings when she saw him close to despair. Everything about this situation said danger, stay away, leave the building, in flashing neon lights. Anyway, she was twenty-seven, he was forty-seven. What possible future could there be?

Looking back, that sense of danger had always been there: danger, desire, and a sort of hopelessness. Had she ever really thought it could work out between them? Did relationships founded on deceit ever end happily? And would she have allowed Harry to come to her, fresh from walking out on his family, to live with her, both of them feeling responsible for that fractured family he'd left behind? The guilt was inseparable from the love. Perhaps she should have stopped to question herself, but it was always up and down, heady and hopeless, with Harry. The problem was that her feelings changed constantly: At times she was jealous of his wife and wanted him all to herself. Other times she felt claustrophobic and trapped by the situation. Still other times she felt an immense tenderness for Harry, and overwhelming love.

When it was all over, when the mistakes had been made and the catastrophe complete, Lily spent a lot of time thinking about that beginning. *It was always there with Harry,* she thought to herself, *this sensation of being on the edge. It was there long before the first kiss.* In all, they had barely two years together, but she felt much, much older than the young woman who had walked into the interview on that day in April.

"AS FOR THE JOB—I DECIDED INSTANTLY," Harry said, twisting linguine around his fork. "The moment I laid eyes on you, it was yours. I don't think I heard a word you said, I just kept thinking how lovely you were, how your brown eyes sparkled and the way you smiled. Even while I was going through the interview questions on the sheet in front of me, all I could think was: *I can't let this woman walk out and never come back.*"

"Harry . . ." Lily shook her head, smiling. "You can't just give someone a job because you find them attractive!"

"*Attractive?* I didn't just find you attractive, Lil, I was consumed. You walked in and I wanted every single inch of your body and your mind. I wanted to talk to you forever, I wanted you never to leave the room. It wasn't a question of attraction."

Lily looked uncertain. It was nice to be appreciated, but she wasn't entirely comfortable with the implications of Harry's words. "And there I was, thinking it was my publishing experience which got me the job."

"Of course you got the job on your merits—your CV and experience were great." Harry took her hand across the dinner table. "I saw five other candidates and you were already at the top of the pile. Plus, if you remember, at the second interview there were two other directors and they asked all the questions. We made the decision unanimously to offer you the job. So there."

Frankfurt was their first business trip away together. It was October, a bitterly cold evening. London was having a mild autumn, so they had been unprepared for the raw German wind. They had lingered in the restaurant long after they finished dinner, partly because of the cold walk back to the hotel, and partly because they had a candlelit corner table and it was too cosy to move.

Lily hadn't been to Frankfurt before; she hadn't expected it to be so elegant. Avoiding the usual publisher hangouts, receptions, and parties, they had found a restaurant in part of the old town.

After dinner, Harry ordered coffee and Baileys. There was an undercurrent of tension this evening; they were wary, savouring and dreading the next steps. They had been leading up to this for six months, and they both knew exactly what might happen next. It was precious and painful, this moment before a love affair was launched. It was the calm before the storm.

PACKING FOR THE THREE-DAY TRIP WHILE Cassie was round at her flat, Lily tried again to convince her sister that there was nothing going on. "I mean, obviously we're close, but just as friends." She held up a handful of lace and silk from her underwear drawer: "What do you think? The Elle Macpherson matching set, the new pale pink silk, or the black lace?" They burst out laughing.

"Right, of course," Cassie said, "because when I go on work trips, my underwear is the most important thing!"

"Seriously, nothing physical has happened. It won't and it can't." Lily threw a handful of the underwear into her suitcase and began to pull dresses from the wardrobe. "It just can't." According to their colleagues, they were already in the throes of an adulterous liaison. Eventually, Lily had given up trying to convince anyone otherwise; let them think what they wanted. The problem was, being unfaithful wasn't just about sex. She knew that Harry's emotional infidelity was far more damaging.

She tried constantly to talk herself out of it. His wife wasn't her responsibility, as such, but she mattered. Anyway, if she and Harry began an actual affair, what could it lead to? On the other hand, how could she stop it? Harry was so wholehearted and committed to Lily, she sometimes forgot he was formally committed to someone else. For all her sensible resolutions when they were apart, being in his presence was another matter entirely. These three days in Frankfurt marked a watershed: Lily knew that if anything was going to happen, it would happen there.

She had talked to her big sister about Harry a lot. Cassie had met him and liked him, but she warned her not to get involved. "I know he cares about you, Lil—I've seen the way he looks at you—but honestly? It's just going to end with everyone getting hurt." The night before she left London, Lily kept thinking about what Cassie had said. How was it possible now to go back, to undo the bond between them? They were like magnets in each other's presence.

The company secretary had booked them on an early flight, so they met at City Airport at six a.m. It felt somehow clandestine: meeting at dawn, having coffee in the airport lounge, reading each other their horoscopes from the newspaper. Harry was wearing jeans; Lily's hair was still damp from her shower; everything felt different from the office. There was an intimacy to the travel routines, taking off their belts and shoes at the security gate, alone together at the back of the half-empty plane. On the short flight across Europe, their conversation was punctuated by moments of shyness; Harry would break off, lost in the middle of a sentence, just looking at Lily, and she'd smile back, questioningly.

———————

THE FRANKFURT SCHEDULE WAS PACKED.
After checking in at their hotel, they had various meetings with
agents about potential rights deals before lunch with authors. Then
it was straight into meetings with a group of French and German
academics about writing a European-style International
Baccalaureate course in psychology. It was an area which Harry was
keen to develop, a potentially lucrative market, and Lily had been
working on the proposal since she had joined Higher Education
Press six months earlier. The International Bac was very different
from the UK curriculum, and it took hours of discussion to agree on
a framework which everyone was happy with. After that, they took
a taxi to a drinks reception for the international sales reps, where
Harry gave a short presentation on the latest company news.

Working like this, rushing around Frankfurt, grabbing food in
between meetings, out of the familiar office environment, Lily felt
even closer to Harry. She was seeing a new side to him, the capable,
sociable—and yes, powerful—strategic director. She noticed the
respect he drew from others. And yet he wore his power lightly. He
wasn't pompous or self-important: he listened to others, discussed
their ideas, and then made firm, clear decisions. He was sharp, and
Lily admired sharp people (Cassie had described her as a "sapio-
phile"). Until Frankfurt Lily had thought she was in control of the
Harry situation, or at least in control of her own actions. Now she
wasn't so sure.

BY THE TIME THEY ESCAPED THE DRINKS
reception, it was after seven p.m. In the taxi back to the hotel, Harry

stretched and rubbed his back, trying not to let Lily see. He was in agony from the flight, then hours of sitting on too-soft chairs, and he didn't have his TENS machine with him.

Lily nudged his knee with hers. "Your back's killing you, isn't it?"

Harry smiled and said: "Oh, it's not too bad. Well, a bit . . ." He'd suffered appalling back pain since his twenties. Nothing cured it, not the two operations he'd had, nor his weekly hydrotherapy sessions. Regular massages helped, and the painkillers of course. At the office the staff were used to Harry's unorthodox habits; even in board meetings he'd walk up and down the room, rubbing his back, unable to sit in the same position for long. Over the years, Harry had also battled major depression, which coincided with the most acute episodes of back pain, the one exacerbating the other.

Lily wished she could help. Although he put a brave face on it, she knew that he was in pain much of the time. Often, it brought him very low. "Harry, you look really tired," she said. "Don't worry about dinner, you need an early night. We've got more meetings tomorrow, and you should rest your back."

"Don't be silly, we don't need to cancel tonight," Harry said. "I've been looking forward to it all day. I'll be fine after a hot bath and some pills. How about we move the reservation to eight o'clock, would you mind? That would give me time for a soak, then I'll be right as rain."

"Are you sure?" Lily said as Harry limped beside her, out of the taxi and into the hotel lobby. "It looks really bad."

"Seriously, Lil, we're not cancelling anything. I'll be better once I've had a drink." Harry smiled and tried to walk normally. He felt like an old man, hobbling along beside her clutching his bloody back. Was this what love did, he wondered, make you feel ancient? "I'll change the reservation, and see you down here at, say, ten to eight?"

Back in his hotel room Harry was like a maniac, pulling shirts out of his bag in an attempt to find his razor, brushing his teeth while he checked his phone. Dammit, there were three missed calls from Pippa.

Lying in a bath as hot as he could bear it, willing the muscles in his back to relax, Harry called home. Daniel answered, and then Joe came on, and they chatted to their dad for a while, Dan telling him about rugby training, Joe interrupting to tell him about his Pokémon progress. Then he spoke to his wife briefly, explaining that he'd been in meetings all day. She asked about his plans for the evening and Harry said he was going out for a meal with his old friend Will, a botanist at the university.

That was the first lie. Changing into a fresh shirt and jeans, Harry asked himself why he'd said that. Pippa knew they were here on business, but since she'd found out that Lily was coming with him she'd kept asking questions. She even demanded to know which hotel he was staying in, something she'd never done before. Thus far, he had not tried to hide his friendship with Lily; Pippa knew they got on well and worked closely together. When they went for drinks after work, he mentioned it, usually. Did Pippa suspect something? Waiting for the lift, Harry wondered whether or not he cared.

Striding through the lobby at a quarter to eight, he realised that the pain had disappeared. The hot water seemed to have done the trick, or maybe it was the double dose of painkillers with vodka from the minibar. Either way, he was a new man. Dinner with Lily. It felt like a date. He asked the concierge to call a taxi, then waited in the lobby. At five to eight, the lift doors opened and there she was.

"Sorry to keep you waiting." Lily had changed into a simple black dress which skimmed her body, the thin straps leaving her shoulders and collarbone bare. Her hair was loose now, and her eyes were touched with just a hint of dark kohl eyeliner and mascara. "Had a quick shower, I feel much better now. And rang my mum too." She chattered away lightly. "How's your room? More importantly, how's your back?"

"Thanks, my back's good—room's good too." Harry was still taking her in. "Are you going to be OK like that? We've got a cab waiting, but I don't want you getting cold." He gestured at her bare shoulders, and in reply, Lily waved her cardigan at him.

They walked through the hotel lobby. Opening the door of the taxi, Harry said, quietly: "By the way, you look beautiful in that dress."

YEARS LATER, LILY WOULD WONDER IF IT was inevitable, their meeting, the connection, and everything which followed. In another world, perhaps they might have continued like that, flirtatious colleagues who never crossed that boundary. But all evening, in that restaurant, they were teetering on the edge. The dynamic had shifted. Harry was no longer just her eccentric boss, who liked to drink and smoke and talk too much. But what, really, could their relationship ever be?

As for Harry, he was sunk. Whatever they were talking about he couldn't be sure, but he couldn't take his eyes from her shoulders, the curve of her collarbone, her clavicle. Through his mind there floated half-remembered lines from Balzac, something about *a woman with a complexion as fine as porcelain, a mouth like a half-burst pomegranate* . . . In the taxi, he breathed in the scent of her hair. When she crossed the restaurant in that black dress, coming back from the bathroom, weaving through a crowd of men at the bar, walking towards him, Harry felt his heart banging in his chest.

Their first kiss was deadly serious. It was nearly midnight and freezing cold. They were crossing the deserted square in front of the town hall when Lily stopped. She looked at him and smiled, and time seemed to stop. Slowly, Harry took her hand and kissed it, just barely touching her knuckles with his lips, drawing her closer to him. They stood there, silent, their faces inches apart. Her brown eyes flashed green in the streetlight as she lifted her mouth to his.

Without words, it was clear that the line had been crossed. Everything up to this point was *before,* and now everything else would be *after.* They walked slowly back to the hotel, not feeling the cold, and sat in the bar, drinking hot, strong espressos, fingers linked, talking. Around two a.m. the bar closed and they wandered across the empty lobby.

"It's late," Lily said as they waited for the lift. "And we have so many meetings tomorrow . . . Whose bright idea was it to drink coffee?"

"Actually it was your bright idea," Harry said. "To sober us up."

"You're right." She smiled. "Dammit. Now I'm going to be awake for hours."

They didn't make love that night. In Harry's room, they drank a nightcap, showered together, lay on the bed, and found *Lost in Translation* on Netflix. Halfway through the movie, Harry realised that Lily had fallen asleep. She was curled up under the sheet, her head against a pillow, one arm across his chest. Gently, so as not to wake her, he reached for the remote and clicked off the TV.

For the first time since leaving London, Harry was properly alone with his thoughts. Here she was, naked, beside him. But he didn't feel guilty. Instead, he felt an uncontainable joy. He gazed and gazed at Lily, young and defenceless in sleep. At one corner of her mouth, the pillow was slightly damp. Harry had watched his boys sleeping this way too, open-mouthed, leaving a tiny patch of dribble on the pillow. Had Lily's father watched over her like this as a child?

Outside, the wind was picking up. It lifted one corner of the curtain where they had opened a window, and showed a grey day dawning. Harry felt the familiar heaviness descending as he considered the future. Everything would change; everything would end.

He wanted this moment to last. He put his arm over Lily's arm, encircling her, and lay awake listening to the gentle rain.

LILY RARELY SPOKE ABOUT HER FATHER, and she tried not to think about him either. But they had all been thinking about him on the day of Cassie's wedding.

The preparations had been complicated, even by Cassie's perfectionist standards. "If I was Cass, I'd be too exhausted to enjoy the wedding after all this," Lily said to her younger sister, Olivia, at the final church rehearsal in Covent Garden. The vicar led them through each stage, walking up the aisle behind their big sister, dealing with the veil and flowers, the wedding poems and signing the registry. All dressed in blue jeans, Cassie; her future husband, Charlie; Lily; and Olivia practised their stately procession to the strains of *Pachelbel's Canon*, imagining the pews filled with hundreds of guests in a few days' time.

ON THE MORNING ITSELF, CASSIE, LILY, Olivia, and their brother James gathered at the de Jongh family home in Hampstead. This was where the four of them had grown up; their parents had bought it decades earlier when spacious, run-down houses in North London were still affordable for young couples just starting out.

De Jongh was their father's name. His ancestors had come over from Holland in the early twentieth century, Amsterdam Jews who made their money in the diamond trade. Celia de Jongh (she had kept her husband's surname) wasn't rich, but after a lifetime working as a dress designer and museum curator, she had saved enough to get by. Despite the exotic heritage on their father's side of the family, none of the children spoke Dutch, nor had they been to Holland. All they had was his unusual surname.

The family joke was "de-Jongh-where-does-that-come-from?" because they could never tell anyone their surname without the question being asked. Although that wouldn't be a problem for Cassie once she was married—Charlie's surname was a good English one: Taylor.

Celia had called a final family gathering before her eldest daughter's wedding. So, before the hairdressing and make-up and pinning of silk dresses began, the five of them sat down to brunch in the garden. It was unexpectedly warm for late spring, a brilliant May morning.

The doorbell rang. "Wedding!" Celia interrupted her oldest and youngest daughters, who even at the ages of thirty-one and twenty-five were squabbling over the last piece of toast. "Are you still planning to get married, Cass, because I think that's the hairdresser at the door." Cassie ran towards the house, closely followed by Olivia, who was muttering something about her dress not fitting.

James leaned back in his chair and stretched, as if he didn't have a care in the world, let alone a sister to walk up the aisle in less than three hours. He rolled himself a neat joint and wandered over to the garden shed. Lily helped Celia carry the breakfast plates and mugs into the kitchen, then joined James for a smoke. The last few months had been a blur, not only of wedding mania, but also Harry. Lily felt emotionally exhausted, raw with love and passion, and uncharacteristically on edge. Before she turned into chief bridesmaid, she needed something to relax her.

FINDING THE BRIDESMAIDS OUTFITS HAD
been a challenge—or as Cassie had said when they returned home
that day, "a complete bloody nightmare." Olivia had wanted something dramatic and busty, possibly in fuchsia or scarlet. Lily wanted
something classy and understated, preferably in ivory or cream.

The problem was finding something which suited them both.
Although they were close as sisters, physically they were completely
different. In fact, the only similarities between them were their
height—both girls were five feet seven—and their identical voices.

Olivia was currently a brunette (she changed the colour quite
often): a glossy, raven shade from a bottle. She had a heart-shaped
face, pale skin, and light blue eyes. She didn't know it, but she
resembled her father Claude in both temperament and appearance.
She was strong and stubborn, a true Taurean, and she had curves; in
previous centuries, she would have been called Rubenesque. Dressed
up or dressed down, Olivia had that knack of looking striking: hair
piled haphazardly on top of her head or shoved into a beanie hat,
last night's make-up still smudged sexily around her eyes. Winter
or summer, she wore layered, strappy tops which showed her cleavage, strong legs encased in jeans or a short skirt, her outfits a casual,
eye-popping ensemble of clashing colours. Olivia smiled a lot, and
she was naturally sunny and sociable. Celia always said that her
third daughter would one day slay a man with those dimples.

Lily had no dimples: instead she had cheekbones. Where Olivia
resembled their father, Lily took after their mother. She had Celia's
slender frame and olive complexion; they both tanned easily and
kept the colour most of the year. She had her mother's large, brown,
oval-shaped eyes which flickered from green to hazel depending on
the light. As a teenager, her hair had been peroxide blonde—even

magenta once—but these days it was natural mid-brown with a few blonde highlights. She wore it long and straight with a centre parting, nothing too high maintenance. Her expression was serious; if you caught her deep in thought, she could look stern. But then she smiled, and those cheekbones changed her expression completely.

Like her hairstyle, Lily's clothes were unfussy: skinny blue jeans, white T-shirts, navy cashmere jumpers, tops in pale blue or oatmeal, smarter trousers in grey. She didn't wear much black—she had lived in black clothes as a teenager and got sick of it.

When it came to the bridesmaids' dresses, it was clear that Lily and Olivia were looking for very different things. Poor Cassie, who was actually getting married, was caught in the middle with just her credit card, trying to mediate between them. Lily wanted classic, Olivia wanted dramatic.

Finally, against the odds, they found a style which suited them both. It had taken hours of searching, first in specialist bridal boutiques, then designer stores, then finally in an upmarket vintage shop in Marylebone High Street. The perfect dresses: pale pink silk, full-length with delicate ribbon straps, elegant but not Barbie doll.

The next miracle was that the dresses could be altered by the first of May. The final stroke of luck was finding two pairs of shoes, in pale pink and white silk. They both struggled to walk in the shoes, but as Olivia said: "Who cares? We just have to get up the aisle behind Cass without falling over. And later at the reception, everyone will be falling over, so that's fine." Hearing this, Cassie wasn't sure that her youngest sister was particularly going to raise the tone of her chic London wedding—but one needed two bridesmaids really, for balance.

"THE FIRST TIME WE HAD SEX? IT WAS IN Frankfurt, not that night—she fell asleep, I watched her sleeping for hours—but in the morning. We woke early, and it was . . . I can't describe it, like waking up and discovering the whole world had changed." Harry looked at Dr. Christos sadly.

"Until the day I die, I'll never forget that morning with Lily. The sex was great, of course, but I mean everything else too, taking a bath together afterwards, watching her wrapped in the hotel bathrobe, laughing, running down the corridor back to her room to get clothes, then meeting in the restaurant for breakfast. All day, being beside her, having this amazing secret between us. Our relationship had gone from a warm glow to a fiery explosion. In the weeks which followed, I swear I'd never been so alive, never experienced life so intensely."

"IT'S FINE—WE'LL KEEP THINGS UNDER control," Lily told Cassie on her return from Frankfurt. "The important thing is that we can still work together, that we like and respect each other."

"And what about his wife?" Cassie asked. "Is she going to be fine with it? What happens when she finds out—is he leaving her?"

Lily shook her head vehemently. "No, things are never going to get that far. No one's leaving anyone. I don't want him to leave his wife, and there's no need."

THE HARRY SITUATION WAS WORRYING
Lily more than she would admit to herself. What she had thought
in winter might be a brief affair was still going strong in spring. She
was more in love with Harry now than at the start. And yet she
knew it was wrong, and she was trying to keep things under control.
His wife wouldn't find out. Everything was fine. Here she was, with
Cassie and Olivia, getting ready for the wedding in her mother's
guest bedroom. Lily began to feel jittery and excited on her big
sister's behalf about the upcoming ceremony.

An old school friend of Cassie's had offered her professional hair
and make-up services as a wedding present. Lily's hair was blow-
dried straight and glossy, with a tiny plait of pink roses around the
crown, and Olivia's hair was piled into an elegant up-do, with red
roses scattered across the chignon. While Cassie's hair was being
done, Lily and Olivia walked up and down the hallway, practising
the walk in their vertiginous shoes.

When all three girls were ready, Celia had a quick go in the
make-up chair. She'd already "put her face on," she protested (they
smiled at the 1960s terminology, and their mum's unique ability to
smudge her eyeliner), so the beautician tactfully tidied it up, added
a dash of base colour, and neatened up her bohemian bird's nest
hairdo. Celia had never exactly been *soignée*, but her cheekbones
and large hazel eyes made up for the haphazard hair and wonky
lipstick.

By this time, Clive the photographer had arrived. He appeared
completely at ease in the bridal mayhem: a tangle of silk stockings
and women's underwear, discarded coffee cups and cosmetics. They
were slightly self-conscious at first, but Clive was so laid-back that
they soon forgot he was there; Cassie later found his series of *getting*

ready photographs with her sisters and mother among the most natural and captivating of all the wedding day images.

The taxi which was to take them to Covent Garden arrived at two thirty p.m. Their hair and make-up were done, their dresses and bouquets were in place. But where was their brother?

When James appeared in the kitchen, they all fell silent. The transformation was remarkable. In between reading the newspaper, rolling cigarettes, and enjoying the sunshine in the garden, he'd taken it upon himself to shower, shave, and change out of his T-shirt and boxer shorts. He was wearing the morning suit Celia had hired for him: black cutaway jacket, pinstriped trousers, dove-grey waist-coat, and white shirt. He looked older than twenty-three all of a sudden, and very handsome. He gave Cassie a quick hug, and they practised a stately march across the terrace.

It wasn't just Celia who thought about what James was doing that day, giving Cassie away in place of the man who should have been there. Even James, who'd never met his father, was thinking of him on Cassie's wedding day.

*   *   *

If he has nothing to hide, why would he lie? Does honesty even mean any-thing to him anymore? I am so confused. I can't work out what's true and what's not, why he never seems to want to be here, whether I'm being paranoid, suspicious, or a total fool. I've just opened a second bottle of red—Harry's "working late" again—and I intend to drink every last drop.

Remember that Frankfurt trip he went on back in the autumn? It's their annual publishing get-together, he's been going for years. Once I went with him, before Dan was born. Actually it was the most boring four days of my life and I flew home early.

Anyway, I know the hotel he stays in, so I ended up ringing them to check up on him—not proud of this but there you go—I asked the recep-

tionist how many rooms were booked for their firm, because of that Lily woman he works with and seems so close to . . . The hotel had one room booked in Harry's name, one in her name, and for a couple of their sales people, so I assumed it was all kosher and there was nothing going on between them.

Then today, I was leaving Waitrose and I bumped into Fiona Parr, literally haven't seen her for years. She's the sister of an old friend of Harry's, a guy named Will who is a professor of botany or something in Frankfurt. Well, I thought he was, but it turns out he moved to Japan quite a while back.

What the f??? I know it's six months ago now—but I specifically remember speaking to Harry in Frankfurt and him telling me he was going out for dinner with Will. It was evening and I'd been trying to get hold of him all day, I wanted to discuss Dan's winter rugby schedule. So there I am, this afternoon, telling Fiona that Harry and Will met up in Frankfurt last October, and Fiona gives me an odd look and says that he's been in Japan for the past three years, that he hasn't been back to Europe since his wife had twins last summer, but they're hoping to see him soon. I actually felt sick when she said that—I garbled something about it being another friend called Will, but I could see she was curious.

So now what? This takes me back to last autumn and winter when he was acting so strange, working late at the office the whole time, and drinking when he was home, detached and somehow distant. I was convinced something was wrong, but was he cheating on me, or having a breakdown, or something else? So I began sneaking around, looking at his web browsing history, trying to listen in to phone calls and find his bank statements, even checking his jacket pockets for receipts—God, I despised myself for doing that. Then we talked and he agreed to go back and see Dr. Christos, and since then things have improved, at least I thought they had. We started having sex again, and he sent me on that amazing spa weekend for my birthday, and he's booked for me and the *boys to go to stay with my parents in Florida next month. But it looks like he lied about Frankfurt, so now there are other things I'm wondering about. The evenings he stays up in London—he always used to get the last train back, no matter how late he worked. His erratic mood swings: sometimes so depressed, then sometimes incredibly happy and full of joy. The constant texting and phoning late at night: yes, he still does. I haven't written much on my blog about it, these past few months, because . . . I'm scared to admit it . . . Harry's always been a bit volatile, he gets low, and he can be tricky sometimes, but what if this is different—what if there's something fundamentally broken in our marriage? I'm scared to do any more snooping, in case I find out—because what then?*

I can't get Fiona's expression out of my mind: sympathetic but pitying. Why would Harry invent that about seeing Will if he wasn't? What was he doing? What's he doing right now?

"I'D LIKE TO PUT IN AN OFFER." SHE COULDN'T afford it. But with Harry's money, she could.

Lily was viewing the Belsize Park flat again, alone this time, and she knew it was perfect for her. This flat at this price was a rarity—by rights it should have sold instantly. The only reason it hadn't, according to the estate agent, was that the owner was very particular about the buyer. "She wants to share her house with someone nice," he said, looking slightly weary.

Lily had been back in the flat less than five minutes when she decided. She wasn't being impetuous: she'd done the rounds of hopeless flats, and she could tell within a few moments of walking into a place whether she could live there. The estate agent was pleasant enough, but his professional patter was wasted on Lily. She wasn't going to be talked into something which wasn't right, even if he was losing patience with her. The flats he had shown her in

Hampstead, Kilburn, and Kentish Town were either way too small or way too expensive, usually both.

This flat was on the second and third floors of a huge leafy villa on England's Lane, a road connecting Belsize Park with Primrose Hill. Huge bay windows meant that light flooded into all the rooms. There were two bedrooms at the top—the larger one with sloping ceilings and a skylight. There was also a small boxroom, ideal for a home office. The kitchen was a little battered but functional, large enough to hold a wooden table and chairs; the living room looked out onto the street, with stripped pine floorboards and lots of bookshelves. Best of all, there was a thirty-foot garden at the back of the house, and a small roof terrace, to which Lily would have access.

Lily loved split-level flats, as she explained to Harry at that first viewing. "I don't know why, but I really like stairs. There's something about being all on one level which makes me feel confined." Lily had already fallen for the flat, but she wanted it confirmed by someone more objective. "What do you think, isn't the light fantastic?"

"It's perfect, Lil." Harry stood in the middle of the empty living room and looked around. "And the cafés and bars along England's Lane are great too." The estate agent was outside in his car this time, catching up on phone calls. "The kitchen could do with some modernising, but it's definitely all here. So much space—and you can really make it your own. And you said the old lady was happy for you to use the garden?"

The "old lady" was Susan Archer—or Lady Archer as Lily had glimpsed on an envelope in the hall. She wasn't really old, mid-sixties perhaps; on her second viewing, Lily had passed her sailing out of the front door in a whiff of Chanel No. 5 and a flutter of Hermès scarves. She had perfectly blow-dried ash-blonde hair, immaculate make-up, and an elegant pair of legs in black tights. Her pink suede kitten heels matched her silk scarf. She smiled, but clearly didn't have time to stop and chat. In the street outside Lily saw her getting into a car with a handsome gentleman in his seventies. All steel-grey hair and navy cashmere coat, he could easily have been a cabinet minister.

Lily was well aware that anyone who viewed this flat, at this price, would want to buy it. Estate agents were masters of persuasion, but when he said there had been a lot of interest, she knew it was the truth. Without working out exactly where it was coming from, she decided to offer the asking price on the spot. Then there was the anxious wait overnight while the estate agent spoke to the Lady.

Until a few years before, Susan Archer had occupied the whole house with Rollo, her husband of forty years. When he died, Susan had moved to the ground and first floors, and converted the upper second and third floors into a large self-contained flat. Her daughter had lived there for a year or so, with husband and children, happy to share the garden with her mother, helping with housework and shopping in return for the odd night's babysitting. Now the family were moving to Dubai for the husband's work and Susan had decided to sell the flat. She had always been privately wealthy, so the selling price was reasonable—ridiculous for Belsize Park, really. In the first week that the flat was on the market, there were nine firm offers, four of them above the asking price. The estate agents were eager to hustle her into a quick transaction but Susan wouldn't be rushed: she wanted the flat to go to "someone nice."

As it turned out, Lily was that person. Susan may not have stopped to chat, but she had noticed the young woman with the estate agent that morning. Something about Lily reminded her of herself at that age: she identified with that quiet, determined look, the anxious, pretty face. Susan's life was busy—she sat in the House of Lords and was out most evenings too. She wasn't looking for a carer or a replacement daughter, but she loved young people and she missed her daughter and grandchildren being around. When they lived upstairs, the house was alive with the sound of footsteps and laughter, comings and goings. Lily was offering the asking price, half in cash, and that was good enough for her.

"ARE YOU SURE ABOUT THIS?" LILY ASKED Harry. He'd booked their initial viewing that day Pippa came home early and almost caught her in the shower. They were sitting in The Washington, a pub on the corner of England's Lane a few minutes from the house. "It's a lot of money, and I won't be able to pay you back for years."

"Lily, forget it. You're not paying me back. The flat's ideal and I want you to have it."

"But how are you going to get your hands on so much money—won't . . ." Lily hesitated to refer to his wife—she'd never said her name out loud. "Won't anyone notice?"

"It's fine. It's my money, I've got various accounts and investments, no one needs to know." Like Lily, Harry avoided mentioning Pippa by name. "But, if you don't mind, I'd prefer you not to tell anyone—not even your family." He knew she shared everything with Cassie and Celia. "I don't want them to suspect me of ulterior motives or anything. It's best kept between ourselves."

Lily nodded. "Of course. I won't breathe a word. And I promise, if there's ever anything I can do—or if I win the lottery or something—I want to repay you someday, Harry."

"Stop it." Harry leaned forward and kissed her lightly. "The flat's yours."

*   *   *

"You know the problem with exercise?" Polly's driving us back to her house after our Friday night Zumba class. We're both red-faced from an

hour's thrusting and twisting to fast Latin music, all of us forty-somethings dripping with sweat inside our expensive athleisure wear. "It makes me unbelievably ravenous."

I nod. "I do worry that the raging hunger after every class cancels out the exercise, Poll."

The back seat is covered in takeaway bags, a large selection of sushi, bento, and salads, but we both know that Itsu's "light bites" aren't going to cut it. Polly's theory is that we should work out together three times a week, getting enthused by new and fun things like Zumba or capoeira, and eat small quantities of virtuous but nourishing food, and by the time the new year arrives we'll be svelte, with glowing skin and abundant energy. But, as my sister points out, exercise makes you so damn hungry.

"So . . . snacks, yes or no? Snacks?" Polly slows down as she approaches the petrol station, our last chance to stock up on carbs, chocolate, and ice cream before we reach the house. We both know the snack stop is coming, and we both know we can't resist. At the crucial moment, I give in: "Yes!" She whoops and swings the car into the forecourt.

Polly's husband, Andrew, and the kids are out at the cinema, so we have the house blissfully to ourselves. We take it in turns to shower, change into cashmere pants, and open a bottle of red. Having devoured all the Itsu in about five minutes, we adjourn to the sofa with large glasses of wine, Love Island on the TV, tortilla chips and dips, a family-sized bag of mini Mars bars, and two kinds of Ben & Jerry's waiting in the freezer.

The subject turns, naturally to Harry, and the latest on this "interfering bitch" at work. (Forgive me, I'd had a lot of wine, but she is a bitch, interfering with my husband.) "Let's google her," Polly says.

Oh my God, we get sucked in. Big time. I should disclose at this point that I know what she looks like. I actually looked at her photograph on the Higher Ed Press website the very first time Harry oh-so-casually mentioned her name. A nice young woman had joined his editorial team, he said, and I knew something was up. It was in his voice. The look in his eyes.

"Forget the boring work profiles," Polly says. "We need to check out her social media." Lily's surname is unusual, German or Dutch or something, so she's easy to find. Her Facebook page is public, the usual mix of cute cats, news stories, uplifting quotes, and pictures of her with her family and friends. Then we find her on Twitter and that leads us to Instagram. Which is where it all goes wrong.

Polly's scrolling through Lily's photos, being loyal and critical for my sake, telling me she's not all that pretty really, and my goodness what's she wearing in that one? Then I spot something and grab the tablet from her hands. Lily is lolling on a rumpled white bed, her hair damp, her skin tanned, wearing nothing but a man's blue shirt. My body goes cold. I recognise that shirt; I picked it out, for God's sake.

I zoom in to confirm what I already know, on the top pocket, a tiny HL monogram in dark blue. I bought this shirt in Italy on his fortieth birthday.

I check the date below the image—September, which I know coincides with a weekend Harry spent in Lisbon. He told me he was at an international publishing convention. Feeling sick I look again at the photo. I don't need to see it's my husband's watch on the bedside table, his glasses. She's tagged the image #portugal #paradise #perfect.

UNLIKE LILY'S PREVIOUS EXPERIENCES OF moving flats, this time it went like clockwork. In the weeks leading up to the December moving date, she found a man-with-a-van on the internet and booked him for the whole day, negotiating an affordable rate by paying in cash. The driver of the van was a young Polish man called Pawel, and he offered to bring a few friends to help with packing as well as moving. For an extra fifty pounds, his girlfriend would give her old flat a final clean when it was empty.

So there wasn't much for Lily to do. She boxed up smaller, personal things in the Camden flat—her clothes, toiletries, essentials from the kitchen—and left everything else to Pawel's team. They packed the contents of the bookshelves into large crates and hauled out the few items of furniture she was taking with her to England's Lane. On the morning of the move, Lily went to work as usual. At six p.m. her phone rang; it was Pawel calling to give her the all-clear. The Camden flat was empty and clean, the Belsize Park flat was full. She took the bus to her new home, stopping on her walk from the bus stop to buy a wintry spray of delphiniums and a bottle of white wine, lingering in the chilly evening air, delaying the thrill of putting her new keys into her new door.

She didn't tell anyone, that first night. Fortunately, Harry wasn't at work—he'd left early for a rare family weekend away. Although she was looking forward to celebrating in the flat with him, she wanted it all to herself in those first few hours.

That weekend, Lily's family descended en masse, in theory to help her settle in, although they created more chaos than order. Her brother, James, came over and helped her paint both bedrooms, and she and Cassie made a trip to IKEA for essential supplies: a large desk, bookshelves, a swivel chair for her new home office. They were barely home with all the flat packs before Cassie was online searching for beds to replace the perfectly serviceable one which Susan had left in the flat.

"But this one looks practically new," Lily said. "OK, it's at the smaller end of double, but I can't really justify buying a new one, can I?"

"It's absolutely tiny," Cassie said. "More like a large single than a double, if you ask me. It may be fine for one person, but as soon as you're sharing it, you'll notice. And trust me, if you don't order a new one now, along with all the rest of the furniture, you'll end up keeping it for years."

"I *have* been wanting to upgrade to a massive bed for years," Lily said, eyeing the spacious super-king-sized models on Cassie's screen. "But they're so expensive—and look, those prices don't even include the mattress!"

"Lily, sleep is essential for optimum health, and you're always saying you don't sleep well anyway." Cassie looked stern. "We spend around a third of our lives in bed, so why wouldn't you give yourself the best? A high-quality bed and mattress are one of the most important investments you can make for your own well-being."

"You know what?" Lily smiled. "You're right. When I think about how much the flat itself is costing . . ."

She had kept her word and told no one, not even Cassie. Harry had bought a quarter of the flat—had paid £150,000 as a cash deposit, in fact. It still worried Lily, not so much the secrecy as the obligation it put her under, the sense of culpability that she was accepting money from a man who was married to someone else.

And yet Harry had been very clear, he wasn't buying a share in it. Even when he transferred the money into her account he said, "This is your place, Lil, I want you to understand that. I'm not expecting to get twenty-five per cent of the proceeds when you sell it, or spend a quarter of my time there or anything like that." Although Lily knew that if she'd asked him to move in with her, he'd be there like a shot.

IN THOSE FIRST FEW WEEKS IN THE FLAT, she worried a lot about the situation with Harry. A few days before Christmas, they had a small celebration: Harry wanted to bring over her presents before he left for his obligatory trip to Pippa's family up north. "I'm dreading it," he said as they sat in front of the living room fire, next to the small Christmas tree Lily had bought. "I wouldn't mind a day or two, but for some reason we have to stay until New Year, it's torture. The in-laws are OK, but mobile reception is hopeless and there are no pubs for miles around. I'll be taking their dogs for very long walks, I think!"

As Harry stretched on the rug talking about Christmas with the in-laws, Lily tuned out, watching the firelight flicker in his eyes. She remembered a line from one her favourite writers Haruki Murakami: "... how people's eyes have something honest about them when they're watching a fire." Harry made light of the family situation, but the strain was etched into his face and the sadness showed in his eyes. Years of depression and the constant back pain he suffered were taking their toll, although he would never admit it. That combination of strength and vulnerability wrenched at her heart.

Harry was a big man—not fat but tall, six feet three and powerfully built. He was robust, what used to be called hale and hearty. In truth, he wasn't healthy. He smoked and drank far too much, and never did any exercise except for the odd game of tennis, but he had that outdoorsy colour of a certain class of Englishman. His skin was tanned, his hair was brown, floppy, streaked like a yachtsman's from the sun. He was in his late forties and looked it: crumpled and handsome and confident.

Harry's eyes were blue; piercing, bright, forget-me-not blue. In the years to come, Lily would always remember those eyes, and see his big hands cradling the stem of a wineglass, cupped around the flame as he lit a cigarette, the span of his fingers across her naked body.

Faint sounds drifted up from Belsize Park far below, people leaving restaurants and wine bars and Christmas parties. Harry wandered over to the window to smoke a cigarette. She wouldn't ask him to move in with her, not until he was free. He was a good man, for all his demons, and she loved him. But she couldn't be the reason for him leaving his wife and sons. She already knew too much about broken families.

Lily picked up their empty wineglasses and moved towards the kitchen to make coffee. She had been thinking more than usual about families recently—about her father, in particular. Perhaps it was her relationship with Harry, or the death of his own father, or just part of getting older. She had started wondering if she might meet her father again one day.

CHRISTMAS HAD BEEN A BIG OCCASION for the de Jongh family ever since they were little, and it was always spent at Celia's house in Hampstead. In the England's Lane flat on Christmas Eve, Lily had wrapped piles of presents, listening to the choristers singing the "Nine Lessons and Carols" on Radio 4 whilst sipping a sherry.

On Christmas morning she woke early, enjoying her solitude in the huge new bed, went for a run on Primrose Hill, and was showered, ready, and waiting for Cassie and Charlie to collect her by ten a.m. Arriving at Celia's house they were greeted with large glasses of white wine from James who had stayed at his mother's the night before. Then Celia appeared, wearing one of her extraordinary velvet gowns, and ushered them into the kitchen. "What can I do, Mum?" Lily said, hugging her mother, noticing how tired she looked.

"I think everything's under control. Although," Celia looked at the overflowing fruit bowl, "maybe you could make a lovely fruit salad, you know, the one you always make? I'm not sure if there's going to be enough Christmas pudding to go round. I've made an apple pie and a rather alcoholic trifle, although I don't know if it's set . . ." She trailed off, opening the fridge.

Lily felt a flash of irritation. For goodness' sake, she'd made a fruit salad once or twice and forever afterwards her mother referred to *those fruit salads you make,* as if Lily had a master's degree in it. But then she caught herself: it was unfair to blame Celia for being vague, today of all days. Hosting Christmas wasn't easy, and their mother did this for all of them, year after year. She had probably been up since dawn defrosting the turkey; the house was warm and welcoming; there were piles of presents under the tree. Festive decorations had been woven haphazardly around doorframes and along bannisters, a string of Christmas cards adorned the mantelpiece, and carol music played in the background. The fridge was groaning with food (far too much, of course) and the bedrooms were made up for any of the children who wanted to stay the night. Celia had a houseful of people and was as welcoming as ever; Lily knew it wasn't fair to get exasperated about fruit salads.

Anyway, her task could have been worse. Cassie was on vegetable duty, peeling mounds of potatoes at the sink, her hands submerged in muddy water and brown peelings. James and his girlfriend drifted into the kitchen to refill their wineglasses, then, seeing there was work to be done, they drifted out again to smoke in the garden.

"How did Mum get hold of kiwis at this time of year?" Lily said, placing an empty glass bowl beside the full fruit bowl and spreading a cloth on the table. She chose the sharpest knife from the drawer. "I thought it was all satsumas and Cox's apples in December." She and Cassie chatted casually as they worked. Cassie was telling her about the service for midnight mass which Charlie had taken her to the night before in St. Paul's Cathedral, and how they'd walked home afterwards. Lily listened, picturing the moonlight on the River Thames.

"It sounds lovely, Cass, really romantic. Do you think Mum will notice if I don't peel the apples?" Lily chopped and diced the fruit, trying to vary the layers of colour in the glass bowl: apples and pears, kiwis and strawberries. She took gulps of wine as she worked, her hands slippery with the different juices on the stem of her glass.

Celia floated back into the kitchen and pronounced Lily's salad a "work of art." They emptied a carton of orange juice over the fruit and covered the bowl with cling film. Then Cassie said that fruit salads had to be lightly chilled so they had to move everything around in the overstocked fridge to make room for it.

Peeling duties over, Lily and Cassie sat at the kitchen table with mugs of peppermint tea, while Celia darted around the kitchen. She looked sublime—"a sublime fire risk," James said—in her trailing feather boa. She basted the turkey which was roasting in the oven, wedged in three baking trays of potatoes, and organised the different pans of vegetables on the top of the stove, ready to be quickly steamed before lunch: Brussels sprouts, peas, carrots, and red cabbage.

By midday everyone had arrived, and once they had replenished pots of tea, cups of coffee, and glasses of wine, they gathered in the living room for the main event.

In the dark red armchair was Celia, resplendent in her velvet and feathers. Cassie and Charlie were squashed together on the small sofa by the fireplace, celebrating their first Christmas as a married couple. Next was James and his girlfriend, Su-Ki, then Olivia and her boyfriend, Giovanni, over from Rome for the holidays. As well as the siblings and partners, there was Aunt Marie, now in her eighties and quite hard of hearing, and Celia's best friend, Carolyn, who was visiting from France. Ten in all, although the conversation levels sounded like twenty.

Lily's phone rang, and she went into the hallway to take it. Harry of course. "Happy Christmas, darling," he whispered.

She smiled. "Sounds like you're hiding in a hedge! Happy Christmas to you too. How's it going?"

"Oh, gruesome, you know. House full of my wife's relatives, the boys have disappeared to play computer games, I'm hiding in the garden with a bottle of whisky."

"Whisky, at this time?" Lily tried to sound shocked. "You're going to make yourself sick."

"I'm already sick with missing you."

"Stop it. Plenty of relatives here too, no whisky as yet." She wanted to say she missed him too, that she loved him, but something held her back. "We're about to start presents, I've got to go."

"OK. And Lil, are you around when I get back, just at the start of January? I'll come into London, I've got a few things for the new place."

She felt a twinge of anxiety at his reference to "the new place," as if it were theirs together, as if they were setting up a love nest. The familiar guilt flooded through her. She wished again that she'd been able to buy it on her own, just so she didn't have to keep thinking about the other woman. "That would be great, text me when you're heading back. Bye, Harry."

"Bye, Lily. Love you."

In the living room, they had started unwrapping one another's presents: books, box sets, clothes, and cosmetics, boxes of chocolate and bottles of wine. Each present was greeted with an exclamation of thanks and hugs. There was a slight hiccup when Olivia received three copies of the same book, and Giovanni's broken English caused a few misunderstandings, but mostly it was high spirited and happy.

They knew one another's tastes and they maintained certain family traditions: Celia always gave them a box of her homemade chocolate truffles; James always bought five bottles of champagne, one for each member of the family, and simply handed them round from a Marks & Spencer carton. At one point before lunch, the noise reached such a pitch that Lily gave up trying to follow the conversations criss-crossing the room, and lay back on the couch. She rested her head against the faded corduroy; suddenly, she felt wiped out. Moving house had been more tiring than she'd expected, and she'd been anxious about Harry and the flat for quite a while now. In the weeks leading up to Christmas, she'd wanted to avoid all this: the chaos and intimacy of a family celebration, the happy couples, and her being alone in contrast. Anyway, she was glad she'd come. She missed Harry, but she also missed celebrating Christmas like the others, as part of a couple. Being someone's *mistress*—Lily shuddered at the word—meant a lot of time alone.

By the time all the presents were opened, the living room was a blizzard of torn wrapping paper, ribbons, and packaging. After a feast of a meal, they sang carols around the piano—another family tradition which had lasted from their childhood. Celia played "Once in Royal David's City" and "Silent Night," and they all joined in. There was more wine, then cognac and Baileys. There was no Queen's speech, for Celia had never owned a television, but in the early evening, Giovanni took over the kitchen and made proper Italian espressos to sober them up. When they started getting peckish again, Lily's fruit salad was a triumph, along with cheese, crackers, and after-dinner mints.

When everyone began to scatter, some to ring friends and settle into their bedrooms, others to smoke cigarettes in the garden, Lily slipped back into the empty living room. The room was dark but still warm, the only light coming from the tiny white bulbs on the Christmas tree. She lay down on the old corduroy couch again, closing her eyes, letting the silence wash over her.

She lay there for a minute until she heard a step and saw Celia standing in the doorway. "Are you OK, darling?" she said, and came to sit by her daughter. She stroked her hair as if she were a child. "Christmas can be a difficult time, can't it?"

Lily nodded and reached up to clasp her mother's hand.

"I remember Christmas Day thirty-one years ago," Celia said. "I had just found out I was pregnant with Cassie." She smiled down at Lily. "It wasn't planned or anything, we weren't married, but I was rather excited. It didn't occur to me that Claude wouldn't feel the same way."

It was rare to hear her mother say Claude's name. Lily held her breath, willing her to go on.

"Anyway, it went a bit wrong. Your father panicked and drove off to see his family in Paris, even though we'd planned to spend Christmas together. I was left to go back to my parents' house in Liverpool alone. Goodness, it was a miserable Christmas! I sat in that sitting room in the middle of Crosby not knowing what to do. My dad watched television all day, and my mum fussed around in the kitchen, and the neighbours came in with gossip and news and idle chit-chat. I was missing your father and sick as a dog with the pregnancy."

"But what happened? Did he come back? What did you tell your mum?" Obviously Claude had come back, since they'd gone on to have three more children, but Lily was intrigued. She'd never heard any of this before.

"Well, I couldn't tell my parents—Liverpool was still a very conventional place back then. My mum and dad were good working-class people and the scandal would have killed them. They hadn't been happy about my moving to London anyway; I could hardly come back a year later and announce that I was pregnant and unwed. I was terribly sick and couldn't stop weeping, with the hormones and missing Claude and all that. I'm sure my mum must have suspected, but she never said a thing." Celia smiled at Lily. "Oh, at times I really wondered what would become of me!"

Lily was fascinated. "But what about Dad—how did you sort things out? And when did you tell your parents?"

"In the end, it was fine. A few days after Boxing Day, we were coming back from church and there was Claude, in his funny old Triumph Herald, parked outside the house. He brought a bottle of whisky for my dad and a Harrods hamper for my mum—a real luxury in those days—and flowers for me."

Lily's eyes widened as she listened; she'd assumed her parents had been a fairly normal couple, but this seemed unimaginably romantic. "Go on, Mum, what then?"

"Well, he just kind of swept in and announced to my parents that we were getting married and having a baby. They were so impressed with him and his car that they didn't stop to tell me off. And I don't think we ever discussed why he'd gone either." Celia stopped abruptly. She seemed lost in the past.

"Actually, Mum, I wanted to ask you something." Lily was hesitant, but the darkness of the living room somehow made it easier to talk. "I wondered if—if you don't mind, that is, I wanted to . . ."

"I know, darling," Celia said. "You want to contact your father, don't you? I've been thinking about this since the wedding— longer, in fact. I think it might be time for us all to try and mend some fences."

"Really, Mum, is that OK with you? I think Cassie, Liv, and James would like to meet him too, maybe. I mean, we've all wondered about him—we sometimes talk about him. But we don't want to hurt you."

"Of course I understand." Celia smiled. "Whatever happened in the past, you should have a chance to know your father. And he should have a chance to know his children too." She leaned down and kissed Lily on the forehead. "Let's talk about it in the morning with the others. Come on, it's late and we're both tired. Time for bed."

Curled up under the duvet in her old bedroom, Lily thought about what her mother had said. She tried to imagine her parents before any of them were born, so young and stubborn and in love, so far apart on Christmas Day. She imagined Celia in Liverpool with her beehive hairdo and mini-skirt, sobbing into the Brussels sprouts, trying to hide her broken heart and her pregnancy sickness. What had Lily's father been thinking of?

From the corridor, she heard her brother's and his girlfriend's murmured voices as they passed, then Cassie and Charlie as they came upstairs to bed. Drifting into sleep, Lily remembered that she wasn't the only one lying there alone. Nearly twenty-five years since their father had left, Celia was still on her own.

*   *   *

Another evening on my own. I feel like a single mother these days, with the added stress of Harry's lies or evasions or avoidance or whatever it is. Is that it—is he just trying to avoid me? Is this home, this family I've worked so hard to nurture, is it really such an awful place to be? I was angry when he rang from London to say he was having dinner with friends and would be back late. That was five hours ago. It's the last few days of the holidays before the boys go back to school and he goes back to work; I thought we'd be spending this time together. Now I wish I'd taken the kids to Cornwall with my sister after all. A whole bunch of them were renting a big house there, at least I'd have had company.

He came away over Christmas, of course, we always go back to my parents for the Christmas and New Year break, but my God he seemed unwilling. The day we were packing to leave for Mum and Dad's, I felt like I was dragging a reluctant child to the dentist. It was clear he'd rather have stayed home alone, or more likely stayed in London with that woman. He seems to think it's enough just to turn up, to come on these family visits, but then he makes no effort to join in. If only he knew how depressing his presence can be—and embarrassing too. Mum asked me several times why Harry was so withdrawn this year, why he was drinking so much, and Dad commented that he was worse than the kids, "glued to that mobile phone of his." He took endless long walks to pubs in local villages and didn't want company, not even the boys. A few days he was sociable and lively, but others I could barely get a word out of him. On Christmas Day, he stood in the garden in the pouring rain trying to get a signal—and you can't tell me that's an urgent work call.

God, what a mess. Harry just rang again and you know what? The anger's gone. I'm tired of it all. Apparently he's missed his stop or his train or something—he sounded so drunk and confused. I feel tired and sad, sad for him, for me, for Dan and Joe, for the whole damn thing. I'm not perfect, I know that. I'm not ageing well, I moan and I nag, I can be demanding and dissatisfied, I expect too much, I care too much what others think . . . But I don't lie to Harry and I don't cheat. I try to make this house a good place to be, when he is here. I just want him to want to come home.

SHIT, SHIT, SHIT. HARRY STOOD IN THE dark car park, waiting for the minicab to arrive. It was raining and the station was deserted, all the other commuters having long since departed. He'd fallen asleep on the last train home, missed his stop, and woken with a jolt twenty minutes later, miles from home. Wiping the rain from his face, Harry checked his watch. It was nearly midnight. Pippa was going to be furious.

He took out his phone and dialed Lily's number. After three rings, she answered: "Harry? Is everything OK?"

"Sorry to ring so late. Did I wake you up?"

"No, it's fine, I'm still up." Lily sounded distracted. "Where are you—did you get home?"

"You won't believe this, but I've done it again. Fell asleep as the train left Marylebone and missed my stop. I'm at Beaconsfield now, waiting for the cab."

"But I don't understand, we left the restaurant before nine, you should have been back hours ago."

"I didn't get the train. I ended up walking around town, found a bar, had a few more drinks. I don't know how it got this late." Harry's voice was slurred. "You know she's going to bloody murder me."

"Hmm. What a nightmare." Lily wasn't sure what to say.

"It'll be fine. The cab driver knows me, he came out last time, charges me a double fare at this time of night . . . But I'm not looking forward to getting home. Anyway, I'll let you go—to bed or whatever. Just wanted to hear your voice. I enjoyed dinner. And we should definitely book that holiday." He waited, but Lily said nothing.

"Holiday?" Lily knew she sounded cold, but she couldn't help it. A year earlier she'd have commiserated with him over the missed train, but now she just felt depressed. Was this how it was going to be, her coming home alone from dinner, him falling asleep on the train back to his wife? They loved each other and the situation was hopeless.

"You know, I mentioned the family's going away? I thought we could plan something for the half-term."

"Oh, yes." Lily shook her head. "Well, February's a long way off."

Harry swallowed. "I'll let you go. And Lil—I love you, remember that."

"Sure," Lily said. "Thanks for dinner. I hope it's not too bad at home. I hope, y'know, it works out."

Harry hung up, feeling confused and vaguely sick. What was the matter, why did she sound so distant? They'd had a lovely evening at one of their favourite restaurants, she'd been relaxed and affectionate at dinner. So why was she being so cold? His dread of returning home to an angry Pippa was replaced by anxiety over Lily. He felt a sudden flash of rage. What a mess everything was. He felt angry and powerless, as if he wanted to punch something.

"Calm the fuck down," he muttered to himself. He heard his cab drive up and took a final pull on his cigarette before getting in.

The sick feeling in Harry's stomach spread on the drive home to Gerrards Cross. He felt tense and weary beyond belief. The pain at the base of his spine was unbearable. It was the to-ing and fro-ing, the long days in London, evenings with Lily, then coming back to these bitter scenes with Pippa. He was falling asleep on the train into work, on the last train too, but when he got home and went to bed, he couldn't sleep a wink. Just lay there beside his wife, wondering what the hell to do.

It was a terrible mess of his own making. He couldn't not spend time with Lily, she was like a drug to him, but this lying and hiding and coming home in the early hours was no good. Ever since Lily had begun working for him, Pippa had been suspicious; it was as though his obsession was written all over his face. This had never happened to them before. He'd never been unfaithful, and nor had she, in all those years of marriage. He had to see Lily, but then he had to come home too, because of the boys. Not that he was any good to them as a father, coming back late, missing dinner, missing their rugby matches and parents' evenings, standing in the doorway of their bedrooms long after they had gone to sleep. What was he doing?

It was as though he had stepped through a door into another world with Lily. Nothing had ever been boring or mundane with her. From the beginning, everything was special because it wasn't real life; they had never argued about taking out the rubbish or worried about gas bills or done the laundry together. It had always been just the two of them.

The cab swerved around a corner a little too fast, turning off the main road towards the village, skidding slightly on the wet tarmac. For a split second, Harry imagined a crash, the perfect way out, an easy ending. He clenched his fists harder. No, that wasn't the solution. He could get back in control of this situation. He'd leave work on time the way he used to, he'd come home and spend time with Dan and Joe, maybe he could patch things up with Pippa. He pulled out some crumpled banknotes and his cigarettes, telling himself he'd sort things out. The one thing he couldn't do was give Lily up.

He asked the driver to pull into the lane alongside the house to avoid the noise of tyres crunching over the gravel driveway. He thanked the man and paid him, trying to close the cab door as quietly as possible, praying that Pippa would be asleep.

As he walked towards the front door he could see a light on in the kitchen. Maybe she'd left it on for him, he thought hopefully, maybe she'd gone up to bed and he could sleep downstairs. There were spasms of pain shooting up his spine now; he was too wrecked for another argument.

As soon as he walked into the hallway, he knew she was still up. She didn't come out, but the air was thick with resentment. Harry eased off his loafers and hung his jacket over the bannisters, dropped his keys on the hall table, ran his hands through his hair, and walked into the kitchen. Pippa was sitting at the table with a glass of red wine.

"So you've come home? Really good of you."

"Pippa, listen, I'm sorry. It got late . . . I had a bite to eat with some friends, then I was walking around London, had a few drinks and fell asleep on the train. Missed my stop and it took ages to get back, sorry. You know, work's been stressful lately, just needed to unwind . . ." he tailed off.

"For God's sake, Harry, don't give me *work's been stressful*, it's the Christmas holidays. Of course I don't mind you going for dinner with friends, of course I don't mind you coming back late and forgetting to ring, once or twice or three times even, but it's the same thing every night." Pippa's face was pale, with red blotches on her cheeks. "I've been pretty patient, I think, but how much more am I expected to take?" She stared at him. "What the hell is going on?"

He'd never seen her this angry. "Nothing's going on, it's just work and—"

Pippa cut in, "Don't treat me like a fool. There *is* something going on, and I'm not putting up with it anymore. Why should I sit here night after night, ringing your phone, leaving messages you never return, not knowing when or if you're coming home. Just go to her. She'll let you move in, I assume?"

"What do you mean, *go to her?*"

"Lily." Pippa almost spat the word out, and Harry flinched.

"Why are you bringing this up again? It has nothing to do with Lily . . ." Harry felt that the best defence was outright denial, but he hated himself. He was a lying bastard. "Lily and I work together, you know that Pippa—and yes we're friends too. She was there tonight, but she left the restaurant before nine and there's nothing going on. Look we've talked about all this: Lily has nothing to do with you and me."

"That's simply not true, Harry. You're lying. You're standing there and you're lying to me and you've been doing it for God knows how many months now."

What had she heard, what had she found out? She sounded more definite than before. "OK, Pippa, you believe whatever you want." He couldn't meet her eye. "So where does that leave us? You told me you didn't want a divorce. You said we should stay together until the boys are older."

"Well, that was before. I've changed my mind now. You're not even here so what difference does it make, we might as well be"— she seemed to flinch at the word divorce—"we might as well be separated. Remember how you used to rush home from work early to collect them from school sometimes, to play in the garden and make their supper." Pippa's voice broke. "You used to want to *be here with us*." She wiped away a tear and shook her head. "You always sneered at weekend fathers but you're not even that . . . Think about it, Harry, when was the last time you helped Dan or Joe with their homework?"

"I helped Dan with his science project just the other night when you were playing tennis with that bloke, Peter. God knows what's going on with the two of you." This was a cheap shot, Harry knew that, and completely unfair. There was nothing going on between his wife and Peter from the tennis club, but he didn't know what else to say.

"Oh, for God's sake, Harry. The reason I have to ask Peter is that you're never here—we used to play tennis together, remember? If you wanted, we could get a babysitter, I'd love us to play, but you're never around. And when you are around it's like you're not. Even if you don't care about me, think about Dan and Joe . . . when you take them out at weekends and ring her, do you think they don't realise, you think they don't *tell* me? When Joe was going to bed tonight he actually asked me, 'Is Daddy in London with his girlfriend?'"

Pippa continued: "And you think I don't notice anyway? The endless work trips, the late nights in London, the way you don't come up to bed with me, the way you stand in the garden talking on your damn phone . . ."

Harry felt sick. He had no ground to stand on. Pippa was right, what kind of father was he anyway? And yet he couldn't live without the boys. But a kind of madness had descended upon him in the last year: he was so consumed by Lily that he'd become reckless. It frightened him to realise that he would do whatever it took to be with her. When he was with her, he was happy, and he didn't think about the rest of his life. He seemed to have a sort of amnesia at the moment. He couldn't seem to grasp the consequences of his actions.

Pippa was still talking: "I'm never sure of anything now, none of us are. We don't know when you're going to be here. And I can't trust anything you say . . ." Harry hated himself for causing this pain; he wasn't in love with her anymore, but he didn't want to trample on her like this. "I'm sorry, Harry, but I can't sit here and take it any longer. Pippa the dependable one, Pippa the reliable, stable one at home, looking after the children. I'm forty-eight next month, and I've had enough. Either you stop lying right now, stop whatever's going on with Lily or whoever it is, and come home to us, properly—or you go."

There was silence in the kitchen. From Pippa's expression Harry knew she was serious. The chaos, the alcohol, and the exhaustion in his brain mounted and he didn't know what to say. Right now, living without either Lily or the boys was unimaginable. They were too precious to lose. But Pippa was right. He was a shit, he was wrecking his family's life with his lies, he had to do something. Staring at the floorboards, unable to meet her eye, he finally spoke: "But, Pip, come on, this is our home, this is where we live."

"Yes, this is where *we* live," she said. "And I'm staying here with the boys—this is their home, this is where they go to school—but you have a choice, Harry. You can be with us properly, as you used to be, or you can go to Lily. But you can't have both anymore."

She couldn't make him choose. "Look, Pippa, I work with Lily, you know that. Don't overreact, it's late, we're both tired. Let's talk this through rationally when we've had some sleep." Harry barely knew what he was saying. The pain in his lower spine was spreading; it seemed to have entered every disc, every muscle and fibre of his body. "Please, can we discuss this tomorrow? We'll have a proper day out, go somewhere nice with the boys and get a pub lunch. Come on, Pip, we can work things out."

He reached into his pocket and pulled out the painkillers he always carried, shook out two white pills, and swallowed them without water. His throat was dry, his head pounding. He needed a cigarette too, badly, but she didn't let him smoke in the house.

"Fine," Pippa said. "We'll talk about it tomorrow. But just so you know, I won't change my mind. I'm not having you seeing that girl again, simple as that. At the moment, you're making my life a misery. Go to her if that's what you want." She pushed back her chair. "You won't have the boys though." He heard her climbing the stairs, then the bedroom door closed.

Harry sat at the kitchen table for the rest of the night. For months he'd been out of control, acting like a madman, ignoring the tsunami heading his way. He was sickened by the mess he'd made of his life, destroying his marriage, neglecting his children. All these years he'd been battling insomnia, depression, the constant back pain; now he was overwhelmed with guilt for what he was doing to everyone close to him.

Despite it all, he couldn't stop thinking about Lily and why she had sounded so distant on the phone. Had her feelings changed?

Harry was still sitting there when the darkness gave way to dawn. Minutes, or was it hours, later, he heard one of the boys moving around upstairs. *Come on,* he told himself, *get a grip.* Take a shower, turn on the coffee-maker, sort yourself out, make them some breakfast, be a father, be a proper man, for God's sake. But he sat there motionless in the grey light, staring at Pippa's empty wineglass. He felt trapped, defeated, and very old.

It's my own judgement day that I draw near,
Descending in the past, without a clue,
Down to that central deadness: the despair
Older than any hope I ever knew.

IT HAD BEEN STRANGE WEATHER, NO longer autumn but not properly winter, when David had reappeared in Lily's life. She hadn't seen him for years, and on the December day she found herself trapped in the flat, a thunderstorm outside and depression within, he was the furthest thing from her mind.

The rain was not going to stop anytime soon. Normally airy and sunlit, even on these short winter days, today the flat felt too small and weirdly dark. It was a Sunday, and it seemed like the rest of the world was somewhere else: Susan had gone away for the weekend, Cassie's phone was off, and Celia wasn't home either. Harry had been ringing, but she didn't want him to come into London, didn't want to be part of the lies he would have to tell his wife, didn't want to deal with his marital angst. After pacing from room to room, then trying to read a book, Lily realised she would go mad if she didn't get outside.

She pulled on her J Brand skinny jeans, a pale pink cashmere jumper, a jacket, and Hunter wellies; grabbed the keys; and made her way downstairs. She needed fresh air and to hell with the rain. Being out in the open helped, and she began to feel calmer. She walked up Haverstock Hill, tempted to stop for breakfast, but decided to work up an appetite first and carried on towards Hampstead Heath.

"Lily?" At the gates of the Heath, a familiar voice made her turn. It was David. He was standing a few paces away near the entrance, locking up a silver sports car, smiling at her. She hadn't seen him for five or six years, and there he was, exactly the same with those dark eyes and that megawatt smile.

"David? I don't believe it!" Lily broke into a smile too, and crossed the gravel path to give him a hug. They stood for a moment beside the car, staring at each other, taking the fact of each other in. Lily had forgotten how handsome David was. She brushed her hair back from her face—at least it was clean—and wished she'd bothered to put on mascara this morning. God, he was gorgeous, had he really been hers for an entire year?

"I can't believe it's you!" David said, pocketing his car keys in a pair of loose, expensive jeans. "You're looking great. Are you living around here these days?"

"Yes, a new place down in Belsize Park, I only just moved in. What about you, still in Golders Green?"

"Yes, still there. Mum's not been well, so I'm staying close to her, and my offices are round there. So what else is new? Where are you working? Are you married or what?" He gave Lily a curious smile, which contained other unspoken questions.

"Are you heading towards the Heath?" She waved a hand at the green expanse. "I was just going for a walk . . ."

"A walk, absolutely," he said. "That's why I'm here too. I've been coding since six this morning"—David was in computer programming Lily remembered—"and needed to clear my head. Shall we?"

The rain had stopped and the sun was shining again. The gravel crunched wetly beneath their feet as they walked. Even though they were so different, they had always been able to talk. *What did they break up over?* Lily wondered as they talked. As far as she could remember, it hadn't been an official break-up, more of a drifting apart, something to do with jobs and travelling. It all came back now, the frank enjoyment of each other's company, and the mutual attraction. They knew each other well enough to feel relaxed, but it had been so long since she'd seen him that there wasn't a hint of familiarity. Every time his bare arm brushed against hers, she felt a rush of desire.

Lily's thoughts were racing. She had forgotten how David made her feel—she couldn't wait to tell Cassie about this! Their conversation moved quickly from superficial small talk to the real stuff: Soon he was telling her about the girlfriend who came after her. They had married two years ago, and now they'd just divorced.

"Literally *just* divorced," he said sadly. "The papers came through this week." A defeated tone crept into his voice when he talked about the divorce. She was going to ask what had gone wrong, but something stopped her. She just listened quietly. He asked again if she was settled, seeing anyone, married with children, in his light-hearted way, but she managed to sidestep the question. She laughed, blushing, saying there were "plenty of interesting men on the scene," and left it at that. She could have told David the truth, he would have understood about Harry, but somehow she couldn't bring herself to say it out loud. Words like "affair" and "married man" sounded so sordid in the cold light of day, and Lily didn't know how she'd found herself in this situation. And she loved Harry. She didn't want anyone judging him.

"Hey, we're near Kenwood—how about coffee?" David said. He sent Lily off to get a table in the window, and bought an enormous chunk of gooey chocolate cake for them to share. After several more cappuccinos, they walked back across the Heath, more slowly now, meandering down different paths, around the ponds, taking each other in with their eyes.

What was happening? Lily intuited from his body language and from the lingering glances that if she was interested, he was interested. After nearly six years. Now there was a dilemma.

If only it were that simple, she thought. If only she could end it with Harry and have an uncomplicated fling with David, or even get back together with him. She had caught sight of her reflection as they were leaving the café and she realised that she was glowing. The anxiety about Harry, the sleepless, anxious look was gone—her eyes sparkled, she was smiling up at David almost flirtatiously. He asked for her phone number, but even as she gave it to him, she knew that it would never work. He was on the rebound from a divorce—and as for her? She was too deeply in love with Harry, too embroiled in the impossible, hopeless relationship they had created. No amount of physical lust could replace that, even with an ex as attractive as David.

She hadn't confided in him about Harry, but she found herself talking to him about Claude, although later she didn't know how it had come up. They were at the car park, and David was unlocking his car. Trying to sound casual, she said she was thinking of writing to her father.

"Your father?" David looked up.

"He probably won't write back, maybe he's moved a dozen times in the past couple of decades, I don't know." She paused. "Anyway, it's not a big deal. I've got along fine without him for all these years. Not even sure why I asked Mum for the address."

David knew what Claude meant to Lily. He was the only boy-friend she had ever discussed her father with. David's father had died just a few months before she met him; he understood what losing a father felt like.

He looked surprised. "You've got his address; you're going to write to Claude? That's huge!"

Lily shrugged. "I don't know. I mean, he's never made the effort to find me . . ."

David shook his head. "Lily, it *is* a big deal. Seriously, write to him. Give it a try. Whatever happens, you'll have made the effort."

Lily realised there were tears in her eyes. She suddenly felt closer to David than to anyone else in the world. He took her hand, so gently. She knew that within the next second they were about to kiss, so she turned her face and brushed away a tear. "I should prob-ably get home, boxes to unpack, floors to wash!"

David smiled, and their eyes locked again. He leaned past her to open the passenger door. "I'm driving through Belsize Park—jump in, I'll drop you off."

LILY GOT OUT OF THE SHOWER, WRAPPED her hair in a turban, and put on her bathrobe. If Harry didn't get up soon, they'd both be late for work.

"Wakey-wakey, rise and shine." She walked across the bedroom in bare feet and flung open the wooden shutters, letting sunlight stream across the bed. Harry lifted his head from the pillow and smiled.

"Come back to bed."

"We don't have time!" Lily disappeared into the kitchen and reappeared with two mugs. "Here, coffee." She set one of the mugs on the bedside table and leaned down to kiss him. "How are you feeling this morning?"

"I feel great." Yet again, Harry had rung on a Sunday afternoon in a bad way; he'd argued with Pippa again, and he was heading into London—could they meet for dinner? Could he stay over? "I feel fantastic now. I don't think I've slept so well in months. Just being here with you—it's magical. This place—we were right to buy it, Lily . . ."

Her throat tightened, and she got up from the bed. "Come on, we're going to be late, we have the acquisitions committee at nine a.m. I'm presenting and I haven't even finished my notes. You need to get in the shower now." She tried to keep her voice light.

Harry groaned, threw back the duvet, and headed for the bathroom. Lily stood in front of her wardrobe, her calm morning mood completely shattered. *We were right to buy it*—had he just said "we"? Every time Harry stayed over, he went on about how good it felt to be there with her, how much he loved the new flat. And now he'd just said "we," as if it was their flat, as if she needed reminding that she owed him a quarter of the price—or rather, since he didn't want her to repay him, he owned a quarter of her flat?

It made her feel panicky, as if she was involved in his family finances, as if somehow she'd been dragged into his marital affairs. Of course it wasn't logical—even though she couldn't talk it through with Cassie, she knew it wasn't logical—but every time Harry said "we" it made her think of his wife. She imagined this woman might find something out, a bank statement, land registry, mortgage documents, something like that. It filled her with insecurity. Could the woman turn up and demand a quarter of the flat's value back? Could she sue her or get her thrown out? Lily didn't know where this anxiety came from.

Stop it, she told herself. *You love this man, and it does feel good being here together.* She had to trust him. *When he says "we" it means the two of us.* They'd had a lovely evening, ordering Thai food from a local restaurant, then Harry had wired up some fancy Sonos speaker system he'd bought her and they listened to old music.

There were so many contradictions in her feelings around him: fear that she was getting in too deep, that this love would hurt them both terribly in the end; anger that she was his secret refuge from his wife; guilt that she was destroying his family; and anxiety that he was going off the rails. Not just the drink, but drugs too—when he arrived yesterday afternoon she was pretty sure . . .

"OK, I'm ready!" Harry stood in the doorway, transformed from the sleepy, troubled man of a few minutes ago to the strong, handsome strategic director she had first fallen in love with. "Lucky I left some fresh shirts here." He took out his phone. "Will you be ready for an Uber in, say, five minutes?"

"Harry, no, I get the bus to work, and we probably shouldn't arrive together . . ."

"Don't be silly. We both need to work on our notes and we're running late. Anyway I'm not leaving you to wait for public transport while I get a cab. We'll get them to drop us around the corner from the office." He fiddled with the app on his phone, then came over to kiss Lily. "Good morning. I'm looking forward to your presentation, Miss de Jongh."

She laughed and pushed him away. "If I'm too tired to think straight, I'll know who to blame! Come on, I'll do my make-up in the cab."

Suddenly it was all OK again. This was the Harry she loved. In control, capable, making decisions and looking after her. Lily fastened the last button on her silk shirt, and they headed for the door.

"I HAVE NO RIGHT. I KNOW THAT, I HAVE absolutely no fucking right to ask her who she's seeing, where do they go, what does she mean by 'friend,' is she sleeping with him . . ."

"It seems to be causing you significant stress," Dr. Christos observed.

"Stress? Yeah, and anger and outrage—I can't help it, I've never felt this jealous before."

"What actually happened?"

"Oh, nothing. She mentioned she'd bumped into an old boyfriend, they went for coffee on Hampstead Heath. That was it, as far as I know, and she says she hasn't seen him since. But I swear it makes me furious. I wanted to find this guy and ask him—I don't know, just look him in the eye and ask him what he wants from Lily—I guess he's only after one thing." Harry stopped, aware how unhinged he was sounding.

"Before the Christmas break, we discussed the possibility of you spending more time at home. Perhaps not going into London over the holidays?"

"That was a failure. The first few days I was at home with Pippa, but the boys were hardly there. I thought I'd go mad if I didn't see Lily. The more I told myself I couldn't, the worse the situation with Pippa got. We just . . . There was nothing to say to each other."

He continued. "Anyway, I started thinking more and more about what Lily might be doing, who she was spending her time with. We had to stay with Pippa's family, but then when we got home, I was drinking a lot, and it became a sort of obsession. To cut a long story short, I started spying on her.

"The first day back, I went to the pub on the corner of England's Lane—she never goes there—I got a double whisky and sat in the window, with a clear view of her flat opposite. It was nearly four by this time, already dark. About fifteen minutes after I got there, a dark-haired man walked up to the front door. He rang the bell, and a few minutes later, the old lady emerged, the one who owns the rest of the house. She gave the young man a hug for a long time, and then I saw Lily coming down the stairs behind them.

"Lily was wearing a sort of sparkly Christmas dress and high heels, she looked fantastic." Harry's face was etched with pain. "I'm not sure, I couldn't see clearly, but . . ."

"Did she know this man?"

Harry sighed. "I got the impression he was a friend of the old woman's, maybe a nephew or something, and she was introducing him to Lily. Who knows? But why was Lily all dressed up like that for someone she didn't know?"

"As an outsider, it sounds perfectly innocent. Festive drinks, perhaps, or a family party."

"You're right. It could have been a party—there were lots of cars parked on the driveway and the ground floor was all lit up. But I wasn't thinking straight: seeing Lily in that doorway, so near to me, smiling at another man . . ."

"And what did you do?" Dr. Christos asked.

"I wanted to hurt the guy, whoever he was, but I didn't do anything. Just stayed in the pub for hours, drinking alone, then I went and bought some coke and did a lot, walking around London, in and out of pubs. I got home very late and had an almighty row with Pippa." Harry made eye contact with his psychiatrist for the first time. "That's why I had to see her over the holidays, it felt as though she was slipping away from me. I had to see her to make sure . . ."

Dr. Christos took a deep breath. "I wonder if this is overstepping the mark," he said quietly.

"What, the drink and drugs?"

"No. I mean waiting for her, watching . . ."

Harry nodded. "It is, isn't it? I know I have no right to do that. I have no right to ask her who that man is, or any man. I'm the one who's married. Some nights lately I've come so close to going round there, maybe just standing in her street, checking on her; I even thought about reading her emails—I could do that through the work server—or putting some spyware on her phone, for God's sake."

Dr. Christos raised a hand. "We're out of time. But I should say, this concerns me." He paused, choosing his words carefully. "This kind of behaviour could be construed as—well, intercepting some-one's personal communications is a serious . . ."

"Look, I won't," Harry said. "I know it's illegal and I won't. It was just a moment of madness, it's been a rough few months, and it's hard, with Lily, never knowing where I am. Because she's so much younger, I imagine her living this wild, promiscuous life, even though she tells me she loves me, and I believe her when she says it . . . But I know, this has to stop. I'm going to take her somewhere next month. The boys and Pippa are going away with her sister for the February half-term. We just need some time alone."

IT WAS THEIR LAST DAY IN SAINT LUCIA, and they were having breakfast on the hotel terrace. Lily came back from the buffet, a plate piled high with fruit and a bowl of natural yoghurt balanced on top. Harry waited for her to sit down, smiled at her, and began eating his scrambled egg and toast.

"Mmm, the juice is good today." Lily took a gulp and gestured towards his glass. "I think it's mango. Or maybe papaya?" They had devoted much time over the previous fortnight to the various merits of the island's tropical fruit juices (mostly mixed with rum).

"Mango, definitely," Harry said. "So, what's the plan for today? Shall we go and visit the sulphurous springs, explore the banana plantations, drive around the island, or what?"

"Or what?" Lily said, smiling. "Or lie on the beach, you mean? Let's see . . . our flight isn't till ten this evening, so we've got all day. Maybe some swimming and sunbathing, and then after lunch, we could see if we feel like being active?"

The likelihood was almost zero, they both knew that. It had been two weeks of doing pretty much nothing except lying on the beach and reading. The hotel was situated on the west coast of the island, in between Saint Lucia's iconic peaks, Gros Piton and Petit Piton, and the guest rooms were actually separate bungalows and villas scattered across the valley, nestled into the jungle. These small villas offered absolute privacy, which was exactly what they wanted.

Being alone like this was a novelty for Lily and Harry. They were used to London life: emails, meetings, trains, and office politics. The change of pace in the Caribbean had taken a few days to get used to. Now that they were winding down, the prospect of returning to the rain and rush hour was far from appealing. And then the other problems, the lies and deception, which awaited them back home. Out here, they managed to escape all that. The hotel was so exclusive that no one seemed curious about Harry and Lily, no one stared or whispered. It wasn't until they got away from London that they realised how nice it was to be left alone like any other couple, to be anonymous and unobserved.

Lily in particular felt the strain at work. Harry was so senior (and bloody minded) that he'd never much cared what anyone thought of him. For Lily it was different—when she first joined HEP she'd been part of the gang. They were all in their twenties, working in editorial, production, and design; they went to the pub every Friday after work, some lunchtimes too. They discussed jobs and relationships and flatshares and, of course, their bosses. Gradually, the others began to notice that she and Harry were spending more time together. They weren't overt, but they didn't hide it either, and when they came in from the park together, or an author lunch, or were spotted in Pret A Manger eating sandwiches (the scandal!), people started to talk.

Months before anything physical actually happened between Harry and Lily, their colleagues had put two and two together and made five. According to the office grapevine, they were torridly, passionately in love. Which meant, of course, that they acted differently around Lily, as if she were a spy planted in their midst to gather secret information and report back up the food chain. They weren't unfriendly, just wary: they no longer bitched about their jobs or their salaries or their managers when Lily was around. Everything at work changed for her once it was decided she was sleeping with the enemy.

Since they got together, Lily had been spending most of her free time with Harry anyway. Even though she told herself that the situation at the office didn't matter, it was a strain. She hated being watched and gossiped about, and she felt frozen out by her contemporaries.

Harry's contemporaries found out too. The other directors and the Managing Director, Colin, were aghast when the news of their strategic director's love affair filtered out. They liked Harry's wife and family, and they regretted this entanglement with a younger member of staff. What would Harry be telling Lily in those intimate, unguarded moments; how could they trust him to maintain professional confidentiality? They felt that he was blurring the boundaries between "them" and "us" in a dangerous way.

However, Harry coped—and Lily knew that he brushed it off when the other directors raised it with him—but she did not enjoy the notoriety. Being away from it all was immensely liberating for both of them. And Saint Lucia was very far away.

By the time Lily and Harry finished eating breakfast and reading the papers, it was nearly ten a.m. They wandered down through the landscaped gardens towards the beach. The sun was already high in the sky and the heat of the day had begun to gather. It drove away the morning chill and dried the dew on the huge waxy leaves of the tropical plants.

On their way down the tiered hotel terraces, they passed an open-air courtyard where a huge chessboard had been painted on the flagstones. Every chess piece was human-sized, and Harry took a photo of Lily grinning between the black bishop and the white queen. Down at the shore, the beach was already filling up with other guests, a few jogging along the sand, others chatting over coffee. Not far away, the morning aqua-aerobics class was taking place in the shallows.

"There you go." Lily waved at the mature ladies in their swimming costumes bending and stretching underwater. "That's what we should be doing. Some exercise!"

Harry, already lying face-down on the sun lounger, murmured in reply, "Definitely . . . exercise later on, I agree . . ."

Lily lay back, feeling the sun warm her face. The sun loungers were huge and soft, swathed in the hotel's monogrammed white towels. "This is heaven," she said quietly. "I could lie here forever."

Harry turned to face her, then leaned over and dropped a kiss on her shoulder. "So why are we going home?" He sat up. "I've got an idea, Lily. Let's not. Let's never go home."

She felt herself tense. Why did he keep doing this? They were having a wonderful time, they had regained the intimacy and trust which seemed to have been lost over the Christmas holidays. Lily was enjoying the moment and not thinking ahead. Then Harry would bring up these impossible questions about the future—how they could be together, what he should say to his wife, when he might leave—and Lily tensed up. She adored him with every fibre of her being. But how could she live with herself if she wrecked another woman's marriage? She wanted Harry all to herself, but to get that she would have to let him walk out on his family. So she went quiet, or changed the subject.

After lunch on that final day, they swam, then went back to the villa, made love, and slept. When they woke, the villa was quiet, and they lay in each other's arms, in silence, under the cool air of the ceiling fan. It was time to pack.

Harry had arranged a surprise for their departure. Lily had expected they would wait in reception for the hotel's four-by-four Jeep to take them back to the airport the way they had come: a long and jolting drive over the island's rutted tracks and potholed roads. Instead, Harry had arranged for a helicopter transfer from the hotel to the airport.

It was eight p.m. and darkness had fallen on the beach. Their luggage was loaded up, and then Harry and Lily ran across the helipad flooded with fluorescent light. The whirring helicopter blades seemed dangerously close above their heads, close enough to touch, and they climbed on board, filled with exhilaration. They were the only passengers flying so late at night, so they buckled themselves into the front seats next to the pilot.

They were used to planes and runways, the gradual gathering of momentum and velocity, but flying in a helicopter was completely different. Taking off, it just lifted straight into the air. Apart from the steel roof and floor, it was plate glass all around, so they felt as if they were floating through the night sky. The pilot made sweeping, swooping turns around the valley and between the two great pitons, pointing out the banana plantations far below. As they banked sharply and passed over their hotel for the last time, Lily and Harry gazed in silence at the dotted lights of the beach bar, the swimming pool illuminated against the dense greenness of the gardens, the tiny bungalows scattered in the dark forest.

Somewhere above the rainforest, Harry turned to Lily and stroked her cheek. "Thank you for this." His voice was barely audible over the roar of the engine.

"Thank you?" Lily said. "There's nothing to thank *me* for! You arranged everything, it's been the most amazing holiday of my life."

Harry didn't smile. "I mean it, Lily. Please remember. Whatever happens, we had this time together."

Lily caught something defeated in his tone, something final and frightening. In the darkness of the cockpit, she saw that he had tears in his eyes.

*   *   *

In the end, it was easy. I didn't need to go looking for the lies or the proof. Everything fell into my lap.

Rewind a few months: my trip to Florida in February with the boys. I haven't updated the blog since then because . . . well, because of what I found out. A few of you left comments asking if I was OK, and I'm grateful—even though I write this anonymously, it still feels like having real friends. I don't know how I got so isolated here, and your support helps a lot.

So, Florida. Harry drove us to the airport and was helping the boys put our luggage through the self check-in. An hour or so later, after he'd gone, we were having breakfast and waiting for our gate number. I got a call from Harry's number—except it wasn't him. A man explained that he'd found this smartphone somewhere in the terminal and was ringing the most recently called numbers to try to locate its owner. Harry must have dropped his phone there or on his way back to the car park. The man was nearby, so we met outside the duty-free shop, and he handed it over.

At that point, our gate was boarding, and obviously I couldn't call Harry to let him know I had his phone. So I left for our fortnight in Florida with my husband's smartphone—which doesn't have a password, surprisingly—and made quite a few discoveries.

1. *He was leaving for Saint Lucia the next morning. Not ten days hiking in Snowdonia as he'd told me.*
2. *He wasn't going alone "to clear his head" as he'd told me. He was taking that woman he works with, Lily.*

3. *She bought a flat in London at the end of last year and he seems to have paid for some of it.*

4. *He wants to leave me (maybe I knew that already) but he doesn't know where to go. She doesn't appear that keen on him moving in.*

So there we are. All my suspicions are confirmed, but worse. Every time he's told me he's been working late or staying up in London, he's been with her. He's been lying for months now, maybe even years, and it took just a few hours, sitting on the tarmac, our departure delayed, while the boys watched movies, to get the whole truth. Texts, emails, photos, bank statements, flight itineraries and hotel confirmations, everything in his phone.

I guess he thought he'd left it at home or at the office because it kept working for several hours—by the time we landed in Florida, it was locked, and I chucked it in a bin. I didn't want to look at any of it ever again. I had all the proof I needed.

So now what? It's May, and I've known since the end of February. For the first few days in Florida, I didn't know what to do. I needed time and space to think. We stayed for a week in Orlando with my mum and dad, taking the boys and their cousins to Disney World. Then me and my twin sister went down to Miami for a four-day spa break on our own. We got tipsy on the first night, sitting by the pool drinking cocktails, and it all came out—God, it was a relief to tell Polly. She understood completely, everything, she always does. In fact, she confided that Andrew had an affair a few years back. She did it properly: checking his satnav, hacking into his emails and credit card details, even following him in the car on the "long bike rides" he claimed to be taking at weekends. She never confronted him, and after a while, she said, "It petered out. The girl moved on to a new job, and Andrew settled back into family life."

Should I do the same? Wait it out?

I never told Harry I had his phone—presumably he thinks he lost it at the airport and it was never found. If I tell him, I have to make some decisions. I have to file for divorce, or forgive him and try to repair our marriage, or something . . . and I don't know what. Half the time I don't feel vengeful or determined or any of the things a betrayed wife is supposed to feel: I feel defeated. I don't want him to leave. I'm scared of what happens next. I hate his constant lies, but is it better to have a dishonest husband than no husband at all? I like our life. I like our big house, and two cars, and living where we do. The boys love their school, and all their friends are in the area. Admittedly, I don't have many friends, but I have tennis and bridge and the WI to keep me occupied.

Which is why I haven't done anything yet. Hearing Poll admit that about Andrew helped, because it reminded me that what Harry is doing is not my fault. It's not just because I'm menopausal and past-it, not just that Harry has fallen out of love with me—according to Poll, "it's what men do." Anyway, she clearly did the right thing since they're still together. Maybe this thing with Lily (it hurts even to type her name) will just blow over, peter out, whatever.

At the moment I'm an emotional wreck—I'm not sleeping and my self-confidence is at rock bottom. Does she know that? Does the "other woman" ever think about that? I wonder. It's Harry I should be angry at, and yet it feels easier to channel my hate towards this unknown girl.

IT WAS THE DAY AFTER JAMES'S BIRTHDAY, and Lily had stayed the night with Cassie and Charlie in Victoria. They had thrown a dinner party for James and Su-Ki, a few of their closest friends, plus the family.

Cassie and Charlie had bought the place in Victoria shortly after their wedding the previous spring, but there was still a lot to be done. It was a large flat, but it needed a facelift, if not a complete overhaul. Lily had agreed to help out with painting, so the post-birthday breakfast found them blearily studying colour charts and assessing the way the light fell.

Cassie had ambitious plans for the flat and had put together a "mood board": swatches of fabrics, torn-out magazine images, even scribbled lines of poetry, to inspire her design choices. It was all about balancing the morning sun with the afternoon shadows, according to Cassie. To Lily, looking at the dark, peeling walls, the mood board didn't make sense. What the flat needed, surely, was a lick of white paint?

She teased her sister, affectionately, at the breakfast table: "How did it come to this, Cass—are you reading *Good Housekeeping* now? Next you'll be stitching birthday cards and stuffing mushrooms!" After toast and marmalade, and several rounds of tea, they finally agreed on the colour scheme for the hallway. Charlie was dispatched to Homebase, with lists of paint colours and strict instructions from his wife. Left alone, Cassie and Lily drifted around the flat and began to analyse the light and shade situation (lots of shade, not much light).

"Well . . ." Lily tried to sound positive. "It's a basement flat, so you don't get huge amounts of sunshine. Maybe it's best to stick to light colours, white and light blue, maybe dove grey?"

"Oh no, that's a myth about light colours making a room feel larger. For this space"—Cassie gestured around the tiny dining nook—"I see reds and ambers, nurturing, warm tones for the heart of the home." She worked as a marketing consultant in financial services, but she loved to immerse herself in "projects." Lily could tell she'd been heavily influenced by her honeymoon in Peru and the interior design magazines—hence the mood board—and this was her latest creative outlet. She loved her big sister for her enthusiasm and determination, even if she did want to paint her basement flat all sorts of unsuitable South American colours.

"OK," Lily said brightly. "I see what you mean—a kind of Incan vibe? You were going to show me those rugs you brought back from Machu Picchu, weren't you. Let's go and unpack some of the boxes."

As they started opening the cardboard boxes which had been stacked in the spare room, conversation turned to Lily's recent holiday with Harry.

"That's a pretty big deal, isn't it, spending a fortnight in the Caribbean together? I don't even know how he manages it," Cassie said. "I'm sorry, but if Charlie was away for two weeks with another woman, I hope I'd realise . . ."

Lily looked at her big sister. Cassie was unpeeling brown tape from a large box, peering in and pulling out some books. "Nope. No rugs here. We should have labelled the boxes; I told Charlie we'd never be able to find anything—I can't believe we're still unpacking. It was all such a rush, selling both our flats, and the wedding, and then going away."

"Cass," Lily spoke in a way that made her sister look up. "There's something I need to talk to you about." Lily wasn't quite sure what she was going to say, but she went on: "You know me and Harry? I'm worried. About us—about him, really." She found her eyes filling suddenly with tears.

Cassie dropped the books back in the box and rushed to her sister's side. "Are you OK? I didn't mean to sound harsh about Harry. What I just said was unbelievably crass, I'm so sorry. I'm not judging you, you know that, right?"

Lily nodded. "Of course, Cass. It's fine, you haven't said anything wrong. I didn't want to fall into this cliché. I thought we could just be friends, he was married—unhappily he claimed, but married all the same. And I've always been clear with him about my feelings, that I love him, but I don't want him to destroy his family."

"But I thought you said he was always threatening to leave?"

Lily nodded. "He does. He talked a lot about that in Saint Lucia. But I can't talk about it with him, Cass. I can't tell him how much I want us to be together, a real couple. I'm so confused; I'm hiding my feelings even from myself."

"What do you mean, hiding your feelings?"

"From the very start, I was determined not to become dependent on Harry, not to expect him to leave his wife for me. We all know this scenario, and it ends badly. I've never allowed myself to dream of a happy ending—that doesn't happen with extra marital affairs; the mistress doesn't win. I'm constantly trying to bury my real feelings, even from myself, because I know this relationship can't happen, shouldn't happen." She paused. "I have to stay strong or it will break me."

"I get it," Cassie said. "Maintaining your independence is a way of protecting yourself from the hurt."

"That was the theory, yes. But it hasn't worked out like that ..." Lily hesitated. "The thing about Harry is that he's so extreme."

"Extreme how? I'm worried about you, Lil."

"No, it's OK. He's not violent or anything. But he gets severely depressed—usually when we're apart—he was pretty bad over Christmas. And he drinks and takes very strong medication, and other drugs, to cope with it all. And the back pain, and the marriage problems." Lily shook her head. "I'm probably catastrophising, but I worry that things are spinning out of control."

"Oh, Lil," Cass said. "You went into it with your eyes open, or so you thought, and now it's got really serious ..."

"Exactly. I'm not blaming Harry for any of this, but I definitely can't let him abandon his wife to live with me. That was never part of the plan. And, Cass, it scares me, the intensity of his feelings, the terrible despair he goes into. I'm stuck between destroying another woman's life and destroying my own."

She shook her head and went on, "The irony is that when he's calm, I love being with him. At the start, before Frankfurt and before we started sleeping together, it was amazing. The most wonderful connection, friendship, enjoyment; we'd talk about books and life and everything."

"I remember, back at the start, you were head over heels for him."

"I was! I still am! But the more he talks about leaving his family, the more anxious I feel. If only we had space to breathe, both of us; if only our relationship could have developed normally."

"Lil, it sounds like he's close to some kind of crisis. I think you need to make it absolutely clear that you don't want him to leave his wife."

"And those two young boys! Not that young, but thirteen and fifteen is young enough. I don't want to be part of breaking up a family."

Cass nodded, staring into space. "We know all about that, don't we?"

LILY FINALLY WROTE TO HER FATHER IN March. She had hesitated for years about asking Celia, but only a few days after their conversation at Christmas, she had Claude's actual address. Talking to her mother had been less painful than she'd expected—exciting, even, to hear what her parents had been like as a young couple. Except, now that she had this vital piece of information, she wasn't sure what to do with it.

Celia had scrawled the address on a piece of blue paper. "I don't have an email or mobile for him, darling," she said. "That shows how long it's been since our last contact. There was a telephone number, but I rang it a few years ago and it was disconnected. Perhaps the area codes have changed. You could probably find the new number on the internet, if you wanted."

"OK, thanks, Mum," Lily said. "I'll look online—or maybe I'll just write." She wondered why Celia had tried to ring him.

She tucked the piece of paper beneath her passport in her bedside drawer. From time to time, she took it out and studied the address. She thought of the letter she might write; she weighed words in her mind. For now, it was enough to have the possibility of writing: even though she wasn't any closer to finding him, she felt as though the first stage had been completed. She was happy and settled in her new flat. The break in Saint Lucia had done her good, and Harry seemed calmer too—less desperate, less reckless.

The arrangement with Lady Archer downstairs was working out too, and they soon established a close friendship. Susan didn't need Lily's help or demand her company, but they were useful to each other in different ways. When Lily went to do a big supermarket shop in her mum's car, she would pick up double quantities of bottled water, kitchen rolls, and washing powder—the boring, heavy stuff—for which Susan reimbursed her. In return, Susan's cleaning lady came upstairs once a week and did a "quick whizz round" Lily's flat, although her whizz round with her vacuum cleaner and mop was far more thorough than any cleaning Lily did herself. Cassie often marvelled at how sparkling the kitchen and bathroom were, and grumbled at the state of her own flat.

Susan was interested and caring, but not intrusive. Lily enjoyed their conversations about politics, family, the weather, or just trivial gossip from the glossy magazines they passed on to each other.

Lily had also taken to gardening, which Susan encouraged. A young man came to cut the grass every few weeks, but there was still plenty of weeding and tidying to be done. In her Camden flat, she'd had no outside space, only a window box, so having an entire garden was a revelation. She wasn't exactly green-fingered, but she was learning. And Susan enjoyed seeing the garden, neglected since her daughter had left, coming back to life. She'd missed the sound of laughter and voices around the place.

As for her sisters, they couldn't believe how lucky she was. "If you weren't my sister, I'd really dislike you," Cassie said. "In fact, I'm seriously jealous. How can my little sister afford to live in Belsize Park with such a beautiful flat and all this space?!"

"Basically, Susan has lots of money and not much time—and Lily has lots of time and not much money," was Olivia's analysis. She was absolutely right, and it suited them both.

Celia, who'd become a devoted gardener since her children had grown up, fell in love with Susan's garden too. On milder afternoons, Lily and her mother dug borders and planted bulbs, pruned the rose bushes and tidied the large terrace. When she was home, Susan joined them outside, and the three women chatted about flowers, children, men, cooking, and life.

One early spring evening, Susan's gentleman friend arrived in his chauffeur-driven car—they were sure he was a high-court judge or former cabinet minister—with an elegant set of patio furniture. He seemed to know his hydrangeas from his hyacinths and was enthusiastic about the latest garden plantings. They had drinks outside and discussed plans for fruit trees, maybe even a vegetable patch at the bottom of the garden.

Lily sometimes sat on the terrace alone in the early mornings with a cup of coffee. It was still chilly but she liked to gaze at the garden and imagine the people who had passed through it over the decades. One morning, some lines from childhood floated through her head: *"And all the lives we ever lived, And all the lives to be, Are full of trees and changing leaves . . ."* Was that her father's voice? Once she had remembered them, she heard these lines over and over, spoken in a low, deep voice.

There were other ways in which Susan and Lily helped each other—taking in parcels or letting in workmen. Lily was happy to feed Susan's cats when she went away, and her presence upstairs helped keep burglars at bay. When Susan had a party with caterers and there was food left over, she always brought it upstairs. "Well *I'll* never get through all this, my dear, and you know I can't abide waste. Besides, when would I eat it, I'm never home!"

It was true: with her House of Lords duties and endless stream of friends, Susan had much the busier social life. Lily found it exhausting just to watch her rushing in and out of taxis, to her gallery openings and blow-dries and manicures, concerts, board meetings, and the various arts committees on which she sat.

One Saturday morning, Lily woke up and knew that she would write to Claude. She dressed in a white T-shirt and grey jeans, pulled on a baseball cap, and grabbed a pen and paper. She walked to her favourite café on Haverstock Hill, bought a mocha flat white, and found a quiet corner table.

Dear Claude,

Excuse me for writing out of the blue. It's Lily, your daughter. I live in London, as do the others, Cassie and Olivia and James, and we're all fine. Mum's fine too. Here's my address and email, just in case.

"Just in case" what? She didn't know what else to say, so she simply signed off, awkwardly:

Best wishes from Lily.

Why was she writing to him? Would he care about her now when he hadn't cared decades ago? Something in the spring air enabled her to swallow the bitterness she had felt for years. She just wanted to let him know that she existed, that they all existed. Beyond that, she wasn't sure.

It was curiously intimate, her own handwriting on notepaper. An email would have been less revealing, a phone call too sudden, even confrontational. She looked at the letter for a long time before she put it in the envelope. She walked to the post office and bought a stamp for the US, then hesitated at the letterbox outside Belsize Park Tube station.

She hadn't told the others about contacting Claude, not even Cassie. They never discussed it much growing up, although from their rare conversations Lily knew that they shared her sense of rejection. James seemed angry when their father's name came up, whereas Olivia was vague and avoided the subject. They were all confused. Nothing had been explained to them, and they didn't want to press Celia for details. Whatever had happened between them, she had obviously been deeply hurt. As young children, they had been protective of their mother for precisely this reason. Even hearing Claude's name brought a veil of sadness into Celia's eyes; they saw this and didn't know what to do.

James had never met his father—Claude had left when Celia was pregnant with him. Cassie had been eight at the time, Lily five, and Olivia just two. Lily sometimes wanted to ask Cassie what she remembered of him. She had only hazy memories: a tall man who threw her in the air and caught her in his arms, bear hugs and rough wool sweaters, but then she wondered if these were father images she'd absorbed later from books or television. Shouldn't she remember any more about a man who had been there for the first five years of her life? She strained to recall some specific details and felt like a failure when nothing came. Once in a while, that low voice in her head, those lines of poetry: *"And all the lives we ever lived, And all the lives to be, Are full of trees and changing leaves . . ."*

Even once she'd posted the letter, she wasn't clear what she hoped for in return. It was enough to have written to him. Now she must put it out of her mind.

LILY WAS STRETCHED FULL-LENGTH ON the sofa in the living room, still in her bathrobe. She'd just finished talking on the phone to Harry. After a difficult few weeks, he was in good form again. "Last night was lovely," he said. "I missed you all the way home, and you were my first thought when I woke up this morning."

"It was a nice evening," Lily said, "I loved the restaurant. And you seemed—I don't know, happier, more relaxed. Are things better . . ." she hesitated. "Are things better at home?"

"Oh, things here are . . . same as ever," Harry said. "In fact, I'm being summoned right now." He dropped his voice. "Apparently, I'm driving to the garden centre. You see my exciting Saturday plans. What about you?"

"Just pottering. Shopping with Cass this afternoon, and we'll probably all have Sunday lunch at Mum's tomorrow."

"Gotta go," Harry whispered. "Love you. Bye."

Lily was used to the abrupt hang-up by now. As she put down the phone, she heard a knock at the door. "Is that you, Susan? Come in!"

There was the clack of high heels being slipped off in the wooden hallway and Susan popped her head around the doorframe.

"The fragrant Lady Archer!" Lily said. "How lovely to see you." This joke about the disgraced politician Jeffrey Archer's wife made them both smile, no matter how many times she said it.

"Have I woken you?"

"Not at all. I was about to jump into the shower, then Harry rang—which is why I'm not dressed. Let me make you a coffee or something." Lily moved to get up from the sofa, but Susan shook her head.

"You stay right there, I've got the hamper waiting in the hall." This was a large wicker hamper from Fortnum & Mason, originally a gift from one of her gentleman friends. She would periodically fill this with fresh fruit and vegetables, homemade soup, artisan bread, and other treats for Lily, and Susan being Susan, everything was of the highest quality.

Whenever Lily protested, Susan shushed her briskly, reminding her of the favours she'd done for her: ". . . anyway, you know I can't cook, my dear. There's some of that couscous you like, and some rather good lasagnes for the freezer, all made by the caterers. I had a party last night and they were cooking all day—it's more than enough for me."

"Now, to business." Susan sat down on the sofa beside Lily. "I'm not going to take up your whole morning, but I've made coffee which we could have with these nice pastries. There's something I want to ask you." Rummaging in the large hamper she produced a silver thermos and a Tupperware box. "Cinnamon whirls from the House of Lords!"

She poured out steaming mugs of coffee. "It's the Colombian stuff we like, freshly brewed. Now, what I wanted to ask, it's about your mother." Susan was always direct when there was something on her mind. "Do you think Celia gets lonely?"

Lily hesitated. "Mum? Lonely? I'm not sure. She keeps busy, but I suppose she might be a bit lonely sometimes. We've never really discussed it. Why?"

"Do you remember a few weeks ago when you and your mother were doing up the terrace? Patrick came round with some new garden furniture, and we all sat outside and had a drink."

"Yes, I remember—the handsome chap with the driver—is that his name, Patrick?" Susan had plenty of gentleman friends, and Lily and Celia had assumed this was another one of her admirers. "He seemed very nice. Are you and Patrick . . . together? Are you a couple?" Lily wasn't sure of the terminology—"boyfriend" seemed inappropriate for a man of his seniority.

"Me and Paddy?" Susan roared with laughter. "No, no, he's my brother, two years older than me. Sorry, I thought I'd mentioned it, that's why he's got the private car and all that. He sits in the House of Lords too, we've both got the family title . . ."

Lily was laughing too by this point. "I didn't know you had a brother, Susan! There was me, thinking he was one of your red-hot lovers."

"Stop it!" Susan rolled her eyes. "I don't have time for lovers, red hot or not! Anyway, ever since Patrick met you both that evening, he's asked quite a few questions—specifically about Celia. I wasn't sure if she liked him, or if she had a chap, or whether she's quite happy on her own, thank you very much. I can't abide matchmaking, there's nothing worse than interfering in other people's lives, but I just wondered . . . well, I thought I'd ask, that's all."

Lily thought back to that evening. She remembered a tall, silver-haired gentleman, who come to think of it did resemble Susan around the eyes. He'd helped his driver to carry the wrought-iron garden table and chairs through from the car; he had seemed vigorous and strong for his age. He and Celia had chatted happily on the terrace while Lily and Susan went inside to get wineglasses. Later, they had strolled around the garden, discussing possible sites for the vegetable patch.

"Let me ask her," Lily said. "As far as I can remember, they got on well. And I think Mum could do with some male company. Or maybe, rather than us saying anything, maybe they could just meet again?"

Susan looked at her, eyes flashing with the germ of an idea. "Aha. You're absolutely right. There's nothing worse than being set up on a date, but if they happened to be here at the same time . . . I'm in the mood for a garden party, especially with this wonderful weather and all the planting you've done outside, you and Celia."

No wonder Susan ran so many committees, Lily thought, she was a born organiser. Already she was reaching for her handbag and pulling out her reading glasses, her slim fountain pen, and her crocodile-skin Smythson notebook. Put her in charge of venues for a party, caterers, and guest lists, and Susan was in her element.

"You have your shower and get dressed, Lily—and then, come downstairs; we'll have a sherry and put our heads together. We've got a garden party to organise."

YOU HAVE NO RIGHT. HARRY GRITTED HIS teeth and clenched his fists. This had become his hopeless mantra whenever the jealousy got unbearable: when Lily referred vaguely to an evening out, or answered a text message in his presence, or left early to meet "a friend." Harry knew it was that ex of hers, David, and he couldn't stand it. He'd promised Dr. Christos that he wouldn't follow her again, but he had, several times, during that spring and summer.

In September he caught the end of a phone call as she walked along the corridor outside his office: "Sure, come over at seven. Of course, I totally understand. You know I'm here for you." Was Harry imagining a flirtatious tone in her voice? Why didn't she speak like that to him? Hating himself, he'd gone to wait outside her flat again that evening, hidden under trees on the opposite side of the road. It was just getting dark, and he could see the lights were on in the top two floors of the house. Just after seven p.m. a silver sports car drew up, and he knew it must be David, a tall, athletic-looking guy in his early thirties. He parked the car and got out, holding a bottle of wine.

Harry had been drinking since he left work, and he had to restrain himself from running over and grabbing the guy. *Who do you think you are? What do you want with Lily? Who do you think helped her buy that bloody flat?* He knew he had to get hold of himself.

They didn't leave the flat. Harry stayed there, across the road, for several hours, getting colder, smoking, looking up at her windows. A Deliveroo motorbike arrived with pizza around eight. He went into the pub on the corner and threw back a couple of whiskies. Hours went by, it seemed, and still the man didn't leave.

"I wasn't thinking straight," he told Dr. Christos. "I waited for ages, then went into the pub on the corner opposite her flat until closing time. I'd drunk three or four double whiskies quite quickly and I was full of anger and booze. I thought if I confronted him— this ex of hers, David—maybe Lily would realise how much she was hurting me."

"Go on," Dr. Christos said.

"I stormed up to the front door and pressed Lily's bell. She was asking over the intercom who it was, but I just kept my finger on the buzzer because I wanted her to come down and talk to me. In the end, David came down, which was the worst thing which could have happened." Harry shook his head. "It was grotesque. I was ridiculous. Drunk, stumbling, shouting at him, did he know who I was, did he know who'd bought Lily that flat, God knows what else I said . . ."

"And your hand?" Dr. Christos gestured towards the large white bandage on Harry's right hand.

"Oh. At some point I was threatening him, and I swung at him and ended up punching the front door, or maybe the wall beside the door. It was when Lily came down. She was dressed but barefoot— she looked so beautiful. I couldn't take it, I was convinced they'd been in bed together, and it made me want to kill the man. I mean, he had his chance with her, their relationship ended years ago, so what's he doing back on the scene?"

"CASSIE, IT WAS AWFUL. HE'D LEFT WORK early and had clearly been drinking for hours, I've never seen him so drunk and out of control. He was shouting at David, throwing punches and lunging . . ."

"Lunging at David?" Cassie couldn't help laughing. "Mixed martial arts and twenty years younger than Harry?"

"I know," Lily said. "And the ridiculous thing is, there's absolutely nothing going on between me and David. We were sitting upstairs on opposite sofas, discussing his ex-wife. He's still really cut up about their divorce, and apparently she's been ringing him, and now they're both wondering if they've made a mistake. We ordered a pizza, discussed David's marital woes, and watched *Newsnight*. You do believe me, Cass, nothing happened with David?"

"Of course I do. I'm more concerned about Harry, though. He sounds dangerous."

Lily got up and closed her office door, speaking quietly into her phone. "He's not dangerous. It was the alcohol more than anything, he was off his head. After I came downstairs and asked him to leave, he started swearing and crying and said he should never have wasted his time on me. He lurched into the road trying to hail a black cab, cars swerving around him and blaring their horns. David was so kind, though. He calmed him down and called him an Uber and smoked a cigarette with him till it arrived."

"What is Harry's problem?" Cassie sounded outraged. "Does he actually think he has rights over you? It's none of his business if you choose to see David, or any other man for that matter. He's the one who's married with children, not you. You're a free agent."

"I know, Cass, I know. I love Harry, but this is wrong. I don't know what he thinks he's seen, whether he's been listening to my calls or what, but I've honestly never cheated on him. It was terrible seeing him crying and pitifully drunk, with that swollen hand, and he wouldn't let us take him to the hospital. I didn't know what to do, how to get him home safely."

"Seriously, Lil, Harry is delusional. I always liked the guy, but this is nuts. You should report him to the police for what he did last night. If it's not assault, it's definitely stalking."

"I don't want to report him," Lily said, her voice flat with exhaustion. "I love him, but he's really troubled right now. After David left, around eleven, I sat there on the living room floor and I felt . . . unsafe. I looked around my flat, wondering if there were cameras hidden in corners, if Harry's accessing my phone and things, you know?"

"I'm sure it hasn't gone that far," Cassie said. "It sounds like last night was a terrible combination of booze and jealousy, but hopefully it was just a one-off. Is he at work today—have you spoken to him?"

"I haven't seen him," Lily said. "We had a departmental meeting this morning, and he didn't show up. His office door is closed and there's no sign of his laptop or jacket. Everyone's asking me where he is. I think maybe he had an appointment with his shrink, but I'm not sure. I'll give it a few more hours and try calling him before I leave here."

*　　*　　*

I thought things couldn't get any worse, after finding Harry's phone and discovering—well, basically everything. All these months I've lived with that knowledge, all the places he's been with Lily, all the lies he's told me, all the money and love he's been lavishing on her, and yet I've said nothing. Why? Because I'm too scared to confront him, I suppose. Because it always comes down to this: I confront him, tell him I know everything, then he says, "Yes, it's true and I want a divorce . . ."

And then what? Remember in Florida when I confided in Polly and she told me that Andrew had done the same thing, but she left it and eventually it blew over . . . I wanted to believe her—and I almost convinced myself in the end that it was the right choice, the dutiful, morally right choice. I was being a good wife, thinking of our family unit, thinking of the boys' future, keeping us together. I told myself that Harry's fling was just a midlife crisis, a last spark of passion as he feels his male virility ebbing away (OK, that bit was from Poll), all middle-aged men do it, boys will be boys, etc.

But it wasn't just a fling, and it hasn't ended. Since I've known the truth, I've become cleverer and he's become lazier. I can read him like a book, the "late nights in London doing work things" are evenings with Lily. I can smell the unfamiliar scent on him when he gets back—her shower gel, deodorant or detergent, whatever it is—a woman knows when it's not from her home. I can see at a glance the hastily rearranged shirt and tie, the damp tousled hair. Don't tell me that's normal at midnight after a long working day. With a couple of checks—on his phone (still no password) and his bank balance—I can see he's spending as much time with her as ever. It still upsets me, of course. But like I said in my last blog, until I decide what to do I'm sort of . . . well, living with it.

And now this. I don't know what to make of it. We had people coming for dinner last night, the house master and his wife from Joe and Dan's school. Apparently it's expected of us, to invite the house master for dinner, everyone does it. The evening had been arranged for ages, and I'd reminded Harry about it over breakfast. He said he'd clear his diary and leave the office early, he even said he'd pick up flowers and wine on the way home.

So much for flowers. He simply didn't show up. He didn't even ring with an excuse. I must have called him ten or twenty times, until our guests arrived, at which point I had to invent a work-related reason for Harry's non-appearance.

They left around eleven thirty p.m., sympathetic and clearly embarrassed for me. I cleared away dinner, trying to work my rage out on the

kitchen surfaces, smashing a few wineglasses along the way. I kept think-
ing what I'd say to Harry when he got back, how he'd let me down yet
again, what a terrible impression we'd made on the boys' house master. I
was so angry but I had no energy for another pointless argument, yet
more recriminations on my side and more lies on his.

It was nearly one a.m. and I was getting into bed when I heard the
familiar crunching of cab wheels on gravel. Harry stumbled up the
driveway and started ringing the doorbell. He had no cash for the
driver, no house keys, and he was holding a bottle of something, whisky
I think. One of his hands was swollen and bleeding, and it looked like
he'd been crying. All my anger evaporated. Harry was drunk and con-
fused and pitiful. In twenty years of marriage, I'd never seen him in
such a state.

I paid the driver and went straight back upstairs. Harry stayed
downstairs all night—I don't think either of us got any sleep. And Daniel
said something strange at breakfast. He said he'd woken in the night and
Harry was standing beside his bed, not saying anything, just standing
there. Joe said Dan was probably imagining it, but I don't know.

IT WAS A FEW DAYS LATER, AROUND HALF
past six, when Harry left the house. He'd barely slept since the scene
outside Lily's place. He'd been drinking his way through the nights,
sitting in the dark kitchen, wandering around the garden smoking,
his hand still swollen and his body aching with despair. He had seen
Dr. Christos but it hadn't helped. Nothing helped.

That morning something inside him shifted. He got into the car
as if driving to the early train to London, but somewhere along the
way he realised he wasn't going there. He skirted the train station,
turned at random onto a road out of town, away from his home,
away from the school, the shops, this familiar neighbourhood where

they had lived for more than ten years. After a while he found himself on the motorway heading for the south coast, the place he grew up, where he had been happy as a boy. He kept visualising the sea and the sky, open space and emptiness. A way out.

He was driving fast on the motorway, gripping the steering wheel tight, beads of sweat on his forehead, his jaw clenched. His thoughts were racing, caught in a spiral: Lily, Dan and Joe, the confusion, needing to sleep, the pain in his back, everything ruined, never seeing them, touching her face, Pippa's anger, Lily's tears . . .

Harry drove blindly towards the sea and the sky, fleeing the mess he'd made of everything. His bridges were burned now and there was no way back. He pulled out a cigarette but he couldn't light the damn thing, he couldn't hold the lighter steady. He needed to put his head in his hands, his head was too heavy, but his hands were shaking, and he was hot, so hot, he was burning up. It was a cold morning but his hands were slippery with sweat and his shirt was sticking to his back.

He found the button for the window, then there was a rush of cold air and the relief of a breeze through the car, somewhere the sound of birds. He closed his eyes for a moment and rested his head against the window frame. He swerved and opened his eyes, gripping the steering wheel tighter, aware that he was driving too fast. The air cooled him and he felt calmer but very weak. The road ahead was a blur. More slowly now, he saw vivid images of the people he'd loved: Dan and Joe when they were first born, tiny and soft and new. The baby daughter who had lived only a few hours. Pippa walking down the aisle towards him, so young and full of hope. His father's face when he was dying. Lily's smile.

He looked away from the road ahead, at the woods, the trees. He saw the leaves in red, orange, and gold, the fiery colours reminding him that it was autumn. Through the fog in his head, the pain rose up again, the shame and guilt of failure, a man who has let everyone down, the panic of a trapped animal. He was nearing the coast: *There, there's space to breathe,* he said, out loud or in his head.

Suddenly there was a shrill noise, jolting him back to the present. He looked down and saw his phone on the passenger seat alongside scattered cigarettes and the lighter. He tried to block the ringing out of his head but it went on and on, like a baby crying, adding to the voices and the chaos in his brain. He picked up the phone and looked at the screen: Lily's name was flashing up.

"No, Lily, no," he muttered. He wanted to answer it—he longed to talk to her one last time—but he couldn't, just left it to ring and ring. It hurt to know that Lily was trying to reach him, but he knew that if he heard her voice he wouldn't be able to go through with this, and he had to, for everyone's sake. There were tears streaming down his face, and Harry was surprised to notice that he was crying. He hadn't realised that letting go would be this hard.

Suddenly the sky opened up, a salty, briny smell filled the car, and he was at the coast. He skidded roughly into a gravel car park, turned off the engine, and rested his forehead against the steering wheel. The phone started ringing again and he stared at Lily's name on the screen, willing her to stop and willing her to keep trying. The voices in his head fell silent and then the phone stopped ringing too. Everything was ending, everything was closing in.

Harry wrenched open the car door, leaving the key in the ignition and the door open, and crossed the deserted, scrubby headland towards the white cliffs. The clouds were racing overhead, the gulls were dipping and wheeling on invisible currents of wind. Everything was bright and the morning sky seemed wide open. The sea stretched away, foggy grey green, and there was nothing visible on the horizon. He remembered lying on the floor of his study with Lily, warm and naked in his arms. They had gazed up through the skylight at the blue skies that first summer:

. . . When I spoke of Patagonia, I meant
skies all empty aching blue. I meant
years. I meant all of them with you.

Had he spoken those lines out loud, or only thought them? He felt she should hear them before he went.

This was the coastline of Harry's childhood; he knew these cliffs like he knew his own hands. Scanning the bay, he saw Dungeness in the east and Selsey Bill in the west. He looked across the sandy dunes to where the pampas grass was waving. This was the place Harry loved, but there was no comfort here today.

Despite the expanse of sea and sky, the darkness closed in again: an inferno of pain in his spine and in his brain. From far away Harry could hear his breathing and his heart pounding in his chest. He was filled with the purest fear and all he wanted was peace. He felt the crumbling ground beneath his feet, the loose stones and chalky cliffs; he closed his eyes and jumped. The screaming of the gulls grew fainter and the wind filled his ears and the waves rushed in.

It was 8.13 a.m. In London, Lily felt something snap.

TWO NIGHTMARISH DAYS LATER, AND HER managing director was calling her at dawn. Lily hadn't slept all night, wondering what to do. She lay wide awake on her bed, staring at her phone. She didn't recognise the number but she knew it was bad news.

On the line, Colin's voice cracked. "There's no easy way to say this. It's . . . it's bad news, I'm afraid. Harry was found, late last night. He's dead. A man walking his dog along the cliffs, down on the south coast, saw a body. He was identified by a family member early this morning."

Lily put her hand to her mouth, silent. What was there to say? She had known that Harry was dead since that moment on Friday morning when something snapped. She knew exactly where he would have gone. She took a few shallow breaths, the room lurching around her. She murmured something, later she couldn't remember what, about it being terribly sad for his children. Colin omitted any specifics, and Lily couldn't ask what she needed to know: *Who had identified him? Where had they taken him?* They ended the phone call as quickly as possible.

Up till now, Colin and Lily's dealings had been limited to those occasional professional interactions. Now, between them was an unspoken mass of problems: that Lily worked for Colin and Harry, that their wives were close, that Lily would be grieving and had no right to, that no one knew exactly how much Harry's wife knew. And Lily didn't forget that Colin had just lost his best friend. To call it a mess didn't come close.

Colin had made it clear that it would be a lot easier for all concerned if Lily stayed away from the office for a while. "Let things blow over" was the phrase he'd used. However, from that first moment, Lily knew she mustn't stay away. If she'd avoided work, she couldn't have gone back, not ever. It was important to face everyone immediately—staying away would only make it unbearable.

Harder even than the scrutiny was going back to Harry's office. Every room in that building was haunted with him, every document held his imprint. In those first few days, she felt his presence everywhere. When the internal phone rang, she automatically expected Harry's extension number to flash up. When the glass door to her office swung open, she'd look up, forgetting for a moment, expecting to see his tall frame filling the doorway.

Early on Monday morning, the day after Colin's call, she had gone into Harry's office before the cleaners arrived. She took the key from where he hid it on top of the bookshelves and unlocked his desk drawer. She removed photographs, letters, airline tickets, three bottles of pills. She reclaimed a pair of silver cufflinks—tiny sailing boats—a present she'd given him for his last birthday. She added a handful of receipts to the pile. This was risky, she knew, and maybe illegal: after a suicide everything was needed as evidence, wasn't it?

Lily didn't care. Illegal or not, she wasn't having her relationship with Harry picked over. These letters and photos wouldn't tell them anything except that the two of them were deeply involved. As for the tranquillisers and other pills, she didn't know exactly what Harry had been taking, but she didn't want him incriminated even more than he already was. Yes, he'd been in a terrible state at the end, but none of that would change anything.

She was aware how futile it was removing these few possessions now, trying to cover his tracks when almost everything was out there in cyberspace. The police would have already accessed his last calls and texts, they would have copies of his bank accounts showing hotel bookings and flights, restaurants they had been to, gifts he had bought her. They would speak to his wife, his sons, his psychiatrist and GP.

She shuddered to think of strangers reading their private messages. She remembered the text he'd sent her that night, at some point after he confronted her outside the flat, staggering around drunk in her street swinging punches at David, even that text—*forgive me Lily, I love you*—a message she hadn't told anyone about, that wouldn't be a secret for long.

She was leaving the office when she noticed the corner of an envelope just sticking out from beneath the desk. It was a thick, cream envelope with her name on it, in Harry's large scrawl, his usual navy ink. Feeling furtive and guilty, she added it to the stack of papers and walked back down the deserted corridor to her own office.

SHE WAITED UNTIL SHE GOT HOME THAT
evening to open the letter. *Dearest Lily,* it read. *I won't be back and I
wanted to say goodbye.* Lily's heart began to thump, painfully. She'd
known he was dead since Friday morning—and Colin had confirmed this—but somehow reading the letter gave her an illogical
burst of hope. *I won't be back* was pretty final, but maybe he was
writing to tell her he'd just gone away for a while? Anything, Lily
thought, any crazy scheme—that he'd changed his identity and
emigrated to Tasmania—would be more acceptable than his death.

*Hopefully, you'll find this letter before they start rummaging
through my stuff because it concerns something only between us: the
flat in England's Lane. I wanted to let you know that it's yours
now, all done and paid off.*

Lily took a sharp intake of breath. She could hear Harry's
matter-of-fact tone even at this moment of stupendous generosity,
she knew him so well.

She realised that a letter was the only way he could tell her about
this, to guarantee there would be no digital record.

*I've sorted everything out with my financial advisor and your
mortgage company. There will be no trace and no trail. I also had
a brief conversation with Lady Archer and she understands the
situation. The deeds are in your name—as I won't be here I wanted
to let you know where you stand. It's only property, Lily, but I hope
it will help. Maybe it will give you the freedom to do whatever you
want, whether that's staying on at work or going freelance or setting up your own business or travelling the world. It's a small*

token of my love for you because you have changed my life. I can't express in words . . . and I think you know already . . . thank you for giving a trapped, depressed, middle-aged fool so much happiness over the past couple of years. I like to think of you in England's Lane, where we had such good times.

Yours always,
Harry

She sat on the floor of the living room, reading and rereading his final words, looking for a clue. Was there something else he was saying, something she could do?

No suicide note had been found; Colin had been clear about that. This letter was the closest thing anyone had to a statement of intent. *I won't be back,* he wrote, but what would it tell them?

Lily stood up and walked over to the window. Her head was spinning. She gazed out across the treetops, seeing nothing. She couldn't make sense of it. When did he buy the flat? When did he write this letter? How long had he been planning his suicide?

She knew that she should tell someone about this letter, but she wouldn't. Already the invasion of their communications, their emails and texts, felt like a violation. Surrendering Harry's letter would also cause practical problems with his wife and family. This letter was all she had now that was truly private. These were Harry's last words to her, and she was keeping them to herself.

LILY KEPT WORKING. SHE DIDN'T TAKE time out from the office and never left early. The situation was a disaster, but she had to keep going somehow. She wasn't sure whether working made things harder or easier, but she refused to let herself think about it too deeply. She showered in the morning and dressed smartly; she drank coffee and attended meetings and gave presentations; she was functioning OK on the outside at least. What was the alternative? It was a relief to work, to lose herself for a few hours writing up a commissioning proposal or an author contract. Then she'd be referring back to a document in the files, and she'd turn a page and see Harry's full name, his handwritten signature, and it would hit her afresh, and she'd find herself staring at the scrawled ink in unbearable pain, tears stinging her eyes (although she never let anyone see her cry). Thank God she had her own office.

As Colin had hinted in that first telephone call, Lily's presence was problematic. Nothing happened for a few days: he convened a staff meeting and announced Harry's "sudden death," supplying few details. It seemed he might leave Lily alone. Then colleagues began to talk, authors rang and asked questions, the trade press got wind of the intrigue and published the story. It was the talk of every book launch and publishing party. A fortnight after Harry's death, the directors conferred, and Lily was summoned to Colin's office.

He spoke to her for barely three minutes, never once meeting her eyes. He asked her to report to the HR department to see the firm's occupational psychologist, whose remit was clearly to find Lily unfit for work. She was pressed in the strongest terms to sign herself off for a while. She was offered leave on full pay and a course of bereavement counselling.

This compassionate, indefinite amount of time "away from the office" was the thin end of the wedge, Lily knew that instantly. Not for a moment did she consider taking it up.

She understood why they wanted her gone. Having her haunting the corridors, wringing her hands like some modern-day Ophelia, would be too inconvenient for words. Every time Colin saw her, he saw Harry, his old colleague and friend. She understood, but she was determined not to resign. Nothing would trigger her depression more than empty, workless hours—she already had entire nights to think about Harry's death; at least for eight hours a day she could sit at her computer and be productive. She missed him with every fibre of her being but she was desperate to stay busy.

And another part of her decision was sheer bloody-mindedness: She enjoyed her job; why should they get rid of her? Did they fear that she would do or say something inappropriate? In those weeks following Harry's death, Lily grew up more quickly than any other time in her life. She learned that many people, even close friends and colleagues, don't want to be around grief. She learned that bereavement is a social embarrassment. On the first day there were hugs of condolence, but in the weeks that followed, she found herself increasingly isolated.

At night, she read and reread a battered copy of C. S. Lewis's *A Grief Observed*: "*No one ever told me that grief felt so like fear. I am not afraid, but the sensation is like being afraid. At other times it feels like being mildly drunk, or concussed. There is a sort of invisible blanket between the world and me. I find it hard to take in what anyone says. Or perhaps, hard to want to take it in. It is so uninteresting.*"

Lewis's words struck home. Without meaning to, she found it hard to take in what was happening in the world around her. She stared at the news on television, unable to understand what the reporters were saying. With colleagues she cast a sombre shadow, like the death's head at the feast, and so they avoided her.

It wasn't that she cared, not really. Death puts things into perspective. Some friends can't come with you to a new reality, that's all. Grief is inconvenient and embarrassing and boring and repetitive. The ones who keep ringing and keep listening to memories and tears and regrets, those are the true friends.

So Lily stayed at HEP and worked harder than ever. Less than a month after Harry's death, she won two bestselling authors from a rival firm, a project the two of them had been plotting for ages. Work was work, and Lily maintained absolute privacy about her loss. She had to harden herself to get through this time. No matter how devastated she felt, she never let the cracks show. At home she allowed herself to fall apart—some evenings she found herself lying on the floor, doubled up with grief—but never once at the office. She refused to let herself be hounded out of a job she was good at. Harry would have approved of her stubbornness.

IT WAS THREE WEEKS AFTER HIS DEATH when Lily realised. She was lying in bed alone in her flat, and she had this thought: it's not goodbye. For a while now, she'd been aware of something physically different. Not wrong exactly, just different. Without following any logical thought pattern, her body simply told her that a part of Harry was still here. He wasn't all gone. After everything that had already happened, somehow this wasn't a shock. She was pregnant.

Lily curled on her side, eyes wide open, staring into the darkness of her bedroom. A gentle night breeze lifted the white curtains at the window. She thought of everything that had happened over the past few years: a wedding, then a suicide, soon there would be a funeral and then a birth. She thought of Harry and wondered what he would make of it all.

LILY HAD COPED FOR SO LONG, IT WAS A shock to everyone when she finally crashed. Throughout the autumn she'd held things together, outwardly at least, going to work, answering the phone, seeing the family and dealing with life.

It wasn't a dramatic crash, more of a thirty-six-hour wobble. She left London and went to the coast. She had realised she was pregnant at the same time as she was starting to accept that Harry truly wasn't coming back. But Lily had had no experience of either situation before and had nowhere to put the emotions they were churning up. A pregnancy was one thing, even an unplanned pregnancy, but this, on her own and without Harry to talk to . . .

She wasn't sure what she believed about death, whether there was anything left of a person after they died. She didn't believe in reincarnation, but since Harry's suicide she had felt his presence very strongly at times. These moments usually occurred when she was lying in bed at night, unable to sleep. That was when she missed him most and felt closest to him. She had taken to getting out of bed, opening the large skylight in her bedroom, and leaning out to look at the stars. The air was much colder now that autumn was here, and she shivered in her cotton bathrobe.

One star was much brighter than the others, and she always felt it was Harry looking down on her.

Give me my Romeo; and, when he shall die,
Take him and cut him out in little stars,
And he will make the face of heaven so fine
That all the world will be in love with night . . .

Lily murmured those lines from *Romeo and Juliet* to herself, looking up at the night sky, aware that talking to oneself was an early sign of madness. But the only escape she found during these nights was in books, it had always been that way. She would drift over to the bookshelves to check the lines in her head and end up reading until dawn.

Looking up at the dark sky, she talked to Harry—not out loud, but in her head—and felt certain that he hadn't disappeared. If he was watching over her, did he know about the baby? She wasn't sure. Sometimes she felt very alone.

Her emotions about the baby were complex too. She was surprised how calm she'd been thus far. Within their family, Olivia was the drama queen, with her endless romantic entanglements, dramatic break-ups, getting sacked from jobs—everything in Olivia's life was a fertile opportunity for a crisis. Now it was Lily with all the drama, and she was quietly baffled where it had all come from. Should she be reacting differently, she wondered, having some kind of breakdown? Maybe it was just that dealing with Harry's death was so damn tiring.

It wasn't straightforward, though. Sometimes she would feel calm all day, and then suddenly find herself gripped by a tidal wave of fear. Mostly she felt very tender towards this unborn baby, grateful to Harry for leaving something behind. It was his unintended legacy, a way for her to hold on to him. He wasn't completely gone and she wasn't totally alone. Then at other times she felt angry with him for being irresponsible, immature, feckless. She would throw all the cruellest accusations she could think of at him, a middle-aged man acting like a teenager, thinking only of himself and his desires, taking for granted his comfortable lifestyle and swanky car, the high-paid directorship. He had a wife providing for him when he bothered to go home, two sons waiting for their dad, and yet he wanted a pretty young girlfriend too, handy with her London flat near the office. Trying to buy her affection with his cash? Who the hell did he think he was? And then, after screwing things up for everyone else, he decided it was too much for him, and checked out of life, leaving her to deal with the consequences.

This anger was unworthy and unfair, Lily knew that. Whether it was due to pregnancy hormones or simply the jagged, uneven process of bereavement, she tried not to dwell on it. She hoped that if

Harry could hear her, he forgave her for the nasty thoughts she sometimes had.

That brief trip to the coast was a frightening blur. She simply left London after work without telling anyone, stayed in a room above a pub for one night, walked along the coast for an entire day. She switched her phone off and had some pretty dark thoughts. Was she going to follow Harry into oblivion? If it had just been her own life, she might have considered it. But she wasn't alone anymore.

Whether it was a sense of responsibility to the baby, her family, or just a life-force, Lily would afterwards never know. She spent hours walking along those cliffs, walking to be closer to Harry, but not to the very edge. Something pulled her through. Coming home, she'd gone straight to Cassie and Charlie's flat, knowing she would be welcome. She spent a few days there being looked after. For the first time since Harry's death, Lily allowed herself to fall apart a little, and it was a relief.

"IT'S OK, MUM, SHE'S HERE." CASSIE KEPT HER voice low even though Lily wasn't in the room. "She arrived about an hour ago, she seems tired and confused, but she's fine and she's safe."

"Oh, thank goodness." Celia sounded close to tears. "Did she say anything? Where's she been? What's she's been doing?"

"She hasn't said much, just that she went somewhere on the coast where she and Harry used to go. I haven't asked too much yet. I'm running her a bath, and she's agreed to stay here for a day or two. Depending on how she's feeling, I could bring her round tomorrow."

"Yes, darling, do. Come for lunch tomorrow, just the two of you, if Lily's up to it. I know it's only been a day or so, but I've been so worried about her. After everything that's happened, I had this terrible dread she might . . . well, you know what I mean."

"Of course. I had the same dread, that she might disappear or do something drastic." The bathroom door opened, and Cassie saw her sister going into the spare room next door. "Anyway, Mum, I'll call you first thing in the morning and let you know. Lots of love."

She gave Lily a few minutes and then made two large mugs of Ovaltine. She tapped gently on the door of the spare room and found her sister sitting on the bed, still wrapped in a large bathrobe, her hair twisted up in a towel.

"I made us both a bedtime drink." She set one of the mugs down on the bedside table.

"Ovaltine! I haven't had this in years, Cass—is this what you and Charlie drink these days?" Lily teased.

"You see what a sad married couple we've become! Although if you want something stronger, I can put a slug of whisky in this?"

"Actually, no, this is delicious." Lily took a sip, thinking how long it would be until she could drink whisky again. She needed to tell her sister.

"Here, and this." Cassie put down a small bar of Dairy Milk beside the mug. "You didn't join us for dinner, and you need to keep your strength up."

"Aha!" Lily tore open the bar and bit into it. "Now this is exactly what I need."

Cassie looked pleased. "I wanted to make you hot chocolate, but we don't have any, so I thought Ovaltine and chocolate would be the next best thing." She was relieved to see Lily. It had been the briefest of absences—barely thirty-six hours—but she and her mother had instantly feared the worst. Silence fell between them.

"I have this memory," Cassie said hesitantly. "I don't know if you remember it too. When we were young, like really small kids, Dad used to take us to Primrose Hill every winter—maybe it was just one winter, I don't know—but I remember snowball fights and building snowmen and sledging down the hill on trays."

"After Primrose Hill, he'd take us to this café, and I'm certain it was in England's Lane. I don't think it's there anymore—probably replaced by a gluten-free bakery or an estate agent's—but it can't have been far from your flat. We'd take off our woolly hats and scarves and gloves, and Dad would buy us these huge mugs of hot chocolate topped with cream and marshmallows. It was sheer bliss!"

Lily listened eagerly, clinging to Cassie's words for a clue, desperate to dredge up some remnant of those precious times but finding a blank. Like all children who have almost no memories of their father, she was desperate to remember something too.

"Oh, Cass. I don't remember any of that. I wish I could. Imagine, hot chocolate in a café with our dad!" She smiled, but a sad smile. "I'm so glad it was on England's Lane, though ... You'll have to show me where it was next time you come over."

Cassie smiled. "And what about you?" She wasn't going to mention Harry, but she wanted to know what was going on in Lily's head.

Lily took a deep breath. "Cass, there's something I need to tell you." Her voice was more serious than she intended, but she went on: "You know me and Harry? Well, since he died, I've realised that we made a mistake. Not a mistake exactly, but something happened ... Anyway, I'm pretty sure I'm pregnant." She smiled, simply, and gestured her arms out to the sides, feeling silly at the dramatic announcement. It was like proposing to someone, she supposed, no matter how you said it: "I'm having a baby" or "Will you marry me?" The words made you sound like a character in a soap opera.

Cassie looked stunned: if Lily had wanted a big reaction, here it was. "Lil, are you sure? I mean, that's amazing, amazing news—are you OK, are you happy?" She threw her arms around her sister, then drew away, worried at Lily's silence. "Seriously, are you OK?"

Until this point, Lily had been keeping herself relatively together. She hadn't cried for over a week. But with the relief of telling someone, and Cass hugging her and showing concern, she found she was smiling and crying at the same time. They both were.

"Yes, I'm OK! I haven't really thought it through . . . I think I'm fine . . . a bit scared, but mostly happy." She paused. "I mean, I don't have any plans, I don't know what I'll do about work or money or being a single mum—haven't got a clue, actually—but I guess we'll be OK."

At that "we," Cassie let out a shriek of excitement and grabbed Lily for another hug. "No worrying allowed. I'll help you make plans, don't even think about it yet. You've got ages." Then she realised she didn't know how long, and looked closely at Lily. "How many weeks are you—when's the baby due, do you know? Listen to us, I can't even believe we're talking about you having a baby!"

"I'm not sure exactly," Lily admitted. "I haven't done a test. I'm just over twelve weeks I think. I know when it happened . . . In fact, it was the last time before Harry died." She smiled. "We were careless."

"And it's definitely Harry's?"

Lily smiled. "I told you, Cass, there hasn't been anyone else. It's a hundred per cent Harry's baby. If I'm actually pregnant, that is."

"You don't know for sure—you haven't checked?" Cassie, who loved a project, sprang into action. "Right, you need to do a test. We could go to the all-night pharmacy in Victoria now?" Lily shook her head, it was far too late. "OK—but let's get a test first thing tomorrow morning. Once we know for sure, we can work things out from there. Have you told Mum yet?"

CASSIE DRAGGED LILY OFF TO BUY A pregnancy test straight after breakfast. The digital display showed that she was eleven to twelve weeks pregnant, "which sounds about right," Lily said, working backwards to a certain careless weekend in August with Harry. Next they rang Celia, inviting themselves to lunch. "We have news!"

Lily was relieved that Cass was involved now; she'd been drifting, unsure what to do. She watched from a distance as her sister made plans, feeling slightly swept away by it all. Cass rang their doctor and secured Lily an appointment for the following day, as well as a date for her twelve-week scan and a "booking-in" date with the midwife, and then drove her to their mother's house in Hampstead.

Any niggling worries Lily had about Celia's reaction disappeared as soon as she told her, as they sat with bowls of pasta in the kitchen. This wasn't the 1950s, for goodness' sake; had she seriously thought that her mother would disapprove? In fact, Celia was over the moon. Like Cassie, she launched into the practicalities with gusto: "So you're eleven or twelve weeks now? Let's see, November, December . . ." She counted off the months on her fingers. "A May baby? Oh, Lily, how wonderful. You funny thing, keeping it a secret. How long have you known?" Celia adored babies and was relishing the prospect of her first grandchild.

With four grown-up children, Celia might have expected to be a grandmother sooner, but they had all taken their time settling down. Cassie was still the only one who was married. James lived with Su-Ki at her flat in West Hampstead, and Olivia was perpetually on and off with her Italian boyfriend Giovanni. Before Harry, Lily had usually had a steady boyfriend, and in the last two years they had accepted the older, married Harry too—he'd come to a few family parties, the odd birthday meal, and everyone liked him. But now Lily was having his baby, and he was gone.

All things considered, Celia was taking it very well. Like Cassie, she seemed genuinely excited. After they finished lunch, she sprang up from the kitchen table. "Come upstairs, both of you, I've got some wonderful things to show you."

From her bedroom, she disappeared into the huge dressing room and emerged with an armful of her old maternity dresses, some beautiful, hippy-style smocks. They were genuine vintage pieces, delicate cottons and silks, mostly midnight blues and forest greens, all embroidered by Celia herself. She held up a wine-red burgundy dress: "I made this one when we were travelling through Morocco. I was pregnant with you, Cass; it was fiendishly hot and I needed something loose."

Both Lily and Cassie were trying the dresses and smock tops on over their jeans, amazed at their mother's skill. "I can't believe you actually made these, Mum!" Cassie said, twirling around in front of a long mirror. "How come no one ever taught me to sew? This stuff is gorgeous, not like maternity clothes at all. Oh, look at this one." she slipped on a purple dress stitched across the bodice with tiny grapes. "Lil, if you don't want it, I'll definitely borrow it."

It was strange to be trying on maternity clothes when Lily's stomach was as flat as Cassie's—at three months there was still no sign of a bump. And she couldn't imagine it happening any time soon. Everything over the past few months had been strange, and she was still taking it in.

When they said they had "news," Lily was pretty sure her mum was expecting Cassie to announce she was pregnant. After all, she was the oldest daughter, and everyone knew that she and Charlie were planning to have a family soon. Lily wondered privately if this was OK with Cass, her leapfrogging the queue with a baby. She felt sad for her sister, and grateful for her support.

*   *   *

What an evening. A memorial service for Harry with his work colleagues, with cocktails and canapés, speeches and a violin quartet. It was beautifully done, in one of the old guildhalls in the city of London, but God I'm glad it's over.

On the train home now, writing this on my tablet. How did he do this every day, twice a day? This journey, I mean: the dirty trains, the fight for a seat, car parks at one end, Tube lines the other. In all those years, I never realised how exhausting it must have been.

Polly offered to come with me, but I said I was fine going alone. I'm getting used to it. The boys were invited, of course, but they were reluctant, and I didn't want to force the issue. They barely knew Harry's colleagues, and it's a school night, and anyway I think they're still in shock from the funeral. All three of us are. You think you understand what death means, but you don't until it happens. This is our reality now, this is what Harry's death means: he hasn't come home and he never will. I'm still really up and down. I have entire days where I think I'm coping just fine, and then the tiniest thing—the way Dan laughs, the expression on Joe's face, or just a song on the radio—makes me fall apart. Some people have been brilliant, my parents, Poll especially, but most of the time I feel like a social leper. At the school gates, those mums who avoid me, pretend they haven't seen me, look away or don't know what to say. It's been over three months now, and I'm just about functioning, getting dressed and driving my boys to school, so why the hell can't they treat me like I'm still a human being? No one invites me to the café anymore, no one invites me to their dinner parties or picnics. I know, I know, a single woman is inconvenient, a widow is an embarrassment, but honestly, bereavement is not a contagious disease.

But a couple of the older women from my book group have been very kind, and also some of the men from the tennis club. They invite me round for lunch or a drink and let me just talk, or not talk, about Harry. About the shock, the grief, the numbness. The anger. My feelings are so up and down.

She *wasn't there tonight. I made sure Colin understood from the very start, since he insisted on organising this memorial, that I wouldn't go if Lily was going to be there. I wasn't having her at the funeral, and I wasn't having her at the memorial. I'm not sure whether I hate her (can you hate someone you don't even know?) or just envy her for having been loved by my husband.*

Some days I hate him, other days I find myself wrapped in one of his sweaters, weeping with tenderness and love. He lied and cheated and made some terrible decisions, and he's wrecked our lives, but he also brought us so much happiness.

But is it all her fault? We'd had some bad patches over the years, all marriages do, but it was when he met her that everything started spiralling out of control. I don't know who to hate, or who to forgive, I just know I'm tired and a bit drunk and really fucking lonely. No husband to collect me from the train station, no one to curl up with tonight. One thing's for sure: if it wasn't for Lily, Harry would still be alive.

ONCE LILY HAD TOLD CASSIE AND CELIA about the baby, they persuaded her to take a few weeks off work: she had accrued a lot of holiday anyway, and the office was quiet at that time of year. Just before Christmas, Colin had held a formal memorial service for Harry, to which Lily was conspicuously not invited, but heard about from her colleagues. Obviously she was aware that it was for Harry's wife, and she wouldn't have gone anyway, but she was relieved to be away from the office during that time.

And it was good to finally stop working and take stock. Cassie came and spent a few nights at her flat in England's Lane; they took long walks on the Heath, did some yoga classes, talked and shopped and cooked—and it helped.

But still, life wasn't simple. A week after Christmas Day, the next hurdle came around: New Year's Eve. Lily spent the day with Cassie and Olivia, bargain-hunting in the pre-January sales. They returned to Cassie's flat for hot chocolate and leftover Christmas cake, and began preparing for the festivities. Olivia was going to a New Year party later on, and Cassie and Charlie were having a group of friends over for dinner. Lily watched Olivia getting ready, and helped Cassie make an apple crumble for dessert, but she'd decided not to join them, despite their insistence. She simply wasn't in the mood. It had been comforting to celebrate Christmas with her family, but she felt too raw for New Year's Eve. It was not quite four months since Harry had died, and she was still adjusting to this new, emptier world.

Lily escaped around six p.m. despite her sister's repeated invitations to dinner, and promised to ring if she changed her mind. Even though Cassie didn't want her to be on her own, Lily knew that she understood.

Coming out of the Tube station, she drifted around the shops in Belsize Park, vaguely thinking she might cook. She bought some food and a good bottle of wine, a white Burgundy—Harry's favourite—although even as she bought it, she knew she wouldn't open it. A small glass would be fine and wouldn't harm the baby, the midwife had told her, but she hadn't felt like alcohol for months. She walked home along England's Lane, passing noisy pubs and restaurants, hearing the music spilling out, dodging the gaggles of revellers who'd started early, feeling removed from it all.

Lady Archer was away with friends at a country house party, so the house was blessedly silent. Lily desperately needed to be alone. Still, she smiled to find a luxurious bottle of sparkling elderflower champagne and a card propped up against her front door: *Happy New Year Lily! Non-alco bubbly to put some fizz in your celebrations . . . Susan x*

She let herself into the flat and exhaled in relief, resting her head against the closed wooden door. She ran a bath and lay there, reading. It was a collection of poetry which Harry had given her a week before he killed himself. It was called *Staying Alive*. On the final page was a poem she kept going over and over, wondering why Harry had given her this, whether he meant her to read it after he was gone. What the hell was he thinking?

I want you to keep
stubbing your toe
on the memory of me . . .

Lily got out of the warm water, wrapped herself in a bathrobe, and poured out a glass of elderflower bubbly. She unpacked the shopping bags—fresh tagliatelle, pesto, parmesan—but didn't feel like eating. She opened the book again, sipping at the champagne, reading that final poem:

I want you to drive yourself crazy
with the fantasy of me,
and how we will meet again, against all odds . . .

In the flyleaf of the book, Harry had written: *Lily . . . love hurts x.*

She went and lay on her bed, staring into the darkness. The loneliness swept over her; she felt almost unable to stand it. For the first time since Harry had died, she found herself face-to-face with the most painful questions: Could she have done something? Had she not cared enough to see what was happening to Harry? Could she have stopped him? Could she have saved him?

Hours went by, her mind taken up with these compulsive, unanswerable thoughts. She must have fallen asleep at some point for when she woke, fireworks were exploding all over London. She sat up, shivering in her damp bathrobe, and turned on the radio. They were playing the chimes from Big Ben; it was just past midnight, just the new year.

She opened the skylight wide and leaned out, the winter air cool against her face. The window was high, but not as high as the cliffs where Harry had jumped. She whispered that she loved him and missed him, that she would do her best for their baby without him. The fireworks went on and on across the rooftops, red, green, and gold from neighbouring parks and gardens; cars were blaring their horns in the streets; people were cheering outside the pub at the end of the road. The sky was ablaze with the start of a new year and Lily was crying because it looked so much like hope.

She drifted through the flat, aware that she was hungry but unable to face food. There were texts and emails on her phone, but she didn't check them. There was only one person she wanted to hear from. Lily thought of the final messages Harry had sent her, from the mobile they would have found with his body.

His dead body. Rotting in a grave. *Stop this*, Lily thought, *just stop this*. Something had opened the floodgates to these terrible images, macabre images, which she had been suppressing for months. The violence of Harry's death frightened her. Lily felt panicky and then more panicky when she thought about being pregnant. She knew this panic wasn't good for the baby. She went upstairs again and lit a scented candle beside her bed. She lay down, trying to concentrate on her breathing and on the sound of fireworks in the distance.

SHE WOKE AROUND SIX A.M. WITH A FEEL-ing of relief. It was over. She looked at the candle, burned down now, the scattered photographs and the book of poetry on her bedside table. She looked again at what Harry had written on the flyleaf: *love hurts. He's wrong*, she thought, smiling sadly. *It's death that hurts, not love.*

Slowly she stood up. She hung her bathrobe on the back of the bathroom door and pulled on blue tracksuit bottoms, a grey hoodie, and a pair of thick warm socks. She went into the kitchen and pulled a cedarwood box from beneath the sink. She took the Valium out of the box—seventy of them now—and wrapped them tightly in a plastic bag. She took the bag down to the rubbish bins outside and stuffed it beneath a couple of black bin bags. She looked up and down England's Lane, silent and deserted. The whole world was sleeping and it was the start of another year. Standing on the front step, her arms wrapped around her, Lily took a deep breath. "Happy new year, little one," she whispered.

IT WAS ONLY JANUARY, BUT LILY FELT AS though she'd lived ten years in the space of a few months. Strange how quickly things could fall apart; strange how quickly one adapted. She was nearly five months pregnant with Harry's baby and he was dead, so what on earth was she going to do? She tried not to think too far ahead, focusing instead on the practicalities of the near future. Making plans for the baby was good; it made her happy, excited. But any further down the line—a year, two years—that was impossible.

Once Cassie had the bit between her teeth, she had got Lily organised. Her diary began to fill up with routine blood tests, check-ups, and scans, and both Cassie and her midwife nagged her to enrol in antenatal classes. Whether it was delayed shock or just denial, Lily found herself putting off the inevitable and refusing to plan for the birth itself.

Thinking rationally, she knew that there was no sense in being frightened. Anticipating a difficult labour and unbearable pain would only make it worse. Hundreds of thousands of women gave birth every day, they had been giving birth since the dawn of time. Their bodies were designed for that purpose, and she would manage it too. Whatever happened when she went into labour, she'd be in safe hands.

The other reason she was reluctant to join the local antenatal class, despite her midwife's reminders, was precisely the element of "joining in." She assumed that all the other women would be with their partners, in a happy heterosexual middle-class mummy and daddy unit. Lily was not ashamed of being a single mother, and she didn't mind what others thought. All the same, those coupley birth classes sounded off-putting.

This was one of the few downsides to Belsize Park. If she'd lived somewhere more appropriate to her means, she probably would have found mums of all social classes, ages, and incomes in her antenatal group. But Belsize Park was an affluent area, and Lily was surrounded by wealthy smugness. In the cafés, delis, and parks, everywhere elegant blonde women held hands with their handsome banker husbands, dressed their pregnancy bumps in designer maternity athleisure wear, and pushed their other babies in expensive Bugaboo prams.

Also, she wasn't desperate to meet people—her life was quite busy enough as it was, what with work and exercise and the flat and her family.

"FOR GOD'S SAKE!" LILY SAID TO CASSIE, mutinously. "She makes it sound like once the baby is born, my whole world will revolve around parent-toddler groups. I'll be condemned to coffee mornings and baby-swim and mummy-massage and we'll discuss nappies and nurseries and that's it—no more real life for me!"

Harry's absence seemed even stronger now that she knew she was carrying his baby. She found herself wanting to talk to him about everything and nothing, mundane daily news, questions she had about work matters, books she wanted him to read, music she wanted him to listen to. In the first few weeks after his death, she had wondered how she'd ever feel whole again. Gradually she began to see that there was a way to carry on without him. Or rather, she just found herself carrying on. No matter how shattered your world was, life went on; you could keep going or you could give up, and that was that.

Then the letter arrived. Lily had almost given up waiting. So much had happened since she had written to Claude, she felt like a different person.

His timing couldn't have been worse. It was a grey Saturday morning, and she was feeling low and aimless, but trying to ignore it. She knew the letter was from Claude because it had a San Francisco postmark. She left it on the kitchen table all morning. Suddenly she was reluctant to open it. Even glancing at it stirred up difficult emotions. Why had she contacted him anyway, what had she been thinking? She'd spent most of her life without a father; why was her long-lost father suddenly contacting her? And how the hell was she going to cope with another abandonment? She didn't want to be his daughter—what was he writing for anyway?

Lily started crying and couldn't stop. She feared the letter in the kitchen and couldn't bring herself to read it. She felt terribly alone. It was a mild day but raining heavily, the first rain for weeks, a strange heavy thunderstorm, and she felt the weight of it pressing her down. She kept thinking about the waterlogged earth and a churned-up grave, filling with water, with mud.

DEAR LILY, SHE READ, LATER THAT EVENING, having cleaned the flat, tried not to think about Harry, worried about the baby, and then about the future and being alone. In the end, she thought she'd go out of her mind with the overthinking. She made herself go out for a walk, shopped for groceries, washed her hair, painted her fingernails, and steeled herself for the letter. *Nine months!* It began. *How can it take nine months for mail to be redirected?* At first she wasn't sure what he was talking about.

Your letter from England has just this morning arrived! Which means that I didn't write back sooner—I wish I could have done. After many years in the same house we finally moved, and it appears to have taken a very long time for this letter to make its way seven blocks north. I'm so sorry.

Lily, I know nothing about you, and probably you know nothing about me. I live in San Francisco with my second wife, Marie, who is a fellow professor at UC Berkeley. She has two grown-up sons (twenty-seven and thirty-three). We divide our time between California in term time, teaching and writing, and France, where we spend half the year. We have a farmhouse not far from Marie's sons. We leave for France in March and we'll be there until the end of September.

I'd love to see a photograph of you—would you email me one? Even better, would you come for a visit? France isn't far away.
Claude

She read his letter again and again, examined the paper and the handwriting (large, generous loops, black ink). She put down the letter, picked up her tablet, and scrolled through possible photos to send him. By herself, with her siblings? She got as far as typing his email address and attaching a couple of pictures before she made herself slow down. She stood at the open window. It was cooler and fresher now after a day of thundery showers. She picked up her phone to call Cassie then changed her mind. She considered ringing Celia, then she thought about going downstairs to see if Susan was around for a gin and tonic. She touched her stomach: damn, not G and T. Herbal tea, then.

For the time being, her thoughts of Harry were gone, the grief replaced with other concerns. Lily felt as though a gulf had opened up in front of her. Did she want to meet Claude? Writing to him was one thing, but she hadn't thought as far as a meeting. She'd tried so hard not to be bitter about the past, but now she was confronted with the possibility of a future filled with—what?

All evening she drifted around the flat, unable to settle. It felt so strange to hear from her father like this. Was she happy or scared? She imagined a possible meeting with Claude, her mind full of conversations, outcomes, reconciliations, disappointments. Could she forgive a man who had walked out on them without a word of apology or explanation? What kind of a man could do that?

David rang and she let it go to voicemail. He had been supportive and kind these past few months. He seemed to understand that in some way she blamed herself for Harry's death, after that terrible final scene outside the flat. He rang her every week or so to talk or offer to pop round, but he didn't pressure her. Her mind was so full of other things.

And now this letter from her father. Lily lay down with the bedroom windows wide open to the darkness, unable to drop off until, around three a.m., she heard the gentle patter of rain.

*   *   *

I actually feel sick. I've just had the strangest, most horrible news. I thought things couldn't get much worse over the past few months and now—this.

So, I had to drive over to Amersham to see the funeral director today. The grave is ready for a headstone—they leave it a few months for the earth to subside, so we just marked it with a wooden cross—now I have to choose a design and work out the exact wording and all that. I'd been dreading that for ages, since the funeral, but actually it was OK: weirdly I find the practical things around Harry's death easier than the huge blank empty spaces. Like, I can talk to our financial advisor about his life insurance and what to do about the mortgage, but sitting here alone in the evenings after the boys have gone to bed, with my bottle of red wine and just one glass and Harry not coming home . . . It's so much harder to bear.

I came out of the funeral director's and went into the deli next door; they do the most divine fresh salads and soups and mini quiches. I had Polly coming for lunch and thought it would be a nice treat for us both. Just in front of me in the queue was Donna, who used to be married to Lee, who's been the marketing director at HEP, like, forever. Lee and Harry were pretty good friends, and back in the day when I used to go to their social events and conferences, Donna and I got on OK—although I never trusted her really. Anyway, she and Lee had a bad divorce a few years ago. We still bump into each other around Gerrards Cross sometimes and always say a fake-friendly hi, although she hasn't bothered to contact me since Harry's death. She looked awkward at first and did the usual "I'm so sorry for your loss" thing, then we both got served at the same time and unfortunately ended up walking back to the car park together.

We were just saying fake-friendly goodbyes when she blurted out, "By the way, have you heard the rumour from HEP?" I went cold all over because I know Donna's way of squirrelling away bits of information and repeating them, and usually her gossip isn't harmless . . .

"Rumour? No, but then I'm sort of out of the loop these days." I tried to sound totally unconcerned and turned away to my car.

"Well, according to Lee there's rumours that Lily—you know that young woman who worked so closely with Harry?—apparently she's pregnant." Donna stared straight at me and my stomach turned over. I clutched my car keys tighter, trying to keep my breathing steady. After a dramatic pause, she went on. "And the thing is, everyone's saying she doesn't have a partner, so whose baby is it?"

She really is the vilest bitch. If I didn't get out of there I thought I might punch her so I mumbled something about it being none of our business and got into my car and drove off. Fast.

Polly was a lifesaver. After lunch, we had a whisky (I know, but it was an emergency) and talked it all through. She calmed me down and reminded me that the worst has already happened; there's nothing I can do now. She really helped me get things in perspective: "If you want to, we can call Colin's wife. She was always a good friend to you and I think she'll tell you the truth—not that Donna-bitch's malicious rumours. But it's not necessarily a good idea."

She poured us both another large whisky. "Clearly a lot of things went on in Harry's life over the past year or so . . . and it's painful and humiliating finding all this out. Maybe you need to draw a line, Pip. For your own sanity now, maybe you should focus on the good times with Harry, preserve those happy memories before things went downhill." She took a sip of whisky. "Forget about Lily, she's nothing to do with you."

She's right, I know. It made sense earlier on when she was saying it—but it doesn't help right now. The thought of Harry making love to someone else, the thought of her carrying his baby . . . I'm the mother of his children, me, us, our family. I've given birth to three of his children, our boys, our little girl who died. I'm his wife, not her. Can it really be Harry's baby? How am I supposed to cope with this?

IT WAS CURIOUS HOW THE REACTIONS OF the people closest to Lily reflected the different emotions she was feeling. Her attitude to the baby was contradictory and constantly changing—equal parts excitement, ambivalence, and fear. It was reassuring that the reactions of her loved ones could be just as diverse as her own.

When her brother, James, heard from Celia that she was pregnant, he had sent a text: *Just heard the news—wow—Mama Lily! Mad props to you, sis. Take care x.* The message was typical of her brother: brief, witty, to the point. Knowing him as she did, knowing that emotional communication wasn't his strong point, she was touched. Celia often said that James was like their father, a man of few words.

Olivia's reaction was at the other end of the scale. They met for breakfast in one of the trendy organic cafés on England's Lane. Olivia was just back from a fortnight in Rome visiting Giovanni— things were back on between them, and she could only be described as "loved-up": sun-kissed, dewy-eyed, and bubbling with plans to move to Italy in the spring. When Lily finally managed to get a word in and told her about the baby, Olivia shrieked and grabbed her sister's hands across the table, almost knocking over their cappuccinos in the process. Her eyes were wide and she kept saying, "Oh my God, really? Oh my God, Lil, are you terrified? That's like, amazing, but so . . . scary . . ."

Lily didn't mind. Olivia was right, it *was* scary. Her little sister was simply, in her own tactless way, bringing up what Lily had been avoiding facing: the whole business of going into labour, the terror of giving birth, the mystery of becoming a mother. The reality of it all. Life *was* scary. Whatever happened next, she'd survive.

PART
TWO

"NOW, I'M GOING TO RUN YOU A BATH."
Susan bustled around the flat while Lily lay on the large sofa feeding Stella. It was early summer and the sun streamed in through the large open windows. "I've got a thermos of coffee in the hamper and some chocolate biscuits, and I'll keep an eye on her while you have a soak."

A soak! Lily smiled. Most mornings, she showered quickly with Stella in her baby seat on the bathroom floor, so to have a bath alone, to put on a facemask, to wash and condition her hair, would be a rare treat. They always shared a bath together before Stella's bedtime, which was one of the best moments of the day, but it involved more splashing than actual washing.

"Susan," Lily said. "Sometimes I don't believe you're real. This flat is heaven and you're a guardian angel."

It wasn't that she was struggling with being a mum—in fact, she was surprised at how much she was enjoying it. Shouldn't it be harder than this? She'd heard so much about postnatal depression, sleep deprivation, the endless, colicky screaming, but so far so good. And being a single parent wasn't as hard as she'd been led to expect, or maybe it was just that she had nothing to compare this to. Yet there were nights when Stella didn't sleep, and Lily longed for someone else to take a turn getting up, someone else to take a turn with nappy changing; there were nights when she just needed someone in the bed beside her, to talk about it all.

Stella had made up for a difficult birth by being a peaceful, considerate baby. She breastfed without biting her mother, she smiled a lot, and she only cried for logical reasons: if she was hungry, say, or her nappy needed changing. Even at six weeks, she was starting to sleep for longer periods—up to five or six hours at a stretch. From the anecdotes of other mothers at the baby group, Lily knew she was extremely lucky.

Still, it was tiring. Even though Stella was tiny, there was no doubt who ruled the Belsize Park household. Everything revolved around her. Since her birth, Lily found it impossible to run around the way she used to. She couldn't just throw on some jeans and nip out to the shops, or go for a long walk, or even read a book. For someone who was used to being in complete control of her life, having a baby had been quite a learning curve.

Cassie and Susan both helped, and Celia came round most afternoons to see them both. Sometimes another mother from her antenatal group would pop by for tea, or they'd meet in a nearby café. Even when it was just the two of them, Lily was so absorbed in feeding, washing, playing, and singing that the days raced by and she didn't have time to get depressed or lonely.

If Lily felt any sadness in those first few months, it was more specific: the sadness of knowing that Harry would never know this precious being he had created. There had been a baby girl, Harry had once told her, but whether she was born before or after his sons, how long she had lived or how she died, Lily didn't know. The pain in his eyes had been such that she couldn't bring herself to ask. But she knew that Harry had always wanted a girl, and here she was, more beautiful every day. With every milestone of their daughter's new life, Lily longed for Harry to witness it. That sadness would never go away.

She couldn't believe Stella was already six weeks old. She had arrived several weeks early, following a dramatic midnight taxi ride to the Royal Free just up the road in Hampstead. The birth, seared on Lily's mind, seemed like only yesterday, but then she couldn't imagine life without her. Sometimes she looked at her and thought she would explode with the intensity of her feelings. For weeks after the birth, Lily felt emotionally raw, with a jagged, fierce quality to her love. She treasured the weight, the miraculous warmth and bundle of her daughter curled on her chest. When Stella yawned, when she smiled or sighed, it was a miracle; it made Lily want to weep.

Susan bustled in the background, getting coffee cups from the kitchen, taking chocolate biscuits from her magic hamper. As if she could read Lily's mind, Stella looked up at her mother and smiled. She had Harry's blue eyes, his exact shade of forget-me-not blue.

HEATHROW WAS FAR MORE CHAOTIC than Lily remembered, despite the fact that it was early on a Sunday morning. With a small baby, it seemed much louder and more hectic than on her previous trips. She hadn't been to an airport since that long-ago holiday with Harry to Saint Lucia.

Once through security, having re-attached her baby, belt, bags, and shoes, Lily headed for the nearest café. By some miracle Stella was still sleeping, so she read for an hour, trying to keep her mind on the book in front of her. The snow had started falling in Oslo and the hunt was on for the serial killer in the latest Jo Nesbo thriller . . .

but it was hard to concentrate on the storyline. She gave up on the book and flipped on her music. Joan Baez was singing "Diamonds and Rust." It was Harry's song and always brought him back painfully, from those opening lines.

"Well I'll be damned, here comes your ghost again . . ."

She should skip this song. She couldn't bear it.
She closed her eyes and gave in to the music.

". . . Now you're telling me
You're not nostalgic
Then give me another word for it . . ."

Lily swallowed hard to keep the tears down. The grief of recent months washed over her, and it was suddenly more than she could bear. And what was she doing now?

Just a few hours away was her first meeting with her father in over two decades. She had been a small child when Claude had left. She had virtually no memories of him, apart from those strange, disjointed lines of poetry, and the images of being thrown up and caught in his strong arms. Gazing at her sleeping daughter, Lily realised she had no idea what a father was like.

LILY HADN'T TOLD ANYONE ABOUT Claude's letter for ages. She hadn't decided whether to visit him or not, then Stella's birth intervened, and when the dust settled, she found herself looking for flights to France. But first she knew she must talk to her mother. With Stella strapped to her chest, she walked over to the house in Hampstead and found Celia in the garden. It was lush and dark green from the overnight thunderstorm, the plants grateful for the downpour after days of muggy heat.

"How lovely to see you both," Celia said, getting up from the flowerbed, brushing damp leaves from her knees.

"Sorry for not ringing first. I wasn't sure if you'd be in but thought we'd take the chance," Lily said, hugging her mother as she handed Stella over.

"You're just in time for coffee," Celia said. "Patrick's coming for lunch so I need to get a lasagne in the oven, but you're very welcome to stay, of course."

They drifted towards the back door, Celia jiggling the baby on her hip, smiling and cooing at her as if it had been months, not days, since she last saw her. In the kitchen, Lily cleared the counter while Celia made a fresh *cafetière* and poured out two mugs of coffee. Then Lily sat down at the kitchen table with Stella while her mother started washing and slicing vegetables for the lasagne.

"So, Mum . . ." Lily began. "I got a letter back from Claude." Celia turned in surprise, holding an onion. "It's quite a short letter—I brought it in case you want to see. Apparently they spend the summer in France, him and his, uh, wife, that is"—Lily wasn't sure how much her mother knew about his life—"and he said would we like to go and visit, go and stay with them, me and Stella, that is." Her words came out in a rush.

She felt disloyal, admitting that Claude had invited them to France. It was as if she was throwing it back in her mother's face, all those years of Celia being there for them, not leaving the way he'd left. She felt as if she was siding with him in some invisible tug-of-war, choosing this fictional father over her real, present mother.

Of course, Celia didn't see it like that. She was taken aback by Lily's news; Claude's departure had been sudden and totally unexplained. She had never put it behind her, not properly. She and Claude had had their ups and downs, like any couple, but they loved each other and he'd enjoyed being a father. She never asked herself how he could have left her but how he could have left the children.

As the mother of three young children and an unborn baby, Celia had found herself suddenly dealing with more financial and practical difficulties than she'd ever expected. School fees and mortgage arrangements, frozen pipes and blocked gutters and car trouble. She wasn't prepared for any of it. But they had coped. She had never wanted to poison her children against their father. Throughout the exhausting years of bringing them up alone, she'd tried not to be bitter.

There had been a few letters from him at first—he was spending time in France, then he was going travelling, then he was moving to America, then silence. No explanations, no child support, not a single visit. The final blow was a package from a divorce lawyer fifteen years ago, some official papers she had signed and sent back to an address in California. She had felt sadness and relief. The initial heartbreak had, over the years, become a dull ache in her heart. A small kernel of pain which she never spoke about.

And now this. The past rushing back into the present, a confusion of memories. Claude wanting to meet Lily, to meet Stella, inviting them to stay with his family in France. She had understood Lily's wish to contact her father—she knew that sooner or later one of the children would—but it was strange how quickly a possibility became a reality. Claude had been out there, living his life, all along. He had married again—she guessed he had, of course, when the divorce came up. Another woman called herself his wife. It was both unthinkable and completely inevitable. Standing at the kitchen sink with the tap running, Celia suddenly felt old.

She put down the onion. "That's exciting, Lil—unexpected! Do you think you'll go?"

"I'm not sure, Mum," Lily said. "I think Stella should have a grandfather, and I suppose I want to meet him too. I don't know, maybe it's a bad idea?"

Celia smiled brightly. "You mustn't worry about me, darling. I support your decision absolutely, I understand why you need to meet him, and I don't mind at all. Let bygones be bygones, isn't that what they say? Life really is too short to hold grudges." The doorbell rang and she went to answer it. "Anyway I'm not sad, lonely Mum anymore. I have Patrick and he's lovely," she called from the hallway.

It *did* make a difference, Lily thought, now that Celia had Patrick. She and Cassie had worried about their mother over the years, more so since they'd all left home, and it was a relief to see her finally happy with someone new. Still, Lily wasn't sure about meeting her father.

*　　*　　*

I'm at a very low ebb. The summer was always Harry's time—he loved the garden and inventing outdoor adventures for the boys during their holidays, taking them fishing and exploring the woods. I remember him coming home one Friday afternoon with a carful of tents and sleeping bags and tinned food; he'd stopped off at a camping shop and ended up buying a load of gear, and we piled into the car and set off for Cornwall. It was the most mad, magical trip. Harry at his best, gathering kindling with the boys, building a campfire, me cooking bacon and beans over the portable stove, doing the washing-up in the stream, then drinking cocoa around the fire late at night.

I miss him all the time, but I'm missing him even more during these long summer holidays. I know the boys are too. I'm trying to be a good mum, support them without pushing them, listen to them without prying into their feelings, but the truth is, I don't know how to be. Are we doing this right? Should they be reacting differently, rebelling and getting into trouble; should they be weeping every day over photos of their dad? We attended a few sessions of family therapy together, but none of us found it helpful. As Joe said, "It's a total waste of time. We don't need therapy, we just miss Dad. It would be weird if we didn't."

Mostly we go on as normal. But the house is so quiet and sad. Our family is broken. Harry was such a presence in the house, in our lives. He held it all together. How will we ever feel whole without him?

SHE KNEW IT WAS CLAUDE IMMEDIATELY, a tall man in his sixties waiting at the arrivals gate. The resemblance to James was startling. They hugged stiffly, then Claude took her bags and led her towards the exit. Despite that slight initial awkwardness, Lily quickly felt natural walking beside him across the car park. Was it his easy West Coast manners or some kind of genetic affinity between them? Claude's wife, Marie, appeared, a small, dark-haired Frenchwoman, and helped to settle Stella in the car. They didn't have a baby seat, so they propped her securely between Lily and Claude in the back.

Marie drove. The journey took them around Lyon, then out across valleys and through small towns, deep into the Burgundy countryside. She explained that they borrowed the car, an ancient Renault, from her younger son, Vincent—he lived not far from them with his girlfriend and two small sons, and ran his own IT company. Her elder son, Julien, three years older than Lily, was an investment banker. He divided his time between London and Paris, but spent most of the summer here in Burgundy, living with Vincent and collaborating on various financial websites. "The boys are good friends now," Marie said, her spoken English a mixture of French and American accents, "but as children they were sworn enemies! I remember when they were very young, I found them in the paddling pool trying to drown each other."

Lily laughed. "It sounds just like our family when we were kids." There was a brief pause.

"And what about now?" Marie asked. "I bet you get on much better as adults, siblings usually do."

At first, Lily felt awkward talking about the family, unsure what to say. She didn't know what Claude remembered of his children, what he would feel able to talk about. But he asked question after question about the four of them: Lily, Cassie, Olivia—and James, the son he'd never met. He seemed hungry for all the details of their lives.

When there were silences, they weren't uncomfortable, just a drawing of breath as if they were marvelling at each other's presence: Lily looking at her father, Claude looking at his daughter. They were finally real to each other. When Lily first mentioned Celia's name, Claude didn't say anything, just nodded. She didn't know if she would ever ask him what had gone wrong, why he had left them—maybe another time, maybe never. Whatever had happened, Lily could see that he hadn't stopped thinking of them during those long years of absence.

The main house was a long, low converted barn of grey stone with large windows and the traditional French red-tiled roof. Marie parked outside a small building next to the main house, "above what used to be the manger for the cattle," Claude explained with a smile. The former manger was now a study and workroom downstairs with converted guest quarters above. Lily was relieved that she and Stella would have their own space during their stay.

Claude carried their bags upstairs and showed her into the main bedroom. "The bathroom's through here," he said, indicating an arch-shaped wooden door into a beautiful blue-and-white bathroom. "I'll leave you to get settled in."

Lily smiled and murmured something about giving Stella a feed.

Claude nodded. "Speaking of food, lunch will be ready in about an hour—something simple, if that's OK; we'll have a proper meal this evening. But come down for a coffee whenever you're ready. I'm in charge of the kitchen!" He put his hand lightly on Lily's shoulder and turned to descend the narrow stairs.

She lay back on the double bed beside her daughter and closed her eyes. So. That was her father. The last few hours had been so intense, it was hard to work out what she was feeling. Did the man himself bear any relation to the memory she thought she had of him? That deep, reassuring voice, the rough-wool sweater and strong arms, that curious fragment of rhyme: *"And all the lives we ever lived, And all the lives to be, Are full of trees and changing leaves . . ."*

Already that memory was fading, merging into the man she'd just met: tall and muscular in his late sixties, tanned from years in California. He was both a stranger and yet familiar. Although she had those blurred images from her own childhood, she couldn't summon any recollection of her parents together. She wondered what Celia would make of Claude now. He reminded Lily so strongly of James, those blue eyes and the wide smile. Of course it made sense that her father would remind her of her brother. But there was something else, a gentle, quiet strength, which brought back her longing for Harry.

Opening her eyes, Lily saw that Stella was gazing at her in silence, concerned. She scooped the baby into her arms, picked up the nappy bag, and carried them into the bathroom, lost in thought. What had happened more than a quarter of a century ago to make Claude walk out on them all?

THEY DIDN'T TALK ABOUT IT THAT FIRST day. They had a long lunch of fresh bread, cheese, salad, and pears from the orchard, sitting on the terrace in blazing sunshine. After coffee, Marie showed Lily her plants—she was particularly proud of the pink and white water lilies in the pond—and then Claude gave her a tour of the orchard and his vegetable garden.

"Of course, it needs a lot of work right now—normally we're out here for all of July and August, but this year we were held up with the move back in the States. The farmer down the lane keeps the grass and hedges cut, but I like to get things back into shape when we first arrive. The orchard doesn't mind being neglected, you saw those fantastic apple and pear trees, but the vegetables are another matter—I need to get digging. The climate here's pretty good: it can be scorching in the summer, but we get plenty of rain too. Very different to California."

Marie filled the small paddling pool by the kitchen door with a garden hose. Claude and Lily sat on the back step and watched Stella splashing about, amazed and laughing as if she'd just discovered water. They had a quiet supper, just the four of them, and by ten p.m. Lily was yawning widely. "I think we could all do with an early night," Claude said, "it's been quite a day." They hugged goodnight.

She was completely exhausted, whether from the simple journey or the not-so-simple emotions she wasn't sure. Lying down, listening to Stella softly breathing in the cot beside the bed, she thought of her brother and sisters. She saw their faces in a new light, their mannerisms and expressions merging with those of their father's as she fell into a deep sleep.

IT WASN'T UNTIL THE FOLLOWING MORN-ing that they really began to talk. Lily and Stella woke around eight a.m. to quiet clattering and low voices coming from the farmhouse kitchen in the adjoining building. Lily ran a bath, emerging from the bathroom to find a cup of freshly brewed coffee had been placed on a low table by the door. She drank the coffee gratefully while dressing herself and the baby.

Downstairs, Marie and Claude were just finishing the newspapers. "Ready for breakfast?" her father asked.

"We certainly are!" Lily smiled.

He set out a warm basket of croissants, butter and jam, a couple of yoghurts, and the fruit bowl. While she ate, Marie and Claude poured themselves more coffee, filling her in on the news headlines. Beneath the lightness, there was something in the atmosphere, a sort of tension. Lily glanced at her father's face and sensed that he wanted to talk.

"Right, I'm off to see Vincent." Marie stood up from her chair, piling plates into the sink and wiping down surfaces as she went. "I need to drop off some books we brought him from the States. I thought we could all have dinner together this evening, now that you're settled in—Vincent and Helene, and their little boys, and also Julien, if that sounds good, Lily?" It was tactful of Marie to make herself scarce. "And maybe I could take this little one with me—if you've fed her, she'll be OK for an hour or two?"

AFTER THEY HAD WAVED MARIE AND STELLA off in the car, an uneasy silence fell in the kitchen. Lily stood at the window, once again unsure of what to say. She always found it strange at first, being without Stella. It hadn't happened often since the birth. Whether she was overly attached because she was a single mother, or just that she was used to having Stella there, strapped to her chest, Lily wasn't sure. And yet she wasn't clingy—on the rare occasions that Cassie or Celia babysat for an hour or two, Lily was delighted to escape for a swim or a wander round the shops, or just to sit in Café Rouge with a book enjoying her own company. As she watched Marie's car backing out of the driveway, Lily's arms felt empty, that unaccustomed sense of freedom returning. For a moment, she wished she could slip outside and avoid the awkward conversation to come.

But of course she couldn't. And it was no good pretending to talk about something else.

"Lily." She turned at the sound of Claude's voice. "It's so good to have you here. To meet you again after all these years. I'm so glad . . . Thank you for coming."

"I'm glad we came too," she said, moving towards the table and pulling out a chair. She smiled at Claude.

"I've been thinking about it all, since I knew you were coming, I wanted to know what—I feel like there's something I should be able to say." Claude looked down at the table, tracing his finger over a chip in the wood. "But I'm not sure there is. I don't have the answer to what happened between me and . . . your mother. Between me and Celia." He hesitated before speaking her name. "I don't have any reasons for why I left."

Lily was holding her breath. Until this moment, she thought she had so many questions—but now every single one had gone clean out of her mind. Whatever Claude could tell her would be more than she'd known before. She just wanted him to talk about that time. She looked at him, feeling like a small child, close to tears.

Without knowing what she was saying, she began to speak: "I would like to know what happened. Why you left. Why you never came back. I know that sounds pitiful, but I'm not angry or blaming you. I just want to understand . . ."

Claude nodded. "OK," he said quietly. "Shall I just talk about what I remember, and you can interrupt me?" She nodded, brushing away a tear.

"I was very depressed," Claude began. "I've had depression since my late teens, I suppose, I've gone through phases. These days I understand myself better, and there are things I can do to manage it: exercise, therapy, so on. Back then I knew nothing about it—depression wasn't talked about as it is now—only that the black clouds would descend, sometimes for a few days, sometimes for months."

He leaned back in his chair, silent for a moment. "I was in my early twenties when I met Celia. We were both in Paris, I'm sure she's told you about those times. We were young and free, both penniless, working in magazines, teaching; she did some modelling; I played guitar and even acted—it was a long time ago." Lily smiled at his wistful tone, trying to imagine Claude and Celia in swinging Paris.

"The problems started after we moved to London. Cassie was born and then you came along—that was wonderful, I loved being a father. Celia and I got married when Olivia was on the way, and we were a happy family. But my depression was worsening—the black spells kept recurring, and each time they seemed to last longer. I felt hopeless, Lil."

Only her close family and Harry ever called her Lil. Now she realised that her father must have called her that as a child because it sounded natural when he said it. As if reading her mind, Claude continued: "I remember one day—it was your third birthday. I was in a bad way. I'd been depressed for several weeks, I could barely leave the bedroom. There was a birthday party in the garden, the sound of children playing, and you came upstairs with a piece of cake for me. It was so bright outside, so dark and gloomy in the bedroom. You put this squashed piece of birthday cake down next to my pillow, and you sat beside the bed and stroked my face.

"I suppose I was getting worse. Some days I couldn't even get out of bed." Lily listened to her father with tears in her eyes. "Then my mother died. She'd had cancer for years, but I hadn't said goodbye, not properly. I felt like a failure as a son and as a father."

Claude took a deep breath. "A month later, Celia found out she was expecting another child—James. I sort of lost the plot.

Sometimes I wanted to kill myself to escape the voices in my head, the crushing sense of panic and failure. I was overwhelmed by responsibility and this house and all these children. I was too young to be a father of four and I felt unable to cope."

Everything Claude was saying made sense. Lily was hurt by it, and yet she understood. She sometimes felt overwhelmed by Stella and she was thirty years old. How would she have coped in her early twenties?

Claude shook his head. "The truth is, I wasn't ready. Celia and I fell deeply in love when we met, but we were so young. And then babies happened. Celia was amazing. She took it in her stride and she was a wonderful mother. But I wasn't ready to be a father. This isn't an excuse, just the closest I can get to an explanation. It has taken me a long time to grow up." They sat in silence for a few minutes.

"You know that Marie used to practise as a psychotherapist before she started teaching at Berkeley?" (Lily didn't know this.) "She says that men usually take longer to grow up than women, and it was certainly the case with me and Celia. I was an only child, and I'd been spoilt rotten. In some ways I was still a child myself, and then suddenly I was a husband, a father of three, four young children." He hesitated. "I felt ... stifled. I adored you all and yet I felt stifled. One morning, I got up early and walked out of the house, and that was it. I didn't know that I was leaving for good—I hadn't planned it—I just walked and walked all through London that day. Eventually I took a train to the coast, then a ferry to France. Kept going for years: Europe, then America. I saw no outlet except running away. Being selfish. Being alone."

Lily nodded. It made sense. Sort of. "And did you miss us?" she asked quietly.

"Oh, Lil, I missed you every minute of every day." Claude's eyes were dark with pain. "There were times when my body ached to cuddle every one of you. I never stopped loving Celia or any of you—maybe that was it; I felt frightened at how precious you were. I was scared I couldn't protect you. Every day I thought of you, wanted to hold you all."

"Then why didn't you . . ." Lily began.

"Why didn't I come back?" Claude said. "I wanted to. I thought about it constantly. But I felt so ashamed at first, and then it was too late."

"It was never too late," Lily said. "Mum never found anyone else."

THEY SPENT THE REST OF THE DAY OUT-doors. Lily lay on the lawn in denim shorts and a bikini top with Stella beside her on a play mat under a sunshade. Marie was knee-deep in the pond, sieving out weeds and stray leaves, while Claude pruned the apple trees nearby. Lily prepared a simple picnic lunch for "the workers" and laid it on a wooden table on the terrace. Afterwards Claude made tiny strong espressos and brought out a bowl of ripe nectarines. The sun blazed down from a cloudless sky, but there was just enough breeze to make it bearable.

"So, tonight." Marie yawned and stretched, leaning forward to clear the table. "I'm planning to make paella for dinner, with a vegetarian version for you, Lily."

"Is that a bother?" Lily asked, jumping up to help stack plates. "I don't want you to cook something different especially for me."

Marie smiled. "It's no trouble at all—in fact Jules is vegetarian too. I simply divide up the paella rice and spices and add extra veg to one dish, and fish or chicken to the other. Couldn't be easier. They're coming at seven, so we'll put the children to bed and then we'll eat around eight. And Claude, don't forget the wine—the winery re-opens at three."

When Claude had driven away, Marie and Lily carried the plates inside. Marie washed up while Lily put the food away in the fridge, and they chatted lightly about this and that, companionable kitchen talk. Neither of them referred directly to that morning's conversation between Lily and her father, but Marie seemed to sense that the air had been cleared.

When the kitchen was ship-shape, Lily picked up Stella to take her upstairs for an afternoon nap. At the doorway, Marie rested her hand on Lily's shoulder. "And what about you—why not run a bath or have a lie-down too? I'll be making some calls this afternoon, answering emails and marking a few assignments. Why don't you have a rest? It's hard work being a mum—you look tired." Her voice was genuine, and it hit Lily just how exhausted she was.

"You're right." She smiled at Marie. "I *am* tired. It's lovely being here, but meeting Dad has kind of taken it out of me. There's a lot to take on board."

She and Stella both felt better after their sleep and a bath. Lily dressed in a white cotton shift and her diamond earrings from Harry, put Stella in a clean Babygro, and went downstairs to help with dinner. "Everything's under control," Claude said, at the stove with a blue-striped dishcloth thrown over his shoulder. "You just sit down and here"—he poured her a glass of red wine and topped up his and Marie's—"tell us all about Stella. Where was she born and when and what are her middle names and what star sign is she and does she have any cousins yet?"

Marie, shelling peas by the kitchen sink, laughed. Claude's delight in his unexpected grandfather status was infectious, and Lily felt a sudden pride in her baby daughter, so beautiful in her white Babygro. "Let's see," she said, "where do I start?"

What her father was really asking was: "Where does she come from, this little girl?" There had been those early emails, saying hello and then arranging the trip to France, but he hadn't asked who

Stella's father was. For all he knew, she was the result of a one-night stand; or there could be a long-term partner in London. But then why had Claude only invited "the two of them" to come and stay?

Lily was reluctant to tell them about Harry's death, not yet, and not with Stella in her arms looking so happy. The atmosphere was so convivial: the warm evening air blowing in through the back door, the pink sunset outside, background jazz playing on the radio, and their glasses of red wine. There would be time for that conversation, but for now she didn't want to bring that sadness into the house.

Lily was saved by the sound of tyres on gravel heralding the arrival of Marie's sons and grandsons. Vincent came through the kitchen door first, one small boy under his arm and the other holding his hand, Helene following with a large bunch of wildflowers. *"Bonsoir tout le monde,"* Vincent said, smiling around at them all. He was around six feet tall, with his mother's clear blue eyes and wide mouth. His hair was brown and floppy, with a few streaks of grey. Helene was small and curvy, with dark curly hair and olive skin, more Spanish-looking than French. They both had that slightly ragged look of young parents who are woken most mornings before dawn.

In fact Vincent appeared even more ragged when his older brother joined them, holding a bottle of wine, having parked the car. Julien was one of those men who wake up in the morning looking immaculate. The physical differences between the two brothers were subtle: Julien was a few inches taller, his hair was darker and neatly cut, his eyes were brown not blue. They had the same build, lean with broad shoulders, the same voice and similar bone structure to their mother.

Lily stood up, smoothing down her cotton dress, the baby on her hip. The brothers came forward and kissed her on both cheeks, murmuring in English how good it was to meet her, making introductions to the twin boys. Helene smiled at her shyly and came forward to stroke Stella's face. Julien was more reserved than Vincent, although not aloof. Lily's cheek tingled from where he had brushed his lips in greeting.

With Vincent and Helene she felt instantly comfortable. They reminded her of Cassie and Charlie—a couple who were obviously happy together but not to the exclusion of others. She could imagine Cassie with a couple of sons, Charlie as a father; she could already see them with their little family in a few years' time. Julien was less easy to read. Even wearing jeans and a white shirt, he appeared almost too smart for the rural setting and the informal family meal. His loafers were Italian and expensive suede, the navy jumper over his shoulders was undeniably cashmere. Vincent spoke English rapidly but with plenty of mistakes and a heavy French accent, whereas Julien's English was faultless. From the slight American accent it was clear he'd lived and worked in the States as well as in London. Lily's French was fluent from several summers spent working in France as a teenager, but now it felt rusty from lack of use. Helene spoke very little English—in the end they alternated between the two languages all evening.

Claude poured wine and Marie disappeared with Helene to put the boys down. Lily tucked Stella into an armchair where she instantly fell asleep. "Any dark corner and she's fine," she said to Julien as she wedged cushions in to keep the baby secure. "I should probably take her upstairs to the cot, but I'm not sure if she needs another feed." He nodded, whether out of politeness or boredom she wasn't sure. Vincent and Claude were at the other end of the open-plan lounge, near the kitchen, examining a crack in the plaster ceiling. Their discussion was animated and complicated, involving a lot of technical French terms, so Lily felt obliged to make conversation with Julien.

"So, have you been out here for the whole summer? Do you work here, or in Paris or . . ." She tailed off, her eyebrows raised in a question.

"I usually spend July and August down here, working on various projects with Vincent, designing websites, meeting investors, that kind of thing. The rest of the year I'm in Paris or London, usually about half-half, with quite a bit of travel in between." Julien smiled, and his whole face instantly seemed friendly, more open. "And you, how do you spend your time?"

It was a non-specific way of asking whether she worked, or just looked after Stella, or was a single mum or married, Lily realised. As someone who *used* to have a proper career, someone who found it hard not working even in these early months of motherhood, she appreciated his tact. It was as if he sensed that Lily's situation was sensitive, coming out here alone with the baby to meet her father. She wasn't sure what Marie had said—Marie and Claude didn't know much, after all. Also the situation between the three of them, Lily and Marie's sons, could have been awkward given that Claude was now married to *their* mother, not hers. So far, it didn't feel awkward with Julien. The way he watched her with Stella, his tone of voice, he seemed interested but not prying.

"Well, I live in London," Lily replied. "I'm an editor in a publishing company, although right now I'm not working full-time because of the baby. I'm still doing editorial work for them a few days a week to keep me sane. And I'd like to write too, maybe some journalism or even a book one day. Something I can do from home."

"And home is?" Julien asked.

"Belsize Park. Do you know London well?" Silly question, she realised, given that he'd just said he spent half his time working there. "I was born in Hampstead, that's where my mother still lives, then I had a flat in Camden, then I moved to my current place in Belsize Park. It's lovely around there, with the parks and Primrose Hill, so green and villagey . . ."

"Yes, I love it too," Julien said. "Actually, my flat is just on the edge of Hampstead Heath. You know that large building which overlooks the ponds? I often go running there at weekends—well, not *that* often, but when I can be bothered."

Lily knew exactly where he was talking about—the large red-brick mansion block which towered above the Heath. "You mean on the west side, just up the hill from South End Green?"

"Yes, across the road from Well Walk." Julien nodded.

"What a great location, and those fantastic views over the Heath . . ." she said, trying not to sound like an estate agent. "We walk there every day."

"So we're practically neighbours!" Before Lily had time to reply, he went on: "We should meet for coffee sometime—do you know Le Pain Quotidien? I go there on Saturday mornings with the newspapers. When I've arrived back late on a Friday night, it's a great way to unwind . . ."

Under the immaculate jeans and shirt, he was human, Lily thought. They hadn't even sat down to dinner and already she liked him.

Marie swept back into the kitchen and started moving pots about on the stove, calling to Claude to open more wine and to the others, *"A table, mes enfants, on va manger tout de suite!"* Helene followed, telling Vincent that the boys had demanded *three* bed-time stories and that she'd promised he would take them fishing tomorrow.

Once they were sitting down with platefuls of steaming paella in front of them, Claude raised his glass in a toast. "Here's to finding my wonderful daughter—and granddaughter!" Lily flushed, looking at him and feeling such closeness since their talk that morning. Although there was still plenty that she didn't understand, she was ready to forgive. As they all raised their glasses, Vincent added: "To families." She felt warm and welcomed.

Julien—or Jules as they called him—was seated at the other end of the table, between Marie and Helene, so they didn't get to continue their conversation. But several times during dinner, she looked up and found him looking at her. Later in the evening, she helped make dessert in the kitchen with her father, slicing up strawberries while Claude scooped vanilla ice cream into bowls. She heard Julien and Vincent laughing in the other room and was surprised that already she could distinguish between the two men's voices and laughter.

Plans for the next day's fishing expedition took shape: Helene would make a picnic lunch, and Lily must come, they insisted. It didn't matter that she didn't fish. *"Moi non plus,"* said Julien. The river was beautiful, and there were walks around the abbey nearby, and the weather forecast was perfect for a lazy day outdoors. Marie said she must go; the abbey dated from the fourteenth century and the little town was wonderful too, so Lily happily agreed.

She noticed that Vincent and Julien cleared away the plates and packed the dishwasher without being asked, even washed up the pans and the large paella dish. While Claude made cups of coffee and served it with bitter chunks of dark chocolate, the boys cleaned up, restoring the kitchen to order, then rejoined them on the sofas. Lily hadn't made it upstairs with Stella after all, but the baby slept on, curled into a corner of Claude's large armchair with her mouth slightly open.

Drifting off to sleep a few hours later, Lily found herself wondering about relations. If Marie was married to her father, what did that make their children? Were Julien and Vincent her stepbrothers, or half-brothers, or no relation at all? There was no blood link between any of them. Vincent made a lovely sort-of brother, but she wasn't keen to think of Julien in the same way.

*   *   *

Getting ready for a date. A man called Robert. I can't even believe I just wrote that—a date—for the first time in what, twenty years? Longer, probably. Polly and I met for lunch and went shopping, I bought a new dress, then we both got a blow-dry and manicure. I've done my make-up and moisturised and perfumed from head to toe, and I'm about as ready as I'll ever be . . . Quite excited actually, wearing red lippy for the first time in a millennium, sipping my wine, dancing to ABBA, I feel almost sixteen again.

Poll and I had this routine as teenagers when one of us had a date: we'd get the train into town, buy something new to wear, just a cheap top or something, then get ready together. Mix tape on, a glass of something strong to share between us—usually smuggled upstairs from Dad's drinks cabinet—dancing around while we did each other's make-up. I met Harry when I was twenty-one and haven't dated another man since. My God, that's actually twenty-eight years.

So, things are happening. It's been a rotten few months, hence why I haven't written much, but I think I'm turning a corner. Not just the date tonight but other things too. I've started working again, part-time at one of the big estate agent's in Beaconsfield. At the moment I'm only helping out with viewings but if it goes well they have plenty of vacancies for permanent roles. I've always loved browsing property online—who doesn't—and looking around other people's homes. It's early days, but it feels good to be out of the house, finally doing something that interests me. I've even done a couple of interior design consultations for friends, and I'm hoping to build up some real, paying clients.

Oh God, butterflies. It's been so long, I don't even know how to act on a date! Apparently letting this Robert come to the house to collect me was a bad idea, what do I know? Poll made me download this app which will track my movements on my phone, so if he turns out to be an axe-murderer or something: "the police will know where to start the search." I don't know where she gets these ridiculous notions. He's not an axe-murderer; we met online after the boys bullied me into joining a dating website. He's the headmaster of one of the local secondary schools. He seems really nice, although we've only exchanged emails.

Joe just stuck his head around the door and said, "Good luck, Mum." God that makes me want to cry! Eek, doorbell. Shoes, phone. Keys. Last sip of wine.

IN THE END, IT WAS JULIEN WHO DROVE them back to the airport. He needed to go into Lyon anyway, he said, and it would be no problem to drop Lily and Stella for their flight home. "And it gives us a chance to discuss London," he said as they all sat in the garden on their final evening, drinking wine on the terrace.

The fortnight in France had passed quickly. After that difficult first talk, things had become easier between Claude and Lily. Just saying those names: *Celia, Cassie, Olivia, James;* just speaking the words: *when I left, after you'd gone, what happened, why?* had cleared the way for them to rebuild something. He hadn't given her perfect answers about the past, but she was starting to understand a little. She had a father now—and that was more than she'd ever had.

On the morning after the paella dinner, she'd gone up to the bedroom and brought down a folder. It contained a stack of old photographs showing the four of them as toddlers and children, and more recently, Cassie on her wedding day, Olivia and James grinning into the camera, Lily with Stella a few hours after her birth. And Celia of course, various images of Celia over the years.

Claude went through the folder in near-silence, studying each photograph for a long time. Again she sensed that he was hungry for knowledge of the family he'd left and the years which had followed. Lily was surprised at how much he remembered: as they looked at the photos, he asked detailed questions about changes to the rooms of the house. Was that the same second-hand car? Where had Celia taken them on holiday? Did they still visit her relatives in

Liverpool? It was as if he'd wondered about them all that time, and now he was finding answers, filling in the gaps, storing away the precious scraps of information.

And she had found something too: a father at last, a face to fill that empty space. She had also found Marie—a woman who wasn't a replacement for her mother, nor even a rival, just a kind, intelligent person who treated both Helene and Lily like daughters. Marie referred to them all affectionately as *"les enfants,"* and Lily enjoyed feeling part of this French-American family. Although Stella would never know her father, she now had an unexpected grandfather, and some half- or step-uncles too. Lily tried to imagine a meeting between the two sides of her family. Claude didn't raise the subject, and Lily knew that it would be very difficult for Celia. Could it ever happen?

Then there was Julien. She was trying to work out why he was still playing on her mind.

AFTER THEY FLEW BACK FROM LYON, Cassie collected them from the airport and drove them back to Lily's flat. Cassie put Stella to bed while Lily unpacked their bags and loaded the washing machine. She ducked into the shower while Cassie rang for a Thai takeaway.

Once Stella was sleeping, they opened a bottle of white wine and collapsed on the sofa. With rays of evening sunshine streaming in the large windows, the flat still held the warmth of the day. Cassie smiled and said: "So. What's he like, this father of ours?"

Having met Claude before the others, Lily was conscious that she didn't want there to be "sides." She wanted her siblings to meet their father. She felt that they would like him, despite the painful emotions involved. As the oldest, Cassie probably remembered more of the past; for James it was entirely different since his father had left before he was born. Would that make him feel more abandoned or less? she wondered. As for Olivia, what did she remember; what did she feel?

Lily found Cassie's question difficult to answer. She remembered how sceptical she had felt until she met their father. It was natural that Cassie should be sceptical too. She really wanted to tell her sister everything about Claude, to share her impressions and emotions from those first few days in France. But then Cassie's question about "this father of ours" sounded sarcastic, almost hostile, and Lily's heart sank. *Please let this not create a family division.*

"He's nice, Cass. He's just a normal, lovely man—and his wife, Marie, is lovely too." Cassie's left eyebrow arched at the word "wife," but Lily ploughed on. "They live in California, but they spend every summer in France—she's French. It's a beautiful house. They were really welcoming, and he wanted to know about all of you. I showed him some of the old photos, also some of your wedding and things like that. He remembers a lot about when we were kids. I think it's been hard for him actually." Lily wondered how much to say about why he left. "He was going through a difficult patch, depression and all that." She hesitated. "He found the family thing too much to cope with." Cassie's face was impassive.

Lily continued: "He didn't make excuses, and I'm not making excuses either, but I think he's a good man. He said he'd never stopped loving Mum and us children, that he was young and immature. He missed us all from the moment he left but he didn't know what to do."

Lily didn't know if Cassie's silence was pensive or angry. They sat without saying anything for a few minutes, then Lily asked: "What are you thinking?"

"I don't know," Cassie said slowly. "I guess people make mistakes. And it must have been hard for both of them, having all those kids while they were still young. But Mum didn't walk out on us, did she?" She stared at her sister for a moment. "Lil, it's just that when he left—I have such vivid memories of that time—it was terrible. I remember him being there, and then I remember the emptiness in the house, and sometimes Mum crying . . . It's really hard to forgive and forget when I remember the sadness he left behind. The whole time you were in France, I was thinking about him, imagining your first meeting." She paused. "Of course I want to forgive. I'd like to have a father too. I just—I don't know if I can."

"I know, Cass," Lily said. "I felt exactly the same, and still do, sort of guilty about liking him, as though I'm being disloyal to Mum. I don't think anyone needs to forget the past—how can we? But maybe forgive a little. And talk to Mum about it. Since Harry died, I think I've changed. The thing is, life's short, isn't it? And family is precious. We have a father, even though he wasn't there. He's there now."

The doorbell rang: the takeaway food. Lily waved away Cassie's money and ran down the stairs. Returning a few minutes later with several large brown paper bags, she said: "Let's eat!"

"Come here." Cass took the paper bags from Lily and reached out her arms. The two sisters shared a long hug. "You're brave, you know that? Losing Harry and having Stella alone and going out there to meet our father . . ." Lily shook her head and refilled their wineglasses. Cassie began opening the foil cartons of steaming rice. "I'm ravenous. Let's eat and you can tell me about the rest of them— what are Marie's sons like?"

Lily wasn't sure what they were like. She could describe Vincent easily enough: an outgoing young Frenchman, intelligent, friendly, and fun. But she was still trying to work out what she thought of Julien. And how could she trust her feelings anyway? After the highs and lows of recent months—Harry's suicide, the grief and guilt which followed, then the shock and joy of Stella's early arrival—she barely remembered what normal, calm emotions were like anymore. When she thought of Julien, she didn't know what she felt, but she thought about him a lot. Anyway, she told herself, she was in no fit state to plunge into another relationship.

With barely a fortnight's acquaintance, she sensed the potential for something more serious between them. Was she completely misguided? She hardly knew him. She didn't even know whether he was single or not. No one had mentioned a girlfriend or partner, but by the time she might have asked Julien himself, it seemed too loaded a question. He referred to friends in conversation, he clearly had a busy social life, but mostly he said "I" rather than "we."

Then again, she had no evidence that he was interested in her on a romantic basis. After that first family dinner in France, he'd certainly been around a lot: whether it was odd jobs, or a meal, or he was "just passing," he had dropped in at the farmhouse every day. He and Lily had gone for a long walk along the river after the picnic with Vincent and Helene. They had helped clear out the pond. They had spent a whole afternoon picking blackberries together, with Stella of course. On the final evening, they had left the baby at home with Marie and shared a bottle of the local Burgundy in the village's only bar. But he hadn't kissed her, nor even flirted with her, as far as Lily could see.

And now? She kept recalling what he'd said that first evening, when they discovered they were neighbours: "We should meet for coffee sometime . . ." But that had been an offhand comment early on; it hardly constituted a definite arrangement. He'd driven them to the airport that last day without repeating his invitation, and they'd said goodbye without swapping numbers or emails. Lily felt pathetic for replaying that fragment in her head.

She didn't tell Cassie how she felt about Julien, how she liked being near him, talking together, the reserved, thoughtful way he had about him. She liked his perfect English with its slight French-American accent; his European clothes and suede loafers;

she liked his dark hair and brown eyes. She liked the musky amber scent of his skin.

There had been hours, almost whole days, in France when she hadn't thought of Harry, hadn't woken with him on her mind or gone to sleep with his image in her head. She had been utterly taken up with being there—with Claude and Marie, their delight in Stella, the sunshine, the food and wine, getting to know her new family and Julien. In Burgundy, that part of her which had been in hibernation since Harry died began to wake up.

Lily didn't say any of this to her big sister because it sounded ridiculously over the top. She hadn't realised herself, until she got back from France, how much she liked Julien. And she didn't even know when he was next in London. Still, these daydreams about him made her happy.

"GOOD MORNING MUM!" LILY UNLOCKED her mother's front door, calling out as she did so. "And what a beautiful morning it is!" She had Stella strapped to her chest, with a large shopping bag in one arm and a huge bunch of flowers tucked under the other. "I've brought you two of your favourite things . . ."

Celia came out into the hallway, smiling expectantly.

". . . your granddaughter, just woken from her morning nap, and some purple flowers!"

"Oh, darling." Celia rushed forward to unburden Lily. "What a treat! Delphiniums! And hydrangeas!"

"Is that what they're called?" Lily laughed, thrusting the blooms towards her mother.

"Oh, they're beautiful. Come through into the kitchen and we'll get these in water. You look wonderful. And you seem, I don't know, you seem different, since France. Lighter, somehow carefree!"

IN THE FIRST FEW DAYS AFTER HER
return, both Cassie and Celia sensed this change in Lily. Her voice
was full of life again, her eyes sparkled, her laughter was spontaneous. The sadness was starting to lift.

Lily felt it herself. She felt hungrier and had more energy. For the
first time in months she found herself looking forward to the future.
She alternated between waiting to hear from Julien—scanning
emails from Claude and Marie for any mention of his name, a
request for her phone number perhaps—to castigating herself for
being so stupid. At night she replayed their conversations and walks,
endlessly trying to analyse the situation. That day they'd walked by
the river, hadn't there been a connection? That last evening, sipping
white Burgundy in the village wine bar, hadn't there been lingering
glances, an unspoken, delicious tension? Lily kept remembering the
way he looked at her. She was sure there was something.

But when she was tired and Stella was crying and she felt overwhelmed and lonely, she told herself that Julien wasn't interested. Of
course he wasn't. He was polite and well-mannered, that's all. He'd
felt sorry for her, a single mother struggling to bring up a child alone.
He was practically her half-brother and he probably had a beautiful,
sophisticated French fiancée in Paris. It had been nearly a fortnight
since she'd come back to London and not a word from him. Why
was she still obsessing over him like some desperate spinster?

This was characteristic of Lily, this tendency to swing between
extremes of hope and despair. She was much harder on herself than
she'd have been on Cassie or Olivia in the same situation. Partly it
was a defence mechanism: she felt it was easier to cope with rejection if she anticipated it, whereas optimism only set you up for
disappointment.

But still that nugget of hope refused to die. Despite hearing nothing from Julien, despite telling herself to stop waiting for an email or text, Lily kept hoping.

AFTER THE INITIAL BUOYANCY OF HER return to London, Lily fell into a slump. She realised that it wasn't just her—everyone seemed down in the dumps. The weather turned autumnal overnight: endless rain and chill winds seemed unreasonable for September. Olivia arrived back from Rome declaring it was over with Giovanni. She couldn't stand living with his family for another day. Cassie found out that she wasn't pregnant again and began to despair. Celia seemed withdrawn too, and Lily worried that she'd hurt her mother's feelings by going to France. The excitement of meeting Claude and her new family had worn off. Then Stella started teething, so they were both sleeping badly. The future seemed bleak.

Then the anniversary of Harry's death rolled around, and Lily was at her lowest ebb. A whole year since she'd last seen him, and now she never would again. She had taken on more editing projects from home for Higher Education Press, keen to distract herself with freelance work, but the manuscripts were dull and complicated. Everyone felt it: the summer was at an end.

During this time—which was only a few weeks, although it felt longer—Lily didn't entirely give up. She was fed up with life, with London, with the rain, sometimes even with her crying daughter whom she adored, but she tried to keep reminding herself that things could change. And finally, a couple of weeks after they got back to London, they did. She was struggling up the stairs with Stella and four heavy shopping bags when Susan popped her head out of the door on the ground floor.

"I've just signed for flowers!" she announced, smiling up at Lily and waving at Stella.

"Lovely," Lily said. "Who are they from?"

"They're for you, so I didn't look at the card. But I'd say it's someone with taste—it's a beautiful selection of roses, lilies, and carnations, all red and orange and autumnal colours. Do you want them now or shall I bring them up in a minute when you've got Stella settled?"

Lily's face was transformed, from rain-drenched and hassled to shining and hopeful. She ran through the possibilities in her mind: the flowers could be from her father and Marie, or from one of her authors to say thank you for the editing, or . . . could it be? How she hoped it was him.

She was still standing on the stairs holding Stella and the shopping bags, although suddenly they weighed nothing at all. "How intriguing. Please do bring them up. In fact, give me a minute and come and have coffee, you haven't been round all week."

When Susan arrived with the flowers, Lily was unable to play it cool. She tore open the cream card tucked inside and let out an audible sigh. *Happy autumn, Lily. Just back from a work trip to Singapore. Would love to meet for that coffee—all three of us? Julien.*

Oh, it was perfect, perfect. Throwing caution to the wind, Lily showed Susan the card and described him in detail while twirling Stella around the room. Once Susan had been brought up to date, they analysed the note and discussed the significance of his precise words. They agreed it couldn't have been more gentlemanly—he was polite enough to include the baby in the invitation, but he sent flowers for Lily which made it romantic too.

"Oh, Susan, I've been longing to hear from him!" Saying it out loud made her realise how much she was looking forward to their meeting. Even Stella seemed to have forgotten her aching gums and was smiling up at her mother. "But now what?" Lily looked anxious all of a sudden. "Does he have my number? We didn't even swap emails. Look, he doesn't mention when we should meet. How is he going to get hold of me?"

Susan shook her head. "Don't be ridiculous, Lily! He's just sent you the most glorious bouquet, so he's managed to find your home address—probably from your father—do you really think he can't track down your phone number? And you're online, aren't you? Just remember how much you wanted to hear from him and enjoy this moment. Let's find a vase for these flowers"—she went into the kitchen—"and then let's work out what you're going to wear when you see this chap."

Lily burst out laughing—it was exactly what her mother would have said. Susan was right about enjoying the moment. It was wonderful to be sitting here with flowers from Julien. The shopping bags didn't matter, the rain didn't matter; with a thrill of excitement she realised she was going to see him again.

The filthy weather continued all week but Lily barely noticed. And by the time she was getting ready to meet him that weekend, the rain had stopped and the sun had come out. By yet another miracle, Stella had slept through the night, so they were both relatively rested on Saturday morning.

Cassie, to whom Lily had confessed everything after Julien's flowers arrived, took Stella swimming. "You've been saying for ages you need to go to the hairdresser, so now's your chance." Lily's hair was still nicely streaked blonde from the summer, but it badly needed a cut—she hadn't been to the hairdresser since before Stella's birth and she was starting to feel like a shaggy dog. While she was at the hair salon, she had her eyebrows and nails done too.

It was amazing what a difference a little TLC made, Lily thought, flicking through a magazine while her hair was being blow-dried. It wasn't a huge extravagance—she had friends who spent hundreds of pounds a month on beauty treatments, handbags, and shoes—and it was worth every penny. Walking back up England's Lane, feeling like a new woman, she resolved to make more time for herself, for simple things like haircuts and the occasional manicure or pedicure.

"Look at you!" Cassie said, barging back into the flat with her arms full of Stella and their swimming bags. "You look gorgeous! I've bought sandwiches, do you have time for lunch?"

"Of course," Lily said. "We're not meeting Julien until four. Thanks for taking Stella, I needed that pampering time. I'll put her down for her nap and then let's eat."

After settling Stella in her cot, Lily glanced in the full-length mirror in the hallway. "Gorgeous" was an exaggeration, but the haircut was a definite improvement. She was wearing dove-grey jeans which fit like a glove, and a black silk top which Cassie had lent her. She had considered buying a new outfit but she didn't want to overdo it. It was just an afternoon coffee; maybe it wasn't even a date. Julien had mentioned that Le Pain Quotidien was very busy at weekends and he suggested instead a new café which had recently opened in Belsize Park.

"Do I look OK?" Lily said, rejoining Cassie in the kitchen. "Is this top kind of low cut?"

Her sister smiled. "Don't be silly! It shows a hint of arms and cleavage but not too much. You still have a great tan from France. And the jeans are perfect—no one would believe you had a baby a few months ago."

"Thanks, Cass," she said. "God, I'm starting to get nervous, my appetite's gone completely."

"You need to eat *something*, I bet you haven't had breakfast. Here, I got us sandwiches from Black Truffle Deli; they do amazing goat's cheese, rocket, and sundried tomato. Don't worry, I avoided egg, hummus, and garlic—no stinky breath!"

"Honestly, Cass, he's probably not interested in that way. And I'm taking Stella with me, so we're hardly going to kiss. Anyway, I'm sure he has evening plans. I wouldn't be surprised if it's a quick coffee and we're home by five p.m."

IT WAS AFTER EIGHT O'CLOCK BY THE TIME Julien walked them home. The time had disappeared: had they really spent four hours just talking? For all Lily's apprehension, the date went beautifully. Cassie had dropped them outside the café in Belsize Park. It had only opened in the summer so Lily hadn't been there yet. There were several large sofas, a play area for children, and low coffee tables with magazines and board games scattered around. The place wasn't packed, but there was a lively hum of conversation: several families, a few people working on their laptops, and an elderly couple reading the newspapers in the afternoon sunshine. Lily forgot her nerves as soon as she saw Julien, who was sitting on one of the large sofas by the window. He smiled and came over to help her off with Stella's papoose.

"Lily, so lovely to see you. It feels like ages, *non?*" He kissed her lightly on both cheeks and drew back to look at her. "You're looking *ravissante*—both of you." He stroked Stella's tuft of blonde hair. "I swear she's grown since France. How long has it been?" Lily could have told him exactly how long it had been, but instead she murmured something about time flying. The waitress arrived and Julien ordered for them both: a large pot of Earl Grey tea and some lemon drizzle cake. Lily settled Stella on the play mat beside the sofa, smiling as Julien discussed the merits of different cake with the waitress.

Stella obliged by finding the soft toys fascinating. She lay there practising her first attempts at crawling, batting at toys, occasionally gurgling up at them. Lily poured out tea, and she and Julien caught up on the past few weeks. "I wanted to apologise for not being in touch sooner," he began. "I meant to email or ring you, but just after you left there was an emergency with work. I was in Paris, then back here for a few days, then in Singapore for a fortnight. The summer came to an abrupt end—I don't think Vincent is very happy with me; I left everything unfinished with him and went rushing off. Anyway, I kept meaning to get in touch."

"Not at all," Lily said. "I've been busy with a couple of big work projects. And I've been looking at nurseries for Stella, which is more time-consuming than it sounds. It was lovely to get your flowers, a real surprise. So, tell me about your travels."

It was only when Julien pointed out the sunset over the London rooftops—a glorious sky shot through with pink and orange—that they realised the time. People began arriving for early suppers, and Stella too needed food. "Are you rushing off or can we get something for her here?" Julien hesitated. He wasn't sure whether Lily was still breast-feeding.

"Actually, she's on to solid food now. I've got stuff for her, puréed carrots, bananas, you know, my usual *cordon bleu*." Lily's limited culinary skills had become a family joke in France. "But here, let me pay for the tea and cake."

"Don't be silly." Julien pulled out his wallet and waved away Lily's money. "You get started on feeding her and I'll get the bill. But I wondered"—he hesitated—"if you like, we could walk on the Heath? The leaves are just turning and it's beautiful up there. If we go soon we'll catch the last of the light . . . unless you're busy this evening?"

Lily felt a rush of pleasure. She hadn't wanted the afternoon to end there. "I'd love that."

"That's great," Julien said, and touched her shoulder. He walked across the café. Spooning puréed carrot from a small Tupperware into her hungry daughter's mouth, she watched him standing at the till. She liked the way he talked easily with the manager, asking about the café opening, how business had been going in the first few months. And his smile, his smell, his hands ... Lily smiled at Stella, feeding her small chunks of banana, and whispered, "Your mummy needs to get a grip." If anything, she felt more attracted to him now than she had in France.

THEY WERE STANDING AT THE HIGHEST point of Hampstead Heath, looking down across London spread out below, when the last rays of light finally disappeared from the sky. "That's my place." Julien pointed. "Over there. That big red-brick building." Lily already knew he lived in East Heath Lodge— although she didn't mention how often she'd walked past it since their return from France.

"Alors?" He turned to look at her. Stella was fast asleep. Julien took Lily's hands. "It's really good to see you again." He reached forward, gently tracing the line of her cheek. "I kept thinking about you, after France and everything. I'm so glad we met." He leaned forward and kissed her, tentatively, on the lips. They gazed into each other's eyes. Then he kissed her again, for longer this time.

Lily could feel herself melting. She pulled gently away. "I should probably get this little one back."

"Of course." He brushed a few strands of hair away from her face and kissed her again. "Sorry, it must be way past her bedtime. I'll walk you home."

As they walked through South End Green, Julien took her hand. "Are you free tomorrow evening? Why don't you come over, both of you, and I'll cook. You can feed Stella and put her down, then we can have dinner and watch something on Netflix? I can drive over and collect you with her cot, that way I can drop you back afterwards and she doesn't need to be woken."

Lily nodded. "OK. Thank you, I'd love that."

*   *   *

So, Robert has invited us to stay at his villa in Spain. Me and the boys, that is. It's been a lovely few months. I never thought a blind date could work out—it certainly wasn't love at first sight, and even for the first few meetings I wasn't convinced. But he's gradually grown on me and I can actually see him being part of our lives. At first I thought he was too old for me—he's sixty-four—too settled, too boring even, but over time I've come to feel very happy with him.

Poll thinks I should go for it. When I told her he'd invited us to spend the boys' half-term at the villa in Marbella, she said something interesting: "You know, Pip, this could work. Robert is everything that Harry was not." I wonder if, in a way, she's right. Robert is reliable, dependable, a man you can trust. He'd never come home late or drunk, or not come home at all.

Do I sometimes feel he's a tiny bit dull? Well, truthfully, no. I like the security. I was anxious over Harry for so long—even before he started seeing Lily—and it was really taking its toll. By the time he died, I was a wreck. My deepening depression, which in fact was a symptom of not working, not having any purpose or career and feeling useless, ditto my constant insecurity over my fading looks, I simply don't feel any of that around Robert. I don't find myself nagging and sniping the way I did with Harry. I don't wonder about the other women Robert works with; he wants to be with me all the time. And I feel ridiculously youthful (the benefits of a fifteen-year age gap), and light and girlish.

Is it too soon? Am I a bad widow for not waiting longer? Am I being disrespectful to Harry's memory? Will it damage the boys? Am I just looking for someone to take care of us? Oh God, who knows . . . who cares? Robert is a kind, funny, and intelligent man and he lifts my spirits. The boys get on brilliantly with him—and his daughters—and beyond that, time will tell. It hasn't been easy. I still miss Harry dreadfully at times, and I'll never be "in love" like that again, the raw physical passion we shared when we first met, those blissful early years of our marriage, the intimacy of our babies being born. He'll always be the love of my life and the father of my boys.

But if his death has taught me one thing it's that life can be brutal. People get hurt, hearts get broken, and sometimes really terrible things happen. Harry's suicide ripped a hole in our family, and I need to rebuild something for the boys, for me. We can't sit in this house forever with this death weighing on us, feeling empty and incomplete.

JULIEN WAS AS GOOD AS HIS WORD, DRIV-
ing over to collect them and taking them back to the Heathside flat for dinner. The baby carrier doubled as a car seat and travel cot, so Lily could leave her daughter sleeping in the corner of the living room. Julien had made a delicious tomato and mozzarella salad, followed by stuffed aubergine with Camargue rice. "This reminds me of being in France," Lily said as they ate. "Your mum's an amazing cook."

"I love Mum's cooking." Julien nodded. "She taught me and Vincent how to make this when we were kids." He refilled their glasses. "The wine's from Burgundy too."

After dinner he drove them home and they sat chatting in the car for a few minutes before she got out. She waved as Julien drove off, and closed the front door quietly. She listened for sounds from Susan's flat, then remembered that she was away for a long weekend shooting in Scotland with friends. She climbed the stairs slowly, Stella still sleeping in her cot. She'd have liked to invite him upstairs for coffee, but she wasn't entirely sure; for now, it was better to take things slowly.

Before Stella was born, Lily hadn't thought about dating with a child. How could you have a romantic atmosphere—how could you even go out—with a baby in tow? Now that Stella was here, and she was entirely responsible for this little life, it felt completely natural. OK, she couldn't be as spontaneous as she was before—a certain amount of planning was required, as well as nappies and sterilised bottles—but motherhood wasn't as limiting as she'd have assumed. Julien had puréed some veg for Stella's dinner, and she'd bathed and changed her in his guest bathroom while he finished cooking. It helped that Julien had only ever known her with a baby; there were no awkward explanations about being a single mother. In fact they still hadn't talked about Stella's father and why he wasn't around.

That autumn they quickly fell into a routine. They saw each other several times a week and spent most of the weekends together. He would come to Lily's flat after work, always with a good bottle of wine and usually with the ingredients of supper. They would cook and talk for hours, late into the evening, curled on the sofa as the room grew dark. It was a great excuse to watch their favourite French films again: *À Bout de Souffle*, *La Boum*, and *Jules et Jim*. At weekends, if Julien wasn't travelling for work, they visited Celia for lunch, met up with Cassie and Charlie, went to art galleries and for coffees in Hampstead or Chelsea, occasionally for drives in the countryside.

For all that Julien adored Stella, Lily was aware that he wanted time alone with her, properly alone. They still hadn't spent a whole night together. It wasn't that she didn't want him or didn't trust him. But a sense of caution, even vulnerability, held her back: she was fragile from the events of the past year. He didn't rush her; they both knew they had time.

For Lily's birthday in October, Julien arranged a weekend away. "I'd like to take you to Paris," he said, arriving one evening after work. "Just the two of us. I spoke to Cassie. She and Charlie will look after Stella from Friday evening to Sunday morning, if that's

OK with you? I've booked a beautiful hotel, and I'll get tickets to the opera. We'll go to some wonderful restaurants, and you can meet some of my friends."

Cassie was more than happy to help out. She and Charlie were still trying to conceive and she loved looking after her niece. "I can't wait, a whole weekend of being parents! Who knows, maybe it will help—they say that being around babies is good for fertility."

The weekend in Paris was the first time Lily had left Stella in someone else's care for more than twenty-four hours. "Oh my God, *romantico!* But are you ready?" her little sister, Olivia, said, when she heard that Julien was whisking Lily away. "Have you been doing your pelvic floor exercises?" Olivia and Cassie found this hysterically funny, and it made Lily laugh too.

But it was strange how little that had come to matter. She remembered the mothers in her antenatal and baby yoga groups endlessly discussing their bodies: stretchmarks and Kegel exercises and how soon they could get back to their "pre-pregnancy weight." Lily hadn't stood on a pair of bathroom scales since Stella was born—she didn't have any in the flat. She must have been weighed by the midwives in follow-up appointments, but she couldn't recall any specific figures. From the fit of her jeans she could tell that her body was back to its "pre-pregnancy weight." If anything, having a baby had made her stronger and leaner.

Still, she enjoyed her birthday present from her sisters. "We decided to give you this early," Olivia said, "so you can get ready for Paris." She waved a large pink gift voucher. "It's a beauty package for knackered new mums: full body massage, exfoliation, waxing, the works!" Lily wasn't sure about being labelled a knackered new mother—it reminded her of those yoga mums, endlessly competing over who got the least sleep and discussing how many calories breast-feeding used up. Then again, it was lovely to be pampered, and she felt like a million dollars after her afternoon at the beauty salon.

JULIEN HAD BOOKED A BOUTIQUE HOTEL in the Saint-Germain district. Lily stepped out of the shower and began to rub body lotion onto her freshly waxed legs. They were smooth as silk; Olivia would be proud of her. It was the morning of her birthday and their second day in Paris. She thought of making love with Julien last night and waking in his arms this morning. She thought of breakfast waiting downstairs: freshly squeezed orange juice, freshly brewed coffee, freshly baked croissants, brioches, and raspberry jam. She thought of fresh air, and sunshine, and all of Paris waiting for them to explore. She thought of Stella's smile and Stella's laugh and of going home to her later that day. She didn't feel like a knackered mum now, she felt like the luckiest woman in the world.

And, like most happiness or sadness, it was entirely undeserved. Lily had never expected to meet someone like Julien. After Harry, after Stella, she hadn't known she could experience such strong emotions again: lust, love, joy.

In the weeks after Paris, the chemistry between them was intense. Lily began to reconnect with her body; she began to feel like a whole person again. As she came back to life, she saw how dead she had been inside, for so long. She hadn't felt sexy since Harry was alive. It wasn't about motherhood, or being "knackered," or her pre- or post-pregnancy body. It was the sadness which had made her lose herself. Until Julien, she had forgotten what it felt like to be so consumed with lust that you couldn't sleep, eat, or think properly. When he'd fly in on the red-eye from one of his work trips, they'd meet for lunch at a gastropub in Belsize Park. They would go back to his flat and lose entire afternoons together.

But her heart was still fragile. Sometimes when Julien made love to her she had to blink back tears. It was barely a year since Harry's death, too soon for anything serious. Sometimes she felt ashamed of herself for leaving Harry behind. She and Julien were falling in love, and she was confused. Strong emotions threatened to tip her over the edge.

But what could she do? Preserve Harry's memory in aspic and never move on—would that be good for her or for Stella? She didn't want to bring up her daughter in an atmosphere of frozen grief, with the shadow of her dead father hanging over them. From time to time Lily thought about Harry's other children, those two boys, and wondered how they were coping. She thought about his wife too, with a deep sense of guilt. Was Pippa still grieving? Would she too meet someone else? And always, those unanswerable questions: How much did Pippa know? How much did she blame Lily? Did she hate her?

From time to time Cassie took Stella overnight and Lily stayed at Julien's flat. One night, unable to sleep, she got out of bed, wrapping a cashmere throw around her. She sat in the large open-plan living room, staring at the embers of the fire they had lit earlier that evening. She recalled a phrase she had read years before written by the mystic Rūmī: "You have to keep breaking your heart until it opens." Her heart was broken, and full, and empty, all at the same time.

IN EARLY DECEMBER THE QUESTION OF Christmas arose. They had been together now for several months and Julien was routinely included in family occasions. It seemed natural enough, during one noisy Sunday lunch, that Celia invited him to spend Christmas with them all in Hampstead. "I can't bear the thought of you spending the day alone, and we'd absolutely love to have you. If I'm cooking for all this rabble, why not one more!"

Julien's answer was polite but vague: "It's very kind, thank you. I just need to work out what's happening over the holidays." He glanced at Lily. "I've sort of made plans . . ." There was an awkward silence. "I usually go skiing at this time of year—a bunch of us, some old Credit Suisse colleagues, a few friends from the Sorbonne."

Lily excused herself and went to the bathroom. Her face was white in the mirror, and her hands trembled. "Get a grip," she murmured to herself. "Get a bloody grip." Later, as they cleared away the lunch table, Cassie cornered her in the kitchen. "Are you OK? Is it about the ski trip?" Lily shook her head and carried on stacking plates in the dishwasher. As soon as coffee was over, she said she needed to take Stella home.

Julien drove them back. Outside their house he switched off the engine and turned to Lily. "Shall I come up?" he said. "I've got an early start tomorrow but I can stay for a few hours. I'd like to ask you about the ski trip." He smiled. "We didn't really get a chance this afternoon."

Lily was already undoing her seat belt and getting out of the car. Leaning into the back seat to unfasten Stella, she said, "No, it's fine. You go and prepare for your meetings—we've got stuff to do." Julien got out of the car to help with the bags but she turned and unlocked the front door with a brief wave. She clasped Stella to her and walked quickly upstairs, wanting to avoid Susan, wanting to get away from Julien. It wasn't until Stella was finally in bed that evening that Lily allowed the hurt to wash over her. Standing in the kitchen, clutching a mug of herbal tea, she burst into tears.

She had assumed Julien would be staying in London for Christmas. He hadn't mentioned the holidays; he hadn't said anything about wanting to go skiing. Why had she been so foolish— why had she imagined he might want to spend his precious free time in boring old Hampstead with her and her small child? What man would pass up the opportunity to go skiing with wealthy banking friends—for all she knew, with ex-lovers and girlfriends? He was probably counting down the days.

Lily also felt humiliated. She wished Celia hadn't invited him in front of the family. It had been obvious that he was embarrassed, and even more obvious that she was upset at his polite evasion. In fact, the whole thing had been a mistake from the beginning. She was a fool to believe that this relationship meant anything to him.

She was just going to bed that night when her phone rang. It was Julien. She pressed "divert call." He rang again, immediately. This time she picked up. "Hi. What is it? I'm on my way to bed."

"Lily, I wanted to talk about this afternoon, about Christmas." He hesitated. "I've been meaning to ask, but I was just looking into things—why don't you come skiing too?"

"Skiing?" Lily nearly laughed. "In case you hadn't noticed, Julien, I have a young baby."

"I meant both of you, all three of us," he said. "People go skiing with babies all the time, we can make arrangements . . ."

"Arrangements? Quite apart from blowing out my mum's Christmas plans at such short notice, there are a few practicalities which you may not have considered: taking a baby to a ski resort, finding childcare, the cost of it all . . ."

"I can cover our share of the chalet, I'd be happy to . . ."

"And flights and ski passes and ski hire and childcare and *après-ski* . . ."

"Lily, honestly, we'll sort all that out . . ."

She cut him off. "Seriously, don't worry about it. Go and enjoy your trip. You work hard, and you deserve a proper break."

"Come on, don't be like that. I wanted to talk about it but there hasn't been time."

"Talk about what? It's fine, honestly, Julien. It would have been nice to know about it a little sooner, but you're a free agent. Now, if you don't mind, I'm tired. Night." And she hung up.

So that was that. They would spend the holidays apart. Lily went about the usual Christmas routines—shopping and wrapping presents, helping Celia decorate the tree—but her mind was far away. She tried to understand what had gone wrong with Julien. One minute they were a close family unit, he was spending all his time with her and Stella, he was taking her to Paris and telling her he loved her, and now he was a different person, off on a ski trip with his Russian and Swiss investment banking friends. Off to lounge around drinking Aperol Spritzes and discussing quantitative easing and derivatives and who had the biggest yacht.

When she had first met Julien in his mother's farmhouse in Burgundy, he hadn't seemed that way. Why had he stuck around if he wasn't serious about her—was she just a way to pass the time in London? She had been naïve to hope that she meant anything to Julien.

Then she started to think that maybe it had started further back, before the question of Christmas had even arisen. Maybe he'd been distant for a while. Had it been after the intense passion of that post-Paris period? Had his feelings begun to cool? She had thought they were in a happy routine, but maybe he found it dull. The rhythm of life with a small child wasn't exactly exciting. Cassie told her she was overreacting, that nothing about Julien's behaviour suggested that his feelings had changed, but still. Lily felt defensive about the life she had managed to salvage from the wreckage of Harry's death—and if that wasn't good enough for Julien, then fine, let him go skiing with his Euro-pals.

In the run-up to Christmas, they still spent time together; he invited her to his company's corporate carol concert in Fleet Street, and they took Stella to the Winter Wonderland in Hyde Park, but Lily began to feel like a burden. Where she used to joke about his busy work schedule and demand that he make time to see them in between trips and airports, she now waited for him to contact her. When he rang, she was short on the phone. When he suggested coming round to her flat, she was diffident. The atmosphere had always been relaxed and easy between them, and now it was strained. She began to lose confidence in his feelings and she withdrew.

The day before Christmas Eve he left to join his friends in St. Anton.

IT WAS NOT A GOOD CHRISTMAS. APART from the previous year, when she'd been reeling from Harry's death, it was the worst Lily could remember. Yet nothing had actually happened. They hadn't split up or even argued—Julien had simply gone skiing for a few weeks. So why did it feel more serious?

Sitting up late with her sisters at Celia's house on Christmas Eve, Lily kept her misery buried inside her. She had a superstition that if she started talking about the end of their relationship, it would come true. Anyway, she wasn't the only one with personal problems, and she didn't have a monopoly on family sympathy. Her sisters had their own lives to worry about.

Olivia had recently returned from Italy where she and Giovanni had reconciled and reunited (again). She was happy but frustrated at the situation: "I just don't know where we go from here. He's talking about getting engaged at some point, but where are we going to live? We can't stay in Rome with his family, their apartment is tiny. Either he needs to move here and get a job, or—I don't know, we just carry on like this? I'm going to be thirty in a couple of years, we can't keep breaking up and getting back together . . ." She paused. "The thing is, I really love him. When I listen to my instincts, I know we're right together."

Cassie nodded. "You have to follow your instincts, Liv. I felt like that about Charlie. Even though he infuriates me quite often, I just know the two of us are right."

They were right about trusting your instincts, Lily thought. The fact that she was thinking this way about Julien was a signal that something was wrong. All her past relationships had borne out this simple truth: feelings were mutual. Positive and negative emotions were there for a reason. When you felt happy and relaxed in someone's company, they were happy and relaxed too. When you felt tense and anxious with someone, as she did now with Julien, they were tense and anxious too.

He didn't communicate much over the holidays. A noisy call from the hotel bar on Christmas evening, clearly in a celebratory mood. She heard female laughter in the background, male voices, the clink of glasses and loud music. She could just picture the scene: bottles of Cristal champagne in some exclusive private members' club, the men dressed in Italian suede loafers and gold signet rings, the women in all-white *après-ski* outfits or stunning little black dresses, with their year-round tans and glossy, shiny manes. Lily would never have that kind of hair.

And yet Julien had always made her feel beautiful. Whether she was wearing jeans and T-shirt or an evening dress and killer heels, she felt good around him, interesting and attractive. What had changed? She brooded over him and his wealthy pals in St. Anton, and felt past her sell-by date.

To make matters worse, one week later he rang from Charles de Gaulle airport. "I'm flying out to the States," he said. "Vincent called to say he was going to see Mum and Claude, and I had this sudden urge for some winter sun." Lily couldn't believe how off-hand he sounded. They had often talked about going to California together to visit their respective parents, and now he was going without her. What a great start to the year.

On New Year's Eve, Claude and Marie WhatsApped some photographs of them all at a fireworks party in San Francisco Bay. *Wish you were here,* they wrote underneath. Did that include Julien, Lily wondered. Did he wish she were there too?

When Julien got back to London in early January, Lily knew their relationship was in trouble. They met up a few times but the magic had gone. That relaxed, easy enjoyment between them was missing and she didn't know how to bring it back. No matter how hard she tried just smiling, being breezy and carefree, the conversation floundered. The more she tried to hide her anxiety, the more strained the atmosphere grew.

She had so wanted this to work: Julien was intelligent, handsome, generous, and kind. She admired his values and respected his opinions and she loved being in his company. But she couldn't make it happen if his heart wasn't in it.

Gradually it dawned on Lily that this ending was inevitable. Why had she been blind for so long? It was time to accept the reality, that they lived in different worlds. She told herself that eventually he would move back to Paris. He'd marry a chic Parisienne with glossy hair and they'd have two immaculate, bilingual children. They would spend the winters skiing in Zürich or Verbier and the summers in Cap Ferrat or sailing around Montenegro in someone's super-yacht. Everything would be chic and well-ordered. *That's not you,* Lily admitted to herself. You're unconventional and sometimes chaotic. You're alone and you have a baby by someone else. You don't fit into the life that Julien wants for himself.

In late January, a few weeks after his return, he stopped calling. An entire weekend passed without hearing from him, and then it was a whole week. One evening, when Cassie was over, Lily broke down in tears.

"I'm sorry," she said. "I've known this was coming for weeks but I was trying to get a grip. It's Julien and me, I think we're over. It's been a horrible atmosphere since he came back—actually, it was like this before he left for Christmas—and it's getting worse. And now I haven't heard from him, I think he's given up."

"But I don't understand, he always seemed besotted with you. Look, you don't have to wait for him to contact you—why don't you ring him now? I'll stay here with Stella, and you can meet up and talk. Surely it's worth a try."

Lily shook her head. "Honestly, Cass, I've gone over and over this one. He doesn't want to be with me, that's clear enough. I don't need to humiliate myself by begging him to meet up. It's strange: Julien was the last person I'd have thought would play games or go cold like this. I simply can't work out what he's thinking or who he is anymore. I feel like a piece of rubbish which has been thrown on the scrap heap."

"You've done absolutely nothing wrong," Cassie said. "Even if Julien has changed his mind, that doesn't make you a piece of rubbish. Can you maybe use this as a stepping stone? Look how far you've come in the past year. After Harry died you thought you'd never be with anyone again. Perhaps Julien was just a lesson, part of the process of coming back to life. Forget about him and focus on the positives: you were dating again, and you had wonderful times together, even if . . ." Cassie shook her head. "I know you're terribly hurt, Lil. I would be too. His behaviour makes zero sense. But remember, you still have me, you still have all of us, and we love you very much. It hasn't worked out this time, but there will be better times ahead."

Despite all the hurt and confusion, Lily knew that her sister was right. Julien's change of heart wouldn't break her; she couldn't let it. She might even look back on their short-lived relationship as just that: a brief, healing romance. Falling for Julien had helped her through the grieving process and reminded her what it felt like to be alive. Perhaps that's all it was.

"Thanks, Cass. I just wish I understood why. If I've said or done something, if he's met someone else or what . . . Anyway, it's all experience." She wiped her eyes and tried to smile. "Enough about me, what about you—you said you had some big news?"

A few days later, Cassie had a miscarriage. Her "big news" had been that she was nine weeks pregnant. They had been for an early scan and seen the tiny form and heard the heartbeat. "I'm actually going to have a baby," Cassie had said, hugging Lily, tears running down her face.

And then she started bleeding. Charlie took her straight into hospital but there was nothing they could do. The doctor was kind but matter-of-fact and told her to go home and rest. It was common enough, he said. Up to one in three pregnancies terminate naturally—she would probably be fine next time around.

Lily was desperately sad for her sister and felt powerless to help. She and Celia took it in turns to visit the Pimlico flat every day, taking fresh food and flowers, a new book or magazine, anything which might lift Cassie's sorrow. She lay on the sofa, pale and silent, her body curled beneath a cashmere blanket. Lily ached for her. She remembered how Cassie had looked after her during those terrible weeks after Harry's death, and she longed to soothe away her sister's pain. It seemed beyond words.

WITH CASSIE'S SADNESS, THE BITTER weather, and Julien's silence, Lily began to feel intensely lonely. She found herself dreaming of Harry again, vivid nightmares which haunted her for hours after she woke. Some days she found herself thrown back into those initial stages of grief, with the fear and the lack of hope. On the days when Celia looked after Stella, Lily would force herself to close her laptop and leave the flat for a few hours, walk across the Heath, go for a swim. She knew she had to keep doing things, anything, because she was slipping into depression.

Work, physical activity, contact with the outside world, she clung to these routines as she felt herself sinking. For the first time since Harry's death she was close to giving up completely.

Ploughing up and down the swimming pool, she tried to talk herself out of it. She was a mother now, for God's sake, was she really going to fall apart over the end of a relationship? It was surprising how little difference it made, being a mother. Those feelings of being brushed off, unwanted, dumped, they hurt as much as they always had. Just like turning eighteen, getting your first mortgage, or casting your first vote, having a baby didn't make you automatically feel grown-up. It didn't make you any less insecure; it didn't make rejection less painful.

What it did, however, was force Lily to keep going. No matter how heartbroken she felt, Stella's basic needs had to be met. Somehow she kept it together: shopping for food, loading the washing machine, smiling at her daughter, taking her out for fresh air and daylight, sharing their bedtime bath. Even this bare minimum felt like an immense effort. Thank goodness for Susan's cleaner, because Lily couldn't bring herself to care about the state of the floors. Some mornings she woke up feeling OK for a few seconds before the weight of hopelessness descended again. Julien still hadn't called, and she knew he wouldn't now; it had been too long. She tried to extinguish the last stubborn flicker of hope.

One afternoon, Lily was walking back from the swimming pool in the rain. She had forgotten her umbrella and the heavens had opened. She was wearing a waterproof jacket and baseball cap, but her jeans, trainers, and socks were wet through. She walked quickly across the Heath, numb with cold, wondering if she had time to go to the supermarket before Celia brought Stella back. There weren't many people out, just a few dog walkers braving the storm.

Coming up behind her, Lily heard laughter, running feet, then a familiar male voice saying something in French. She froze, forcing herself not to turn around, forcing herself to keep walking. She kept her head down, staring at the path, until they had passed by—it was Julien, she knew it. For a few seconds, Lily saw his face in profile, mid-sentence, smiling. Wearing black shorts and a black T-shirt, he was running beside a young woman in fitted capri pants and a hot pink crop top. Her hair was wet and sleek down her back, her limbs were long and lean, tanned and lightly muscled. Even from behind Lily could tell that she was beautiful.

She stopped walking, for a moment feeling as if she'd been physically punched. She watched them running in easy rhythm, two perfectly matched figures in black Lycra and that splash of pink. Their voices carried clearly through the empty air. She heard the girl's pealing laugh again, heard her exclaim, "Jules, *non!*" They ran fast, enjoying the rain and each other's company. They were heading up the hill, parallel with East Heath Road, in the direction of Julien's flat. Lily knew what was coming. She kept her eyes fixed on them in the distance, unable to bear what she was about to see. They were going home, to his home, together. The girl shrieked at something Julien said and pushed him, he ran after her and caught her round the waist. They disappeared in through the gates of his building. Lily turned away, sick to her stomach.

Thank God he didn't see you. Thank God, thank God, Lily repeated to herself, over and over, as she trudged home. In a daze, she barely noticed the roads she was crossing, the shops and people she was passing. The rain was getting heavier but she didn't care. She walked around Belsize Park until she was soaked to the bone, shivering, unable to face her mother or her daughter.

Lily had thought she was unhappy over Christmas when Julien was away, but that was nothing to this. She burned with jealousy, she ached with betrayal. But *thank God he didn't see me, thank God,* she kept saying, clinging to this pathetic mantra which meant nothing at all. When she pulled herself together and returned home, mercifully

Celia had fed and bathed Stella and was in a hurry to leave. "She's all ready for bed. I'm so sorry I have to rush off, it's choir practice tonight. You look very cold, darling, you need a hot bath."

Lily could barely tell if the water was hot. She sat motionless, staring at the white tiles on the bathroom floor. Her body was a shell of misery. Until this moment she had been hoping, half believing, that Julien still loved her. Despite his silence, despite what she'd said to Cassie about giving up on him, she'd kept thinking it was just a matter of time. Late at night, when she lay in bed missing him beside her, she'd actually thought that he was lying there a few streets away missing her too. Until today she hadn't even been sure they were properly broken up. Now she had to face the truth. He was with someone else. It had been only a month. How quickly he had forgotten.

What hurt the most was how obviously happy the two of them were together. She couldn't recall Julien laughing like that with her for a long time.

The running girl played on a loop in Lily's mind all through that night and for days afterward: the playful laugh, the springy step, the sleek hair down her back, that tanned, toned physique. She was made for Julien, they were perfect together. No one went running on Hampstead Heath in weather like that, but they did, because they were super-fit and in love. Even though she hadn't seen her face, she instinctively knew everything about the girl: that she was French, that she was in her twenties, that she was child-free, that she was spontaneous and adventurous and everything that Lily wasn't.

Some days she didn't want to leave the house in case she saw them again. She took Stella to the playground in Primrose Hill rather than risk going near the Heath. She dragged herself around the supermarket at odd times, feeling mundane and domestic, hating everything in her basket and despising herself. One morning, standing in front of the bathroom mirror to apply her eyeliner, she suddenly thought, *What's the point?* The girl was tall and slim, with long dark hair and tanned skin. Her name would be Virginie or Aurelie, something pretty and sophisticated. She wouldn't need make-up. Lily felt dreary, sallow, and old.

How long had they been together? Had they met while skiing? More likely they'd known each other for years, probably from Paris. Perhaps they were childhood sweethearts, or university lovers. Lily didn't want to know and wished she hadn't seen them, and yet she was racked with not knowing. She carried on, for Stella, going through the motions: shopping, cooking, singing, splashing in the bath, and reading her favourite bedtime stories. Animals could sense if humans were sad—could babies sense it too? She hoped she wasn't damaging Stella, trying hard to smile whenever her daughter was around. She edited the manuscripts she was sent on autopilot, taking no interest in her work. She stopped making plans to meet up with friends, avoided the other mums after baby yoga, and abandoned her beloved swimming altogether.

She worried about Cassie too. She and Celia tried to think of ways to lift her spirits, to distract her from the sadness. "Losing a baby, no matter how early, is indescribable ..." Celia said. "There's nothing we can do except keep her going. It will take time." The only thing which seemed to help was Stella. One afternoon when Lily had a work meeting near Victoria station, she left the baby with Cassie. When she got back to collect her, Cassie looked happier and more alive than she had for weeks.

January turned into February, and winter clung on. "Isn't it supposed to be spring by now?" Olivia grumbled at one of their family lunches. "I'm beginning to think that moving to Rome is a good idea after all." Suddenly there were Valentine's Day roses, champagne, and heart-shaped chocolates in all the shops.

Lily was shocked by how quickly everything had fallen apart. She kept thinking back to when she had been a member of the happy tribe, holding Julien's hand, strolling on the Heath, watching him feed Stella, laughing in their local café at weekends, shopping for three in the supermarket. Their little family had been perfect for a time. Why had she taken that happiness for granted?

The fourteenth of February came in silence, of course. When she passed couples and families in the street now it hurt so much that she had to look away. She gritted her teeth, clung to the daily routine, and took refuge in Stella's sweetness. She told herself that spring would come and things would change. She couldn't go on like this.

IT WAS CLAUDE WHO CHANGED THINGS, unintentionally. They had been in regular contact since her trip to France, mostly emails and the occasional Skype chat. Claude had even offered to pay for their flights to San Francisco at New Year, although by that point Lily had been too unsure of the situation between her and Julien to take him up on his offer. Perhaps it had been silly not to go; perhaps she had every right to visit her father, whether or not Marie's son was there too. She wasn't sure what Claude knew about her and Julien; now that things had ended like this, it was awkward.

In April, an email from Claude arrived. As usual he was brief and to the point: *I'm giving keynote at Imperial College conference 8–15 May. Marie will be in London too doing some research, catching up with J etc. Can we meet? Dad xx*

Lily emailed back immediately: *Fantastic news, Dad! We're around and can't wait to see you. L xx*

Then she added a postscript: *Do you and Marie want to stay with us? You'd be very welcome xx*

———

THEY ARRANGED TO MEET FOR LUNCH ON the day that Claude landed. His hotel was right in the heart of Bloomsbury, and Lily and Stella took the bus into town. They found him standing in the lobby, looking as fit and lively as ever. "I booked the restaurant here, if that's OK?"

"That's great, Dad," Lily said. "You don't seem jetlagged at all! How do you manage it?"

"I've got used to it, I guess," he replied. "Flying between Europe and the West Coast over the years, usually having to deliver some kind of lecture the same day, I just try to sleep on the plane and then keep going. In fact, a hot shower and strong coffee sorted me out—I feel fine now." Claude smiled, signalling to the waiter that they were ready to order. "And look at this one, I can't believe how she's grown." Stella was sitting in a high chair between them, sprinkling crumbs of artisan focaccia on the white linen tablecloth. She gazed at her grandfather as if she half recognised him but was trying to remember where they had met.

"I'm free until the evening reception, can you stay a bit?" Claude said as he signed for the bill.

"Of course," Lily said as they headed for the lift. Stella was heavy-eyed, on the verge of nodding off in Claude's arms. "If we take her upstairs, she can have a nap and we can have a proper catch-up."

She tucked Stella into the huge bed, wedged in securely with pillows, while Claude ordered coffee and cakes up to his suite. "Yes, cakes," he said, when Lily rejoined him in the living room. "You need it. Sounds like you've been burning the candle at both ends with all your editing work and looking after Stella. We need to feed you up!"

It was true, Lily had lost weight, although not intentionally. "Honestly, Dad, I'm fine. It's been a busy few months." Since the shock over Julien and the running girl that day on the Heath, Lily had completely lost her appetite. She pushed it out of her mind and smiled at Claude. He handed her a cup of coffee and gestured towards the tray of chocolate éclairs.

"So listen," he said, sitting beside her on the sofa. "You know Marie's here too—obviously she's dying to see you both. When my conference finishes, we're planning to stay on a week or so, catching up with London and old friends. I wondered about the others—Cassie, Olivia, James—do you think they might be up for meeting me?"

Lily hesitated. "I don't know, Dad. I can ask them if you want, I'm not sure how they feel . . ."

"Sorry," he said. "It's a big thing to spring on them, I should have given you more notice. I've been hoping that if I was here anyway, we could just get together for dinner or something, keep it low-key, you know?"

"I understand, Dad . . . but you have to understand too, this *will* be a big deal for them, if they do decide to meet. It's been a really big deal for me." She wanted to prepare Claude for the possibility that his children might not want to see him at all. As far as Lily could tell, none of them felt particularly conciliatory towards their absent father. In fact, Cassie was the only one who had even considered the possibility of meeting. Olivia hadn't shown any interest in seeing him, and James, who had never met Claude, was downright dismissive.

"As you say, Dad, it's really short notice. I don't know if they're ready to play happy families."

"OK. Thanks, love. I know I haven't exactly earned a place in their lives." He smiled sadly. "In any case, are *you* free next weekend? Marie's longing to see Stella, and she'll be staying just near you, with Julien. Actually, that's the other thing . . ."

"Dad," Lily said. "I wanted to say something about this. I don't know if you heard about me and Julien, but I should probably fill you in. After I came to France last summer, we met up in London and then we started seeing each other."

He nodded. "Yes, I know. We were really happy for you, Marie thought you were perfectly suited."

Lily felt tears rise in her throat. "I did too. Anyway, things haven't worked out. Everything was great until December, we were spending all our time together, and he and Stella adored each other. Then Mum invited him to spend Christmas with us, and instead he went off skiing with his friends and then to California to see you guys for New Year, and since then . . . I don't know, he became sort of distant. For some reason, it just fell apart."

"I don't understand," Claude said. "I thought you changed your mind. I thought you decided you weren't keen . . ."

Lily looked puzzled. "*Me* not keen? Not at all, Dad. When Julien came back he cut himself off—I keep asking myself what happened, whether I said or did something, or if he met someone else while he was skiing." She was saying more than she should—she hadn't intended to talk about Julien at all—but suddenly she didn't care. It was a relief to let it out. "I guess he lives in a different world to me, all those ski trips and Swiss bank accounts . . . Of course, I can understand the single mother thing might be off-putting—it's a lot to take on another man's child. But he was brilliant with Stella, and he seemed to enjoy being around her . . ."

"According to Marie, he misses Stella like crazy," Claude said. Lily looked confused. "He seemed a bit low when he came out at New Year. But we didn't discuss it, it didn't seem appropriate. I think he spoke to his mother." Claude looked vague.

"Wait, Dad," Lily said. "Are you saying that Julien was depressed in California because I had lost interest? That's completely illogical. Mum had just asked him to spend Christmas with us and I wanted him to be there. He went away to St. Anton and everything fell apart between us. Anyway, it's irrelevant. I'm pretty sure he's met someone else, I heard something . . ." She shrugged her shoulders.

"Met someone?" Claude said. "I haven't heard anything about that."

"Dad, are you sure?"

"Oh honey, I really don't know. I think you're better off speaking to Marie, why don't you two go for a coffee when she gets here?"

"OK," Lily said. "I'll give her a call. Look at the time, we should make a move, I need to get Stella home for her bedtime. And you need to prepare for your evening reception."

"I'm starting to feel the jetlag catching up with me," he said. "Thanks for coming into town, and we'll see you next weekend? Saturday, for sure—either dinner with me and Marie, or with the whole gang, depending on what happens." He raised his eyebrows.

"Don't worry, Dad, I'll speak to them." Lily could tell how much he wanted to see his other children. "I'll let you know as soon as I can."

He walked with them as far as the bus stop on Tottenham Court Road and hugged her before she left. "And, Lil, I hope I haven't confused matters further—about Julien, I mean. I really don't know what's going on, but I think you guys need to talk."

Having slept all afternoon, Stella was full of beans on the journey home. Lily listened to her chattering away, smiling at her daughter's nonsense language. As the bus idled in traffic in Camden Town, she stared at the long line of cars ahead, trying to make sense of what her father had said. Why was Julien depressed when he got to California? Was it anything to do with her, and if so, what had she done? And what about the running girl: was that a new relationship or just a fling? Just as Lily was finally starting to forget about lying, cheating Julien—as she sometimes thought of him—here he was, filling her head. And she missed him as much as ever.

After she had fed and bathed Stella and settled her, Lily went into the kitchen to find herself something to eat. On her phone was an email from Claude:

Lil, one more thing I remembered. There's some issue with Julien's father (more father issues, eh?). Sorry I don't know exactly what happened, Marie doesn't talk about it, but tread softly. I know you will. Wonderful to see you both today. Vivement Samedi! Dad xx

Lily read the email several times, trying to make sense of it. She didn't even know there *was* an issue with Julien's father. She remembered in France, one night at dinner when she told Marie and Claude about Harry's death, Marie had mentioned her first husband. All she said was that he had died when the boys were young. Because of this, Lily had never asked Julien about his father. She assumed it was a painful subject, and she didn't want to pry.

Why had Marie mentioned her husband when she told them about Harry's suicide? Were the two things connected?

Lily leaned her head against the fridge door and closed her eyes. Suddenly she longed to be close to Julien. She wondered where he was tonight: probably just a few minutes' walk away from here, perhaps cooking dinner for Marie and the running girl. She wished she could talk to him, but at the same time she hated him for the speed with which he had replaced her. Was that girl still around? The more she thought about it the more confused she became. She should go to bed. Her chances of sleep tonight were looking increasingly unlikely.

Around four a.m. she gave up trying to sleep. She pulled on her bathrobe, made a cup of tea, and took it through to the living room. She stared out at the night sky, thoughtful but not unhappy. Again, she heard her father's words: "I think you guys need to talk."

SUNDAY DAWNED, CLOUDLESS AND HOT.
Lily dressed Stella in a sundress and hat and took their breakfast down to the garden. While Stella practised crawling on the grass, Lily scribbled a to-do list on the back of an envelope: *Ring Cass, Olivia, James re Dad. Ring Marie re weekend—when/where?* Then she wrote: *Julien?* She stared at his name, blankly, and added another question mark.

Of her siblings, she opted to call Cassie first, since they had talked about their father a few times already. It was lucky Claude was here now and not at the start of the year, Lily thought. Cassie had been devastated by the miscarriage and would have been in no state to meet him. Now she was pregnant again, just safely past her three-month stage, and radiant with relief.

Cassie answered immediately. It turned out that they were all at Celia's house, Cassie and Charlie, Olivia and James, and James's girlfriend, Su-Ki, having brunch and reading the newspapers in the garden. Lily felt a pang and wished she were there too.

Cassie put her on speakerphone. "Olivia, James, come and listen. It's Lil and she wants to talk."

Lily realised that Celia would be there too, presumably within earshot. She plunged in: "It's about this weekend. Well, it's about Claude. He's in town, and he'd love to meet you all. We could have tea round at my place, or maybe a pizza somewhere local, just a quick meal ..."

Her words had come out in a jumble. There was silence at the other end, and Lily held her breath. What were they thinking? Suddenly she really wanted this to work out. Claude was genuinely sorry for what he'd done; wasn't it natural that he'd want to meet his own children?

James spoke first. "I don't mind, Lil. I can't imagine we'll have much in common, but I'll come if you want." Lily's heart leaped. Then Olivia: "OK, if James goes I'll go. And Cass, you have to come too." Cassie's voice: "I can't do Saturday afternoon, but the evening's fine."

Lily realised she had been pulling up handfuls of grass. She exhaled and unclenched her fist. "That's great, guys! Thank you. I promise we'll keep it low-key, nothing heavy. And Mum"—she hesitated—"are you OK with this? You'd be very welcome too, if . . ."

One of the barriers to any relationship with their father had been their feelings of protectiveness towards their mother. Since their earliest childhood all four of them had been aware that he had abandoned her. As they grew into young adults they had witnessed her loneliness and felt a mixture of anger and humiliation on her behalf. However nice Claude might be, however remorseful about the past, Celia was their priority. But over the past two years Patrick had come into Celia's life and changed things. At long last she had found happiness with someone else, and now they worried far less about her.

"It's fine, darling." She could hear that her mother was smiling. "I'm at a dinner party with Patrick on Saturday. I'm not averse to meeting at some point, but it's probably best for you to get to know your father first."

Lily could hardly believe it had been that straightforward. James's and Olivia's reactions had been less than enthusiastic, but they had said yes. That was all that mattered. Lily had brokered this reunion and after that—well, it was up to Claude.

His phone was off, and she realised he was probably onstage giving his keynote speech. She sent a text: *Just spoke to the others, they're OK for meeting Saturday dinner. I'll book a local pizza/pasta place if that sounds good xx.* Then she rang Marie and invited her to the flat on Saturday morning. "We can go for a walk and potter round the shops," Lily said. "It will be lovely to see you—Stella's been missing her sort-of grandma!" She felt relaxed around Marie now. They might even have the chance to discuss Julien. She wondered if he was in the background, if he could hear his mother talking to her.

THE WEEK PASSED QUICKLY. DESPITE SEVeral more sleepless nights, and a gnawing anxiety about Julien, Lily finished two of the editing projects she was working on. Miraculously, none of her siblings pulled out of the meal with Claude. On Friday evening, Lily popped downstairs for a glass of wine with Susan after Stella had gone to bed, the baby monitor clipped to her jeans.

Lily related her confusion over Julien and the strange fragments of information from Claude. She told her about the scene on Hampstead Heath, how she'd witnessed Julien and that beautiful girl running through the rain. It was a relief to talk to someone outside the situation, although it didn't resolve anything. "You don't know who that woman was," Susan said. "It could have been a friend, a neighbour, anyone. I agree with your dad: the two of you need to talk."

It was wonderful to see Marie on Saturday morning. She admired Lily's flat, enthusing over the light, the high ceilings and wooden floors. Lily trusted Marie's sense of style—she had restored the farmhouse in Burgundy beautifully—and they discussed various layouts for the living room and a possible upgrade of the kitchen. No one knew, but since Harry's last bequest Lily was entirely mortgage-free; for the first time in her life, she actually had money to spend.

For Stella's first birthday, Marie had brought a luxurious set of white bath towels and bedsheets, one hundred per cent Egyptian cotton, from Harvey Nichols. "Rather than more toys or baby clothes, I thought you could do with something for the flat," she said. "I know what it's like when they're young, one's endlessly doing laundry and things can get a bit ragged." Lily was touched she had remembered Stella's birthday and delighted with the present.

They were finishing their coffee and getting ready to leave the flat when Marie dropped the bombshell. She spoke so casually that Lily almost missed it. ". . . and it's been lovely to see my niece again. She's been in London lately looking at various graduate courses at Imperial College." Lily was searching for Stella's socks and didn't make the connection at first. Then Marie said something about this niece staying with Julien. She felt a wave of relief wash over her. Keeping her voice as casual as she could, she said, "Your niece? Have I met her?"

"My younger sister's daughter, Melisande. We pretty much brought Meli up, so she and Jules are very close. They're more like brother and sister than cousins." An image of the running girl flashed into Lily's mind again: the same colouring as Julien, the same laugh. Of course, they were related. No wonder they seemed so easy together.

Lily's heart soared. The running girl wasn't his lover after all. She was his cousin. They had grown up together, as close as siblings. She didn't mind how beautiful and athletic the girl was now—they weren't sleeping together and they weren't in love. She blinked back tears. She must resist the urge to hug Marie, the bearer of this stupendous revelation. She must stop herself from confessing all her paranoid suspicions, all her unfounded rage and bitter jealousy. With those few simple words, Marie had changed the entire future.

Steady, she told herself. You and Julien still aren't speaking, and this is no guarantee that he hasn't met someone else. It was no guarantee, but it was everything, everything. The past few months had been so hard. Giving up the hunt for Stella's socks, grabbing a pair of tiny sandals, Lily thought she might burst into song.

They set off for Belsize Park. Marie had a long list of special British requests from friends back in California: PG Tips, Marmite, shortbread, honey, all of which they could get at the local supermarket. Lily floated around the aisles, smiling at strangers, feeling as though she had been born again. After buying everything on Marie's shopping list and more, they strolled towards South End Green for a walk on the Heath.

Marie was carrying Stella in the papoose, and Lily felt deliciously unburdened. The weather was hot and sunny, as it had been for weeks, and she was wearing a black silk shift dress, bare legs, and jewelled sandals. *It must be fate that I wore this dress today,* she thought, walking beside Marie. Julien had bought it for her birthday in Paris the previous autumn, and this was only the second time she had worn it. She had found it at the back of the wardrobe this morning. She must have shoved it there, out of sight, in the midst of her despair. She remembered trying it on in the tiny Parisian boutique, and how Julien had said, "That's it. That's the dress." That evening he'd taken her for dinner at his favourite restaurant, Le Cherche Midi on the Left Bank, and she'd worn the dress. This morning, rediscovering it, she felt able to put it on.

They waited to cross the road. Marie asked about Cassie's pregnancy, how it was going and whether it was a girl or a boy. "She's decided not to find out," Lily said. "Charlie says he'll be happy with either, and Cassie's just relieved to have got past the three-month stage. I think she's finally starting to relax ..." Abruptly she stopped speaking. Standing at the crossing, directly opposite them, outside Le Pain Quotidien, was Julien.

Lily pushed up her sunglasses, blinking in the brightness. It was definitely him. Now what? She could hardly run away or pretend she hadn't seen him. Marie noticed him a moment later and waved. It was only ten or fifteen seconds until the traffic lights changed to red that they stood there facing each other, but to Lily it felt much longer. They walked forward, awkwardly meeting in the middle of the crossing, and then Julien retreated, joining them on their side.

"Hi, Lily, hi, Mum." He leaned over Stella and stroked her hair. "Hello, sweetheart." (What did people do without babies to diffuse tricky situations? Lily thought.) They looked at each other, saying nothing, until Marie broke the silence. "Here's an idea. I'll take Stella to the park—I need a walk and she needs some fresh air— then the two of you can have a talk . . ." She looked from her son to Lily. "How does that sound? I'll ring you in an hour or two."

THEY WATCHED AS MARIE WALKED AWAY, neither of them sure where to start. "How about we go back to my place?" Julien said. "The cafés are really busy at the moment, usual weekend rush . . . I've got all this fruit from the market," he said, holding up some brown paper bags. "I'll make you my special Californian smoothie."

Lily smiled. "Your special Californian smoothie? How could I resist!" They didn't say much, walking up East Heath Road, but it felt good to be by his side. She couldn't believe the timing. If she'd run into Julien twenty-four hours ago, if Marie hadn't told her about the niece, Lily would have cut him dead. Everything about today was miraculous: the dress, the weather, the news about the beautiful sporty cousin, Meli-something . . . Whatever her name was, she wasn't his girlfriend.

As they turned into the gates of his building, Lily recalled the two of them running through the rainstorm. What did it matter now? She had clearly been losing her mind.

"You're going to love this," Julien said, ushering her into the kitchen. He reached into the cupboard and lifted out a top-of-the-range silver Vitamix. "I got it when I was visiting Claude and Marie. It makes juices, smoothies, soups, everything." He emptied the paper bags onto the counter, pulled out two chopping boards and two gleaming Sabatier knives. "Can you prep me some carrots?"

She had always enjoyed messing around in the kitchen with Julien, prepping the vegetables for a salad or stir-fry while he masterminded the actual cooking. It was a good place to talk, or at least a way to relieve this tension in the air. He sliced a couple of apples and dissected a large mango, added her chopped carrots, spinach leaves, a handful of ice cubes, and some grated ginger on top.

Julien's flat was cool and spacious, but it wasn't a day to stay indoors. They sat on the balcony in the sunshine, overlooking the Heath. "I hope you like it," he said, pouring out two tall glasses of the Californian smoothie. "I've got a whole book of different recipes. This one's my favourite."

She took a sip. "Mmm. That's delicious. Much nicer than anything you get in the shops—you can really taste the mango and ginger."

"So . . ." Julien put down his glass and looked at Lily. She had forgotten those flecks of green in his brown eyes "I should start by apologising. Whatever happened with us, for whatever reason, I shouldn't have cut myself off . . . I think I got the wrong end of the nettle." Lily smiled at this mixed metaphor; just once in a while his flawless English let him down. "I know we should have spoken."

"Julien, hold on. Can we start from the beginning? As far as I remember, we were OK in December—and then you went away and after that we weren't OK anymore." The girl might not have been Julien's lover, but Lily still needed to understand what had happened before that. "Did you change your mind while you were skiing? Did you meet someone else?"

"No, to both those questions. I didn't meet anyone else and I didn't change my mind." He paused. "I thought *you* had changed your mind. I cut myself off because I didn't know what else to do. By the time I wanted to talk to you, it seemed like it was too late, you'd lost interest."

"Lost interest?" Lily said, more sharply than she'd intended. "In what way, lost interest? I've been here all along, you're the one who went away. I just couldn't understand why things went weird between us, why we stopped seeing each other . . ."

"I don't understand either," he said. "At least not entirely. Remember in London, we were having lunch at your mother's house and everyone was there? She invited me to come for Christmas, but I'd arranged to go skiing with my friends as usual. Anyway, I really wanted us to spend the holidays together, so I asked if you'd come to St. Anton too, but you didn't seem keen." He took a deep breath.

"Here's the thing, Lily: I had it all planned out. I spent weeks looking into the baby-friendly areas of the resort. I found out about daycare and ski schools. I even booked a chalet with a separate loft apartment for the three of us, so we'd be away from the others and it would be quieter at night." He shook his head. "I really got excited about you and Stella coming along. But when I finally got around to asking, you dismissed it out of hand. I felt like a fool—we'd only been together a few months, I was obviously rushing things. Then I started thinking: Well, it's not surprising, after all she has other priorities, she has a child. Why would she want to come skiing with a bunch of people she doesn't even know?"

"You actually wanted us to come?" Lily said. "I thought you were asking to be polite—I thought it would be an absolute pain, having us tagging along, cramping your style. I'm not the world's best skier, and I didn't know how it would work with Stella, and to be honest I was worried about the cost too. And then you rang and casually mentioned you were off to California; after all those times we'd discussed going together, you must have known I'd be hurt. After you left, Dad invited us out for New Year, he even offered to pay for the flights, but by then you'd gone silent and I didn't know what was going on. I didn't want to turn up in San Francisco, as if I was chasing you out there."

"I wanted you to come, Lily. I thought it would be wonderful to visit Claude and Mum together. I honestly felt like an idiot. I thought you weren't serious about our relationship."

"I *was* serious about our relationship, of course I was," Lily said, shaking her head. "Have you any idea how I missed you, how confused I was . . ."

"No. I had no idea," Julien said. He looked angry for a moment. "You seemed so distant. I went away and I tried to get everything out of my system—you, Stella, everything. I skied a lot, and I drank a lot, and I felt miserable."

Lily stood up and walked to the edge of the balcony. She stared across the Heath, then turned to face him. "OK, here's what I think. We are both very proud, very defensive people. We're a terrible mix of confidence and insecurity. I thought you didn't want to spend Christmas with us, so I withdrew. You thought I didn't want to come away with you, so you withdrew. I thought you were bored of me and Stella, that you preferred partying with your wealthy ski friends. The more distant we were with each other, the worse it got. We were being defensive because we were hurt. Don't you see?"

"I don't think I'm defensive," Julien said, and then laughed. "OK, yes. Maybe I am. I couldn't work out what you were feeling."

"My feelings never changed," Lily said, her voice quiet. "I liked you from the moment we met in France. I thought we had a future together."

He came over to her and took both her hands. "We do." He leaned forward and kissed her lightly. "We do have a future." He touched her shoulder, smoothing the silk folds of her dress. "Isn't this . . . ?"

"Yes, the dress we got in Paris. Do you like it?"

"It's beautiful," he said. "I've been a complete fool. I'm sorry, Lily. Can we try again?"

They kissed for a long time on the balcony, oblivious to the joggers and dog walkers on Hampstead Heath behind them. Julien scooped Lily's hair up, kissed her neck, and led her inside.

Afterwards they lay in bed, half-covered by a white sheet, enjoying the slight breeze through the open doors. "Stella!" Lily suddenly said, sitting up. "How long has it been—what time did we leave them?"

Julien lazily reached out an arm. "Don't worry," he said. "She's with Mum. They'll be having a lovely time."

Lily ran out of the bedroom. "I completely lost track of time!" She found her phone in the kitchen. "Oh you're right—they're fine. There's a missed call and a text message from Marie: *Have kidnapped your daughter! Having picnic in park. Will bring her back to J's around 2ish xx*"

Julien glanced at the clock beside his bed. "It's nearly three." He laughed. "I think Mum's being tactful."

"I COULD REALLY DO WITHOUT THIS tonight," Lily called to Susan through her open bedroom door. "Obviously I'm glad they've agreed to meet Dad, but I've had enough drama for one day."

"But you're happy?" Susan said. "Things are back on track with Julien?" She had come upstairs to babysit for the evening and was playing with Stella in the living room while Lily dressed.

"I think so." Lily stood in the doorway, eyeliner in one hand and hairbrush in the other. She looked tired but radiant. "He said he's had a horrible few months too. It was just a major breakdown in communication, both of us assuming the worst and retreating into our shells."

"Did you tell him about seeing him with the running girl?" Susan asked, smiling.

"No!" Lily said. "God, I feel like a fool. Talk about getting the wrong end of the stick. Or as Julien says, the wrong end of the nettle."

"All's well that ends well."

"But, Susan, think how easily it might not have ended well. If Marie hadn't mentioned that her niece was staying in London, if we hadn't run into Julien in Belsize Park, if we hadn't spoken . . ."

"If, if, if . . . Don't waste time with what-ifs, Lily, life's too short. The important thing is that you both feel the same way."

"You're right," Lily said. "We should have talked ages ago."

"Well, it sounds like you've had quite a day. And now a de Jongh family reunion to oversee."

"I know." Her phone began to ring. "It's Cassie, they're down-stairs. I'll just buzz them in."

THEY HAD DECIDED ON NO PARTNERS for dinner—just the four of them. Walking through Belsize Park to the restaurant, Lily noticed that James looked nervous. Even Olivia was subdued. She thought back to France and her first meeting with her father at Lyon airport that day with Stella. She had felt sick with nerves on the flight, and then, as soon as she'd met him, instantly OK. She squeezed Olivia's hand and murmured: "It's going to be fine. He's really nice."

Claude was already at the restaurant, sitting at a large table in the window. He stood as they entered and came forward, arms open. He kissed the girls and shook hands with James. Lily watched the two men and was struck again by the similarity. They were the same height and build and had the same blue eyes, but it was more than that, something indefinable. Standing next to each other, they could only be father and son.

"I've ordered champagne," Claude said. "As it's a special occasion." No one said anything. The champagne was an attempt to be jaunty, even jovial, but he seemed nervous too. Lily thought he was paler than usual, his voice strained. He looked like he hadn't had much sleep. Cassie, Olivia, and James were polite but guarded with him, and Lily knew how desperate Claude was to make this work. Couldn't they at least smile, put him at his ease? There were three of them and only one of him—she was surprised to find herself on his side. It wasn't a battle; there were no "sides". Just that he seemed so vulnerable, in the face of these silent children. Lily's heart twisted with love for him.

"Thank you so much for coming tonight," Claude said. "And I might as well say it now: I'm sorry. Sorry for leaving when you were little, sorry for missing your childhoods—your birth," he added, to James. "Sorry for hurting your mother . . ."

A waiter appeared and hovered by the table with the bottle of champagne. Claude nodded at him to pour and they sat in silence, watching the man fuss with flutes and ice buckets, mopping up spilled drops and adjusting napkins.

"Anyway," Claude continued. "I don't know if Lily has told you what I told her, or if you want to ask me questions, or not talk about it at all? Or I can tell you what happened?"

"Sure. You can tell us about it," James said, his tone cold.

So Claude told them again what he had told Lily the summer before: that he had been deeply in love with Celia, but it had all happened too fast, too young. "I was struggling with depression at the time too and still pretty immature. We had one child—that was you, Cassie—and then we had two, three, and then a fourth on the way. You were all deeply wanted and loved, but we hadn't planned to have so many children so quickly. I suppose I panicked at the weight of responsibility. But I honestly never meant to leave. I thought I'd go away for a bit, to get some headspace as they say, but weeks turned into months . . . The longer I had been gone, the harder it became to come back."

Lily thought of Julien's words earlier that day: *I cut myself off because I didn't know what else to do. By the time I wanted to talk to you, it seemed like it was too late* . . . Her skin burned at the memory of his touch, how gentle he'd been, and how he'd brought her close to tears.

Before this afternoon, she had almost convinced herself she was going to be OK without Julien. After such a miserable Christmas, and then his silence all through January, she had to pull herself together. She was a mother, not a lovesick teenager; Stella needed her, and she had no right to fall apart. She hadn't fallen apart when Harry killed himself and she wouldn't fall apart over Julien. She had toughened up, gritted her teeth, and tried to put him out of her mind. Now, just when she'd rebuilt her life without him, here he was again. Until he'd kissed her this afternoon, she hadn't realised how lonely she'd been.

She forced herself to focus on the conversation. James was interrogating Claude about Marie.

"So you walked out on Mum and then found someone else to replace her?"

"It wasn't like that," Claude said. "For a long time I was on my own, or having brief, meaningless relationships. There was no responsibility, no commitment. I was lost. For years I couldn't settle to any job, to any relationship, I couldn't even stay in one country."

James frowned. "So you just drifted around, doing whatever you wanted?"

Claude nodded. "Pretty much, I suppose. But not quite the way it sounds. I was unhappy for a very long time. More than once I thought seriously about ending it . . ."

Lily felt sick. She took a gulp of champagne.

"None of this is an excuse," he went on. "I'm not asking for sympathy. I brought the situation on myself, I know, and there's nothing I can do to change that. I'm just telling the truth."

Olivia had been listening, silent. "But Marie, she had children?"

"Yes, she has two boys—obviously you know Julien"—he smiled at Lily—"and a younger son, Vincent."

James cut in, his voice harsh. "That's what I don't understand," he said. "You say you couldn't cope with your own children, but then you settled down with a woman with two kids of her own . . ."

"You replaced us with a different family," Olivia added.

Claude shook his head. "It was never like that. I didn't meet Marie until fifteen years ago, at Berkeley. We'd both been through some difficult years. At first we were colleagues, and for a long time it stayed that way, just colleagues and good friends. Her boys were teenagers by then, at university back in France."

"And we were nearly teenagers too and we had no one." Olivia had tears in her eyes.

"Mum had no one," James said.

"I know," Claude said, in a low voice. "I know."

Lily had to look away, her heart was so full of love and sadness. Over the past few days, she had been worrying more about Claude than about her brother and sisters; she hadn't realised how much they were hurting too.

There was silence for a moment. Then Cassie, her arms resting lightly on her stomach, said: "But you found happiness in the end, Dad?"

She said that final word so quietly, Lily wasn't sure if Claude heard.

Gradually the atmosphere thawed. They had needed that bloodletting, but once the hard questions had been asked, the air cleared. Claude wasn't looking for sympathy or even forgiveness. Just to know his children.

They ate large pepperoni pizzas, plates of calzone, tagliatelle; Claude ordered red and white wine, and more sparkling water for Cassie. He insisted that everyone should have dessert. Lily went to ring Susan to check Stella was OK, and when she came back to the table they were all talking: James was arguing with Claude over the relative merits of Liverpool and Chelsea, Cassie was showing him some of the baby scans on her phone, and Olivia was asking if anyone would share the profiteroles with her. Thank God, Lily thought, it was going to be fine.

"AFTER THAT FAMILY DINNER, I THOUGHT I'd survived the worst of it," Lily said. "But I can't actually believe today."

She was sitting on the kitchen counter, dressed in pyjamas bottoms and a vest. Next to her, Julien chopped basil for a pesto sauce. The events of the weekend had taken their toll on them all; even Stella had fallen asleep the moment Lily put her in her cot. Julien had driven Claude and Marie to the airport for their flight to the West Coast and then come back to the flat with fresh pasta, salad, and a bottle of wine.

"You look exhausted," Julien said. "Here." He poured her a glass of red. "Go and lie on the sofa and I'll bring dinner through." Lily could see that the weekend had been a strain for him too.

She lay on the sofa, her eyes closed, listening to the stirring of pots and pans in the kitchen. She felt emotionally worn out, but happy. A few days ago, none of this was on the cards. No matter how much you thought you were in control, you weren't, she thought. Life had a way of doing this, just unfolding in front of your eyes, for good or ill.

After the tension of Saturday's dinner with Claude and the siblings, on top of her own reconciliation with Julien, Lily had been looking forward to some peace. Then something which had not happened for over twenty-five years took place: a meeting of Lily's parents—an actual meeting of their entire family.

It wasn't planned. On Sunday morning, her head a little foggy from the champagne and wine at the restaurant, Lily had been planning a quiet day with Stella. They were finishing breakfast when Susan popped upstairs to ask for Lily's help tying up some roses in the garden. They were still in the garden, chatting over cups of coffee, when Cassie and Charlie rang the doorbell with James and Olivia in tow. "We ended up staying at Cassie's last night," Olivia said, "since she wasn't drinking and had the car."

"They came crashing in around midnight," Charlie said. "It was like a herd of elephants. This father of yours is clearly a bad influence."

"Yes, I blame Claude," James said. "How's your hangover, Lily?"

"You all deserve your hangovers!" Cassie said. "I feel incredibly smug and clearheaded. Lil, we're on our way to Kenwood for a picnic, and there's a concert later—why don't you come?"

Lily ushered them through to the garden, and Susan insisted they stay for coffee.

Lily had run upstairs to her bathroom to get some Nurofen for James when she received a text from Claude: *Just having breakfast at Jules's place, are you home? Marie wants to see Stella before we go—and Jules wants to see you! xx* Lily smiled and texted back immediately— *YES.* Then she noticed another text, sent half an hour earlier, from her mother: *Beautiful weather! Am driving over with Patrick to bring cuttings for Susan.*

Oh God, Lily thought.

She went back outside and asked the others what to do.

"It's fine," Olivia said. "They're grown-ups. They'll cope."

James agreed. "It's been going on far too long anyway." They both seemed to have forgotten that, until the previous day, they had been actively avoiding meeting their father.

"Leave them to it, I reckon," Olivia said.

"Water under the bridge and all that," James added. "Let bygones be bygones."

Lily looked at Cassie in disbelief. Her sister rolled her eyes.

It was too late to put any of them off. Claude, Marie, and Julien walked up the front path as Patrick and Celia were parking their car outside.

"It was terrible timing," Julien said. They were sitting on the sofa, too tired to lay the table or even watch TV, eating plates of spaghetti. "I was standing outside your house with Mum and Claude, and I saw your mum getting out of the car and suddenly realised—I didn't know whether to try and warn you, or stand between everyone, or what."

"I know," Lily said. "I kept looking at Mum, and I was so worried she'd think I'd arranged it on purpose, like we'd secretly engineered this situation to force her and Claude to make up."

"Thank God they were adults about it," Julien said. "I thought Celia was utterly gracious."

"It really helped, having Patrick there. She didn't look some lonely spurned wife. And Marie was so kind—she assessed the situation and got everyone talking."

"And she got on so well with your mum! It was lovely, seeing the two of them playing with Stella, discussing the roses, acting like everything was fine. Poor Claude, though. It can't have been easy for him."

"Yes, poor Dad. He looked like he wanted the ground to swallow him up. Of course, he's the one who caused the whole mess in the first place—but there isn't much he can do about it now."

"I guess he's doing the only thing he can," Julien said. "Saying he's sorry and showing he's sorry. It was good that they talked—your parents, I mean."

Lily nodded. "It was strange, seeing them together for the first time." She paused. "Maybe not the first time, I must have seen them together as a child. But I don't remember it."

"I know," Julien said. "My memories of my dad are hazy too. Sometimes I don't know if I remember him at all anymore. If I'm making things up."

Neither of them said anything. Julien took their empty plates, set them down on the coffee table, and gently pulled her head down to rest on his shoulder. From the sofa, they gazed out the window, watching the evening sky turn dark.

"Julien, can I ask you something?" Lily said. "What you just said—about your father?"

"Of course."

"I don't want to rake over the past or force you to talk about something which is painful. It's just something Claude mentioned, and what you said just now. We've never talked about your father. And we've never talked about Harry either—Stella's father."

She could barely see his face in the shadows. It was a moment before he spoke.

"You're right, we should talk about all this. What I said yesterday, when we discussed why things went wrong between us—well, it wasn't the whole truth. The whole truth is that I talked to Marie while I was in California. As soon as I got out there, she could see I was upset, and she guessed it was about me and you. I hope you don't mind, but I was so confused about the situation—if your feelings had changed, or if I'd done something wrong—and I thought that Mum might help. Then she told me about Harry, I mean how he died. I had no idea."

"Yes. He killed himself," Lily said. "I suppose there was never a good time to talk about it. When we first met in France, you were just one of Marie's sons. I assumed we'd be sort of half-brother and sister."

"We're not related in any way." Julien smiled. "You do know that, right?"

"I know, I know." She smiled too. "But it was never the right time to tell you about Harry, certainly not in France. Then we came back to London, and I didn't know whether you were interested in me in that way. Actually, I never know what to tell people when I've just met them, about me and Stella, about what happened to her father. It seems either too little or too much . . ." She sighed. "Does that make sense?"

He nodded, stroking her hair.

"I assumed that Marie or Claude would tell you, or maybe I was putting it off—I didn't know what to say. The whole thing about suicide, even the word, it's like a taboo. It's such a big concept for people who haven't been through it—"

"That's the thing, Lily," Julien interrupted. "I don't know if Claude said anything—I don't even know if he knows—but my father committed suicide."

"No." Lily was shocked, despite her previous conjecture. "No, I didn't know. I'm so sorry. Dad didn't say anything. When—what happened?"

"It was years ago, nearly twenty now. I'd just turned thirteen. My father wasn't well—I guess he was depressed—but no one realised how bad it was. I came back from school one day; Mum and Vincent had gone to a carol concert. I found him, hanging, in the garage." He paused. "It was worse for Mum than for us. Children are pretty resilient, aren't they. We had friends, we had school, all that. Mum took it very hard though. She never talks about that time, but the next few years were truly awful; I think she had a sort of breakdown."

"Poor Marie. I can't imagine how she coped, bringing you two up alone."

"That's why we left Paris for a few years," Julien said. "We moved around, staying with family in the US, then in Europe. Later Mum moved back to the States and started working at UC Berkeley, where she met Claude."

"I don't think Dad knows about it," Lily said.

"She never talks about it, or almost never. Anyway, California has been good for her. She loves teaching, and the sunshine, and meeting Claude—meeting your dad—was the best thing that could have happened. Selfishly, I'm really glad they met."

"Not selfish at all," Lily said. "They're an amazing couple, I'm glad they're together too. But what about you, how did you cope with losing your dad?"

"I'm OK," he said. "For years afterwards I had this dream, it was a replay of that afternoon, coming home and finding him in the garage, trying to get him down, trying to get help. The same dream every time. But it doesn't come often now." He smiled. "But it happened just before Christmas, so that tends to be a really shitty time of year for me. That's not an excuse, but it sort of explains what happened in December. Why I lost the plot."

"I do understand. September—when Harry died—will probably always be like that for me too, full of memories and sadness."

"And regret," Julien said. "If only I'd asked him if he was OK that morning, if only I'd come home earlier that day or found him sooner . . ."

Lily shook her head. "There are a million things you could have done differently—perhaps you could have avoided catastrophe, perhaps you could have saved him that one time—but the fact is, it happened. I feel the same way about Harry. There were so many warning signs. Now when I look back, I see how desperate he was and I wish I'd got him some help. But it's no good thinking that way. It happened. They're gone. There's no way of changing the past."

Julien nodded. "I know. But what you said yesterday, when you called me defensive or insecure, you're right. When Dad died, I felt such—such betrayal as I've never felt. Because if the man I loved more than anything in the world could do this thing, then nothing made sense anymore. It was like the ground beneath my feet had literally been torn away. I didn't know where I could stand and be safe."

"That's terrifying for a child."

"And you're right, it probably *has* made me insecure."

"I was calling us both insecure," Lily said. "When someone who looks after you takes their own life, it makes you feel utterly abandoned. You think they'll always be there and then they leave, and you feel you can never trust anyone ever again. My overwhelming feeling after Harry's death was abandonment. When I found out I was pregnant, I felt it even more."

"He never knew about Stella?"

She shook her head. "I felt very alone at first. I was angry with him too . . . Even now when I watch her, when she learns something new, when she started crawling and talking, I feel sad that he's not here to see it. That he's missing all these moments."

"It makes sense," Julien said quietly.

They stared at each other in the darkness. Strange that in that moment, both so alone with their memories, Lily felt closer to Julien than she ever had before.

"Come on." He stood and held out his hand. "Time for bed."

*   *   *

Dear Harry,

It's strange to write that. We haven't spoken for so long. I'm writing this on my blog but I'm not sure if I'll publish it or whether it's a private message to you—but where would I send it? Your last email address? Even when you were alive we didn't use email, did we? It was usually just a text or a quick call.

Remember when we first met, you'd hide love letters under my diary at work or in my top drawer for me to find during the day. And when the boys were born, you'd leave little cards with the nurses on your way out of the hospital after visiting hours, so I'd have something from you before bed or with my breakfast. When I tell the boys that we met before mobile phones, before emails and WhatsApp and the entire internet, they look at me as if I'm a dinosaur. I'm certainly getting old—I can't believe I'll be fifty next year.

The boys are amazing, I wish you could see them now. The other day, I was trying to explain the concept of "landlines" to Joe. "But why would you attach a phone to the wall? What if you needed to walk around, or leave the house, how would you take the call?" He's so funny, Harry. They've changed so much since ... since you died. They're young men now, tall and strong. Polly reckons Dan is taller than you already. Joe's been learning Spanish, and he's going on a school trip for a week to Barcelona. Dan's working hard at his A Levels and he's in the rugby first team—and he's got a girlfriend! I miss you so much when things happen with the boys and you're not here to share it.

So I wanted to talk to you somehow, and I guess writing this felt like it might be a way of communicating? We saw a family therapist for a few sessions back at the start, until the boys went on strike. She was pretty rubbish, I admit, but she talked a lot about disbelief and anger, forgiveness and acceptance. Those "stages of grief" are a bit simplistic—I've had those different emotions about your death sometimes all at the same time—but I wanted to say some things.

First, Harry, I think I'm going to sell the house. I know it was our dream home, and I stayed here initially out of shock and ina-

bility to think about moving, and to give the boys some stability, and also out of respect to your memory and wanting to cling to the past. But I think it's time. I need to start afresh and I can't do that with your presence all around me. You fill every room, Harry. The garden, your study, our bedroom, you're everywhere.

Second, I've met someone. He's a good, kind man, older than me. The boys get on well with him, and he looks after us. I haven't thought too far ahead—when and whether we move in with him when I sell this house—but I won't ever marry again. The vows I made on our wedding day will always be sacred to me.

Lastly, Harry, I forgive you. I know you were unfaithful to me. I know you broke those vows with your body and your heart. I know you fell in love with someone else and would have left me for her—but I don't want to hold on to the anger anymore.

I'm sad that I couldn't make it better for you, that we couldn't make our marriage last longer, that you couldn't find what you needed here at home. I'm so sorry you were driven to suicide, Harry, that I didn't see the torment you were going through.

But I'm letting go of the bitterness and blame and jealousy. None of this should have ended the way it did. It was never meant to cost you your life. We were happy for a long time, and we made these two amazing young men, and you'll always be my husband and the love of my life.

*   *   *

"HEY, LIL." JULIEN TOOK HER HAND. "DO YOU ever think about the future?"

They were walking back from dinner in Belsize Park. Cassie and Charlie had taken Stella for the night, and they were enjoying a rare evening off.

"The future?" Lily said. "No, of course not. Never give it a moment's thought."

"Very funny. You know what I mean—where you want to live long term, where to bring up Stella, and all that."

"Yes. I've been thinking about it a lot recently."

"And . . . ?"

"And . . . there are various decisions to be made, I guess."

"And have you made any?"

"Yes and no. Still thinking . . ."

"OK," Julien said. "If you don't want to talk about it . . ."

"It's not that. Just that I'm still thinking."

They turned into England's Lane. At the flat, Lily kicked off her shoes and went to change out of her dress. When she came out, wrapped in her bathrobe, Julien was in the kitchen making coffee. They opened the large windows in the living room to let in the night breeze and the distant sounds of the city below. Julien smiled at Lily and handed her a mug of coffee.

"I've had an idea. It could involve you, if you want."

"OK . . ." She smiled.

"It's about London. It looks like I'm going to be heading up the Europe team from now on, so I'll be travelling less—that is, I'll still be travelling but mostly short-haul or the Eurostar. And I've been thinking about a permanent base. Remember I said my neighbour was putting his place on the market? Apparently in the first week he had five offers over the asking price."

"Property prices are completely out of control . . ."

"Right. So I started looking at houses—just online, I haven't gone to any viewings. There are some beautiful places out there. I'd definitely stay in the area—you know I love Hampstead and Belsize Park—but first I wanted to ask what you think . . ." He paused. "At the moment it seems crazy. We have two flats in London, barely a mile apart."

Lily raised an eyebrow.

"I wondered whether you might consider a house too—with me. And Stella, obviously." He laughed nervously. "The three of us."

"Oh." Lily went silent. "Can I think about it?"

"Yes, of course. If you're not keen, there's no pressure . . ."

"I mean, yes, I'd like to. Living with you would be wonderful. Actually"—she paused—"did you know Susan's thinking of downsizing? Her brother Patrick has a great little flat in Westminster, and if he moves in with my mum, which he may well do, Susan might take on Patrick's place. It's convenient for the House of Lords, fully serviced, and I think the garden here's getting too much for her . . ."

"Are you kidding me?" Julien took Lily's hand. "That would be amazing—having this whole house I mean—nothing like this ever comes up in this area! Maybe we should talk to her about a private sale?"

"Hold on, hold on," Lily said. "She's not doing anything immediately, and she promised to talk to me before putting it on the market. Before we start making plans, can you give me a few weeks?"

"Sure," Julien said. "No rush."

"I love the idea too. Just that there are a few things I need to take care of." She kissed him softly on the lips. "A couple of loose ends . . ."

*   *   *

I saw her. Or rather, I saw them. Today, at the cliffs, I saw Lily and her baby. And there's absolutely no doubt that she is Harry's daughter.

It's his birthday today. A few months ago, on the anniversary of his death, we went to the graveyard: me, Polly, and the boys. We took flowers, and Polly said a prayer at the grave. But for his birthday I wanted to do something different. This morning Dan suggested going for a drive, and Joe said he'd come too. After breakfast Robert asked if I'd like him to

come along, "for moral support or as a driver or whatever," but I said I
thought I'd just go with the boys, and he didn't mind at all. (It's one of
the things I love about him: his tact, his trusting nature, his constancy. I
can't recall a moment of tension or conflict since we met.)

Anyway, we got in the car, and I started driving and found myself
heading for the south coast. The boys were very quiet on the way, they
didn't ask where we were going, or demand snacks or rest breaks or any-
thing. Dan put some music on and amazingly Joe didn't change it or tell
him it was shit. We all just listened and looked out of the window and
kind of remembered Harry, I guess.

We got there in less than two hours. The boys knew where we were. I
parked up by the cliffs and they set off ahead of me, giving me space. I
watched them, walking close together, and thought how strong they've
both been. I wonder if they talk about their dad with each other. I hope
they do. I've tried my best as a mother, but I haven't been much good as a
replacement father.

We'd walked for nearly an hour along the headland and were heading
back to the car park, the boys now lagging behind me. It was a beautiful
day and my spirits had risen; I felt closer to Harry than I'd felt at any
point since his death.

Then something changed. I was in the car park, slowing down to wait
for the boys to catch me up, and I saw a young woman standing by her
car. She was around thirty and had a baby strapped against her chest. I
can't explain—she was a stranger, but it was like every nerve in my body
was aware of her presence even before I got close enough to see who she
was. Then I saw the baby's face: a little girl so like our daughter I could
have cried out. I didn't need to look at the woman's face to know. I could
see she'd been crying, and there were shadows beneath her eyes. It wasn't
just the tiredness of new motherhood. There was a deeper sadness too. I
was standing still now, a few feet from my car and hers, unable to walk
on but unable to say anything. Her eyes met mine, and for a few seconds,
or was it minutes, we looked at each other in complete frankness.

I knew who she was and she knew who I was. Neither of us said a word. I gazed at the face of her daughter, remembering my daughter in those brief hours we had her before she died.

I found myself in the car, the boys in the back, driving home. The strangeness still hasn't left me, hours later.

I hadn't allowed myself to think about her for months. Hearing that she was pregnant was such a shock, by far the worst of all Harry's betrayals, so I tried to put her out of my mind. I had no concrete proof it was his child, but from the rumours and everything that came out after his death, it seemed pretty certain. Polly kept reminding me that the worst had already happened and I'd survived; thinking about them together and her having his baby would only make it worse.

Seeing them today was all the proof I needed that it's Harry's child. And yet . . . the anger I expected to feel isn't there. Perhaps I'm beginning to understand that she must be hurting too.

Having his baby on her own, what was that like? How has she coped? I'm not pretending that I'm overflowing with compassion for her because when you mess with other people's marriages you get burnt. But it can't have been easy for her either. I'm done with the rage and the blame. Lily didn't wrong me—I have to admit that. Lily didn't make our vows and she couldn't break them. It was Harry who betrayed me, and day by day I'm learning to live with that—and not to hate him. Maybe one day to forgive him.

I wonder what she's thinking right now. I hope she understands what I'm trying to express here, clumsily. That the jealousy and anger are gone; that we both deserve peace now.

THEY WERE HALFWAY TO THE COAST before Lily realised it was Harry's birthday. *Strange,* she said out loud, glancing at her sleeping daughter in the rear-view mirror. Lily hadn't told anyone where they were going.

As she drove, she tried to work out what this journey was about. It had been prompted by Julien's suggestion that they should move in together, but it had been on her mind for a while. It was something to do with closing a chapter, or asking permission to open a new one. *Permission for what?* she wondered. Stella was Harry's child. Lily needed his permission to take this next step. *Not his permission—his blessing.*

She had decided to bring Stella, not to the cemetery where her father's body lay, but to where he had last been alive. She couldn't take a baby to a grave. It was early afternoon and the car park opposite the cliff path was almost empty. Stella stirred as Lily turned off the engine, opened her eyes, and gave a sleepy yawn.

It had been overcast in London, but here the clouds were scudding fast across the sky. Every so often a strong shaft of sunlight streamed down, warming their faces, illuminating the endless, shifting expanse of blue-green ocean below. Here at Beachy Head, under these vast empty skies, Harry's presence was strong. Lily felt it as she walked along the white cliffs, her daughter warm against her chest. She wondered what he had seen on the day he came here. She wondered where he had jumped.

It was more than two years since she had last seen him. There had been terrible moments during that time, but she was still here. And now, was it OK to leave him behind? She thought of the book of poems Harry had given her two days before his death. She remembered what he had written in the flyleaf: *Lily . . . love hurts x.*

Those were the words she had read on that lonely New Year's Eve when she decided not to die, but to live.

As she walked, peace settled over her. Harry wasn't here and he wasn't gone. He was alive in Stella and in Lily's memory. It was OK, she realised. It was OK to move on; it was time. She stood on the high cliffs, looking out to sea. Stella gazed at the gulls wheeling and screeching overhead and waved her little hand. Lily turned and retraced her steps along the cliffs, holding her daughter more tightly against her.

She became aware of two boys and a woman walking towards them along the clifftops, also heading for the car park. The boys were in their mid-teens, tall and gangly, the woman middle-aged, small and dark-haired. Lily got a strange sensation all over, like fear, without knowing why. As the boys drew closer, she took a sharp breath. The likeness to Harry was unmistakeable. They were the right age, and their mother—she glanced at the woman—yes, it was her. She had seen photos of Pippa and there was no doubt. She looked older now, with grey hairs in her black bob and deep lines etched into her face.

It was too late now to avoid her; Lily stood by her car, her eyes fixed firmly on the ground, fumbling in her jeans pocket for the car keys. The older boy called something to the younger one—it was Harry's voice—and they ran ahead towards a Lexus at the far end of the car park. The woman stopped a few metres from Lily. She was looking directly at Stella. At Harry's blue eyes in the baby's face. She looked at Lily, recognition dawning, and time stopped between them. She seemed to be about to say something; then she walked on.

Lily somehow got Stella out of the papoose and buckled her into the car seat. She sank down onto the back seat beside her, the car door still open, her hands shaking and her breathing uneven. She watched Pippa's small figure receding in the distance. She felt shocked and ashamed. She put her head down and wept.

All this time she hadn't thought properly about Pippa and her sons, but there they were: another family who had lost a husband and father, just like her, like Marie, like Celia, like Julien ... It had been so hard just keeping her own head above water, rebuilding her life and looking after Stella. She hadn't comprehended the ripples of Harry's death, the way the waves of hurt had touched so many. These parallels, these circles of pain and betrayal and loss: Pippa's sons, Marie's sons, Celia's children, and now her own daughter, all without their fathers.

Through her grief, Lily realised that now she had this second chance, this precious chance to start over with a new love, maybe even another baby, another family . . . She sat there for some minutes, tears running down her face, until she felt Stella's tiny fingers patting her cheek.

She turned and smiled at her daughter and took her hand. "It's OK. We're OK." On the passenger seat, her phone started ringing. She leaned forward and saw that there were four missed calls from Julien. She answered immediately.

"Lily, where are you? I've been ringing all day."

"Sorry, we just went for a drive. I'll tell you about it later. We're on our way back now; we'll be home in a couple of hours."

"But are you OK?"

"We're fine. Everything's going to be fine. And—Julien?"

"Yes?"

"I'm ready if you are. Those loose ends, I think they're all tied up. I'm ready to begin again."

ABOUT THE AUTHOR

EMMA WOOLF is a writer, journalist, and broadcaster. Born in London, she studied English at Oxford University. She worked in psychology publishing before going freelance and becoming a columnist for *The Times* and *Newsweek*, TV presenter on Channel 4, and commentator across the BBC. She is a radio and arts critic in the UK and speaks internationally at literary festivals from Cheltenham to Mumbai.

Emma's non-fiction books have been translated around the world, including the bestselling *An Apple a Day* (2012), *The Ministry of Thin* (2013), *Letting Go* (2015), *Positively Primal* (2016), *The A-Z of Eating Disorders* (2017), and *Wellbeing* (2019).

Emma is the great-niece of Virginia Woolf.

WEBSITE: WWW.EMMAWOOLF.COM
TWITTER: @EJWOOLF